We were 50 light years from Old Earth when the ship's computer network alerted us. Every screen flashed three times, and Saul Gilpin's voice sounded a warning.

"Listen carefully. The Universe is alive with beings whose minds can and do reach through the space you are now in. It is not concepts that they project, but raw emotion. No matter what comes to your minds, you must not echo, you must not be afraid."

We sat there in silence. I felt chilled. I thought of mind-tendrils, reaching out to me, out from the burning suns, the icy darknesses...

GILPIN'S SPACE

REGINALD BRETNOR

ACE SCIENCE FICTION BOOKS
NEW YORK

Book I of this novel, now called *Owl's Flight*,
appeared in the February 1983 issue of
Fantasy & Science Fiction, under the book's present title.

GILPIN'S SPACE

An Ace Science Fiction Book/published by arrangement with
the author

PRINTING HISTORY
Ace Science Fiction edition/June 1986

ISBN: 0-441-28837-5

Ace Science Fiction Books are published
by The Berkley Publishing Group,
200 Madison Avenue, New York, New York 10016.
PRINTED IN THE UNITED STATES OF AMERICA

BOOK I

Owl's Flight
Geoffrey Cormac

1

IT WAS STRANGE that until he disappeared I never realized that, even though we were friends and he at least nominally worked under me, I really knew next to nothing about Saul Gilpin. He was a fey little man, with a big nose, bigger ears, and a dun-colored squirrel-tail moustache, and I knew—or at least I had assumed—that he was a chemist. (Who but a chemist, for God's sake, would name his only daughter Polly Esther?) I'd simply taken him for granted, mostly because of that discreet PH (no chemical pun intended) next to his name on the roster, meaning that he'd been personally hired either by Admiral Endicott, when he was still alive, or by Laure, his widow, neither of whom ever made a mistake about a man. In the Navy, I had been the admiral's aide, and now I was her general manager. It never occurred to me to ask questions about Saul.

But there is no better way to get questions started than for a man to vanish while there's still daylight, and not by himself alone but with his entire lab, especially when that lab is an eighty-foot still-experimental submarine safely moored between her two recently completed sister ships at the yard where they'd been built, with all three just about ready for their sea trials. Because it was past closing time and we'd shut down, only two people saw it happening: Rhoda Durfee, Laure Endicott's confidential secretary, and Dan Kellett, our chief of security. They were more or less engaged, and he'd been walking her to the parking lot. The ship didn't disappear abruptly. There was no implosion or anything like that. The blue-gray skin of *Cupid's Arrow*—the cute name Gilpin had given it—began, almost imperceptibly, to pale. Then its texture seemed actually to *thin*. Then it and everything inside it was seen to turn momentarily transparent. Then it was gone. Like that. Instantly, the bay surged in to fill the hole, splashed back and

3

forth a bit, then stilled. Nothing remained—nothing but the pier, and surgically severed hawsers, and her two sisters, *Owl* and *Pussycat,* now with only that frightening emptiness between them.

Dan and Rhoda had reported immediately to Laure Endicott, as usual still in her office, and her phone call had caught me before I got past the guardpost at the gate. I wasted no time getting back to her.

She sat behind the huge, polished rosewood desk she had inherited from the admiral—just as she had inherited Underseas, Ltd., and his shipyard, his library, his gun collection, his hunting dogs. If she had not inherited his ability, it was because she had no need of it. He had died owning one shipyard. Five years later, she had three, an additional one in Ireland, and one in Brazil, all building cargo subs and tankers. She had been born French-Canadian, educated in Paris and in England, and she was one of those rare, rare women who carry all their beauty with them as they age. Her face was a seventeenth-century face: a patrician nose, slightly arched brows over cool, piercing gray eyes; she wore her silver hair in one of those beautifully impossible arrangements that must take a personal maid at least half an hour to arrange. Though she was not really tall, I always felt she was towering over me. The first time Janet, my wife, met her at a party, she watched her for a while, then turned to me and said, "Geoff, tell me—your Mrs. Endicott is more than old enough to be my mother, much more, and yet every man in this room—and that includes you, my love—can't keep his eyes off her."

When I told her that she herself was much more beautiful, and that it was just *noblesse oblige,* she kicked me in the shins.

Now Laure Endicott smiled at me, a friendly smile, but with no humor in it. She gestured me to my accustomed chair at the corner of her desk. Kellett and Rhoda Durfee were already seated, facing her, Dan looking like a harried quarterback, Rhoda working her capable, shapely hands against each other in her lap.

"I shall outline what has happened," said Laure Endicott, "and then you can question Rhoda and Mr. Kellett, who both witnessed it."

Dispassionately, as though she were giving me a routine rundown on the weather, she told about the disappearance of

Cupid's Arrow. She turned to them. "Can you add anything to that?"

"You've covered it," said Dan, obviously impressed. "Every bit of it."

"Except for one thing, Mrs. Endicott," Rhoda put in hesitantly. "There—there was no *sound.* It—well, it just melted, and there was nothing *left."*

There was a touch of hysteria in her voice, and Laure Endicott soothed her expertly. "Rhoda," she said, "that's why I'm sure it didn't simply melt or anything like that. It couldn't have, not without a trace. It was, if anything, *transferred,* sent somewhere else. We'll have to try to find out where and how."

Almost in an instant, I had experienced utter shock, cold realization, and half-acceptance of the unbelievable.

She leaned toward us. "In the meantime, we've other fish to fry. Before too long, one of Dan's boys is going to realize that *Cupid's Arrow* has disappeared, and once the word's out, the whole yard will be swarming—local police, federal men, then the media, and God only knows who else following. Geoff, what do you think we ought to do?"

I hesitated, juggling choices. "I think our best bet's a cover-up—at least for now. That may give us a chance to find out what happened. Otherwise, government—" We exchanged glances, thinking of the people who had come to power in Washington. "Otherwise, they'll really make a mess of things, and we'll have nothing left to get our teeth into."

She sat back, smiling grimly now. "I was hoping you'd say that. Dan Kellett here tells me both the ship's hawsers were cut off razor clean. Could we give their ends a quick laser burn to hide the fact?"

"No reason why not, if no one sees us."

"I can manage it if we can keep our own men off my back," Dan told her. He stood up massively. "It's lucky Saul wouldn't stand for any automatic security devices when there was anyone aboard. If he had, the fat'd be in the fire. Right, Commander?"

"Right, Dan."

He took his intercom out of his pocket and called two men I knew would be nearest.

"Sousa! Myers! Kellett here at the office. From the window it looks like maybe there's steam or smoke out near the end of the north slip. Probably nothing, but better chase on up and check it out."

We waited till they got back to him that they were on the way. Then, quickly and quietly, he left the room. I looked inquiringly at Laure Endicott.

"You're wondering why I'm so anxious to make things look as though the boat's been stolen?" She smiled. "Partly, Geoff, it's because of the people we'll be dealing with. But there's something else. Saul told me about a week ago that he'd accomplished something sensational—a major breakthrough. He halfway hinted at a preview—he called it a *première*. The only other people present were to be his daughter, and his Chinese girlfriend, that pretty Lillian Yee, and you, and Franz Andradi because, after all, he did a lot of work on it with Saul. I don't want the powers that be even to suspect that there might be more involved than some minor improvement in the drive or power plant—and, Geoff, there *was*."

We sat there looking at each other silently, hoping Dan wouldn't be too long with his "Mission accomplished!"

He wasn't. It took him eight minutes by the clock. Finally his voice came back to us. "Commander Cormac? Looks like it's time for me to button up. I've a dinner date, but I'll come back and make a quick check around midnight."

Our intercoms were scrambled but Dan was spooked. Well, so was I. "Good boy," I told him, playing right along. "See you tomorrow."

We looked at each other, Laure Endicott and I. "Well," I said, "now the shooting starts. We'll just have to face up to whatever weirdos our new government sends down to bug us."

Rhoda was crying very softly—beautiful, loyal, dedicated Rhoda. She had a worthless brother, Arley, estranged except when he came begging her for money; and a grandmother, an inoffensive, ineffectual semi-alcoholic living in a protected retirement complex, whom Rhoda visited sadly and dutifully. None of us realized how dreadfully vulnerable she was going to be because of them. Laure Endicott and Dan were the only real family Rhoda had. I went and patted her on the shoulder. "I'm glad the admiral didn't see these so-called Individualists take power," I said. "He really *was* an individualist—and these apes are against everything he stood for."

His widow nodded. "He recognized them immediately for what they were. 'Their individualism,' he told me, 'means only that everyone's free to be like every other individual—and they'll define *that*. When they talk about private enterprise, they simply mean you're free to buy a share or two in one of the great conglomerates, but if you succeed by yourself you're a public menace. Like me.'"

She did not allow her bitterness to affect her voice. The admiral had been relentless in his opposition to the Individualist People's Party, in his cutting denunciations of their heavily funded charismatic leader, Breck Dugan—Good Ol' Breck—and their entire program. Both she and I felt that when his private plane slammed into the Cascades, killing him and his copilot, there'd been dirty work afoot. But there was no way to prove it, and anyway, by that time IPP influence had grown to the point where they could have hamstrung us. Since then, they had swept the country. Good Ol' Breck was now our President, and his movement was spreading into other countries, south of the border, through what remained of the British Commonwealth, even behind the Iron Curtain, where Marxist ideologues had found a spiritual kinship between their repressive collectivism and his own—it reminded me of the Hitler-Stalin pact at the start of World War II. The death rate among independent industries had soared, and so far Underseas had survived only because Laure Endicott seemed to know even more than the Japanese about economically building first-class cargo submarines.

Rhoda dried her eyes. "Hadn't I better be going home, Mrs. Endicott?"

Laure Endicott stood up. "Please don't," she answered. "I need you both. I'm going to take you out to dinner, somewhere where we can't be found too easily. Geoffrey, why don't you phone Janet and see if she can join us at—let's see—how about Les Trois Mousquetaires? Rhoda can go and freshen up while you're phoning."

Rhoda looked at her gratefully, and went out, and I reached for the phone, but Laure stopped me. "A moment, Geoffrey! Rhoda and Dan Kellett can go together. You can ride with me because I want to talk to you. I want to brief you on some things you don't know—about Saul and *Cupid's Arrow*. Janet can drive you home after dinner—and you'll probably either find the phone ringing for you when you get there, or else one of our people waiting to rush you to the yard."

I called Janet at the hospital, and waited while they had her paged. We'd been planning to have dinner out together anyhow, and she was delighted to go to a restaurant that was so quietly famous. She'd meet us there.

Laure was a good driver. We left the yard behind us, and she turned her swift, silent car onto the access road leading to the freeway and the city.

"Geoffrey," she said, "have you ever wondered exactly what we've been paying Saul Gilpin for? Of course, it was to develop better and cheaper ways of doing things, but that wasn't all by any means. John never believed that very profitable myth that only corporate or university or government-owned think tanks can come up with anything original—that everything's become too complex for the individual genius who just can't or won't fit into a think-tank slot. Years ago, he said, 'Someday Saul's going to come up with something really revolutionary, something the whole world's been waiting for without knowing it. My money's on him.' Geoffrey, Saul was working on a new drive."

"I knew that," I said, "but I just assumed he'd worked out a new way of converting the nukepak's energy to electricity. Maybe he wasn't a mad scientist, Laure, but he really played the part—living aboard *Cupid's Arrow*, actually setting up housekeeping there the last few months, bragging to everybody that he was working on the world's fastest sub. It was just lucky that sub-killers have made submarines so vulnerable that they're militarily worthless—otherwise, the government would have plucked him out of here long ago."

"Lucky for him—and us. His new drive wasn't as simple as he made it sound. It was based on concepts that, quite literally, nobody else could understand. Franz Andradi told me he couldn't, even though he's a nuclear engineer. Once I asked Saul to explain it to me, and he replied, '*Chère ma tante*, I would be delighted to, but no—there is no way. It echoes the poetry at the heart of process, that's what it does! But I promise you—it will succeed! Indeed it will, and then you can throw the greatest party of all time to celebrate, even if I'm no longer there.' Then he bowed, and walked off chuckling to himself."

I was beginning to catch on; a new and even more disquieting dimension was being added to the vanishing of *Cupid's Arrow*.

"Do you mean," I asked, "that Saul's new drive did more

than just *drive?* That it shifted *Cupid's Arrow* into—into—
oh, hell!—into a different universe or something?"

"Or something," she replied. "Yes. And that's why I'll do
anything—and I mean *anything*—to keep Good Ol' Breck and
his people from finding out about it."

"What about Saul?"

"He must've been aboard—he and his cute Lillian Yee, and
probably Polly Esther, too. He'd never have let himself get left
behind in that kind of an experiment. And he wouldn't have
gone off without them."

"Do you suppose that's what he meant when he talked of
celebrating even if he were no longer present?"

"Probably. God only knows where they are now. They may
no longer even exist. Anyhow, I intend to find out what happened. Are you with me, Geoff?"

"All the way," I told her.

"And Dan Kellett?"

"He feels the way I do—about you and about the IPP. What
about Franz? How much *does* he know?"

Momentarily, she smiled. "Probably more than we do. By
an odd coincidence, he went off backpacking in Montana—at
least ten days, he said, up in the high country where no tele-
phone can reach him."

The freeway crossed the river, and we looked down on the
city turning on its lights, and I found myself wondering what
was going to happen to it under Dugan's rule.

"Thank God," I said, "that some of the creeps Good Ol'
Breck's appointed to high office aren't too bright. Still, we'd
better cover all bases."

"Do you remember how John used to put it? 'The first
contingency plans you make are for when somebody sinks your
unsinkable ship.'"

"Well, let's suppose we can keep them hoodwinked," I asked.
"Then how do *we* go about finding out what and how?"

"I'll know more after we talk with Franz," she told me.
"Right now I haven't even a shred of an idea."

"Didn't you keep copies of Saul's records—you know,
equations, diagrams, blueprints, parts lists, all that sort of thing?"

"Geoffrey, Saul didn't work that way. He never offered
them. I never asked for them. We'll have to depend on what
Franz can tell us when he gets back. At this stage, maybe it's

just as well. There literally isn't anything for anyone to find."

That I couldn't argue with.

As we wound down into the city, she told me what immediate action she was going to take. "We both know how the Individualist People's Party operates," she said. "Their goons used terrorist and KGB tactics, the whole immoral arsenal, during their drive to power and in their interparty rivalries, but we can't waste energy getting scared. We'll go on the offensive. We'll report it to the local police immediately, and to the state and federal agencies. We'll blame it on industrial espionage and sabotage. We'll scream to all the media—theft of our supersubmarine, possible kidnapping of its inventor and his daughter! We'll raise the roof and keep on raising it. Of course, they'll have the Coast Guard and the Navy out, but when they don't find *Cupid's Arrow* they'll simply think she slipped away. Only sub-killers would be dead certain, and even *they* wouldn't dare to use those—not in peacetime, and with all the international traffic."

"Okay," I said, grinning at her. "The minute the yard gets in touch we'll get to work."

2

LAURE WAS ONE of those rare, wonderful people who not only can relax and enjoy themselves even when they know the world may fall in on them tomorrow, but who can transmit the feeling to those around them. All through dinner, she kept anxiety at bay, soothing Rhoda, gradually teasing out my own worry lines, carefully briefing Janet on what had happened without alarming her. Of course, the fact that it was a splendid dinner, superbly served, did no harm; and when finally, at about ten-thirty, we went our separate ways, knowing we'd see each other again in less than half an hour, we were actually lighthearted.

It didn't last. As Janet and I drove up to our apartment, we saw the company car waiting at the entrance. It was Sousa, who'd been trying to phone me all evening. He'd figured we'd gone off someplace, but took the chance we'd come on home. Somebody had stolen *Cupid's Arrow*—

I made appropriate noises of shocked disbelief, and he blurted out what they had found. What with Saul living right aboard with a phone and his own kinky alarm system, they hadn't bothered to check on the small subs for nearly an hour after they came back from the north slip—and then—well, the ship was *gone*. They'd called in to the office and told Ordway, who was in charge with Kellett gone, and he'd told them not to disturb anything and to get in touch right away with Mrs. Endicott or me.

"Come up to the apartment," I told him. "We've got to call the cops."

We hurried. I got through to city police harbor detail—and found that Laure had phoned them a few minutes before and they were on their way. She hadn't had as far to drive as we. So then I called the feds, and some nasty bastard—a new IPP appointee by the sound of him—told me Laure had called them,

11

too, and I'd better get my butt down to the yard on the double, and what kind of amateur job were we doing down there anyhow, letting somebody steal a friggin' submarine?

I gave him a soft answer, and took off after Sousa. When we roared in past the gate guard, I saw nothing but police cars, sheriffs' cars, federal cars, and lots of media cars, with everyone snorting around and shouting orders. I pushed through to Laure's office, and found a couple of the new federal boys trying to browbeat her and getting absolutely nowhere. I looked them over, and decided that their qualifying experience must've been either as jail guards or inmates. They seemed to figure they had the problem solved: Was Underseas, Ltd., having money problems? And was this weird sub insured? And for how much? And how about the Gilpin guy, was he aboard? And who stood to collect *his* insurance?

Laure was playing with them, giving them deliberately evasive answers, getting them more and more fouled up in their own confusion, and generally managing things so they'd believe what'd be best for us, so I went down into the yard again and got Dan alone for a moment. "How's it going?" I asked.

"Fine! They've been stomping around over absolutely everything, even each other. Believe me, if I left any evidence when I used the laser—by the way, I took care to leave a few burns on the pier—it's either gone by now or so kicked around it's meaningless."

"Let's hope so!"

"There's one guy worries me." He frowned. "A brick outhouse sort of character named Whalen Borg. He's not running with the pack, and he's got a look on him like he's out to burn a heretic." He saw the expression on my face. "Know anything about him?"

"Too much. He's a displaced ayatollah. But not stupid— no way. While he was working for the party his business *was* burning heretics—or at least working them over pretty nastily. And that's not the worst. I knew him in the service. They found him pulling rough stuff on enlisted men—and women—and it was the admiral who brought charges and made them stick, but strings were pulled and he ended up out on a psychiatric discharge. He'll have forgotten none of it, and he'll be remembering that I testified against him, too. And now he's a fed?"

"Buzzer and everything. He doesn't act like he's in charge,

but also he doesn't act as if anyone's in charge of him. And he's been asking the wrong questions."

"Such as—"

"Such as what kind of drive was Saul working on? And how come he was getting such special treatment? And when could his records be made available for inspection?"

"Dan, Borg changes the whole picture. He's a personal enemy—not just of mine, but of Mrs. Endicott's because she's the admiral's widow. From now on, we can't forget him for a moment, especially if things quiet down and he seems to fade into the background. It could be we'll have to fight a little private war, and if we do there won't be any rules. Catch on?"

He nodded, so I gave him a slap on the back and went up to Laure's office again. Now she had even more company— media people, agents, cops—all milling around while the agent in charge, another new appointee, sounded off about how he had the whole case in the bag. He was a gangling, school-teacherish sort of man with an abrasive sideshow barker's voice, and he was promising the media the greatest story of the year. Of course, he had to keep it under wraps until he'd had everything checked out, but they could go ahead and tell the world that it was significant—*most* significant—that this Saul Gilpin's girlfriend was *Chinese*. And they could also say that neither he nor the administration took any stock in Mrs. Endicott's accusation that perhaps one of the major conglomerates had stolen the submarine. Now possibly some other irresponsible small entrepreneur . . . He left the suggestion hanging for the media people to bite at; and Laure Endicott, ignoring him, smiled at them regally.

Then, in the opposite corner of the room, I saw Whalen Borg staring at me. He was enormous—almost grotesquely so because to match his chest and shoulders he should have been a foot and a half taller. His thinning hair was combed very carefully across his tub-shaped head. His round, colorless, cold eyes protruded slightly, drawing attention from his undistinguished, heavy face. He stared at me, smiling very slightly, and I stared through him for a moment before I let my glance drift on.

A few minutes later, it was over. The agent in charge dismissed the media; he herded his own people through the door; he didn't even bother to say good night. And Whalen Borg, never taking his eyes off me, was the last to leave. The first

late, late newscasts were telling all about it—the suspected
Chinese involvement, and how Saul Gilpin had a record of
mental instability, and how taxpayers' money was being wasted
on an unimportant incident which could never have occurred
at a conglomerate yard.

On the surface all was going well. There was only that one
fly in the ointment, and I didn't need to point it out. Laure had
seen him, too.

The next two weeks were raucous. Individualist People's Party
senators and congressmen shouted about the danger of letting
"fly-by-night speculators" play games with industries vital to
the economy; they demanded investigations; they introduced
bills which—even though destined to die quickly in committee—showed clearly what the future held in store for us
once both Houses were purged of our last friends. The media,
of course, yelled just as loudly. *Cupid's Arrow* could not be
found? Their inside information said she'd been destroyed—
again, for insurance—or gobbled up whole by a huge Chinese
naval cargo sub like Jonah in the whale, or (God help me!)
stolen by Saul Gilpin for a protracted sex orgy with his girlfriend *and* his daughter.

The cops kept pestering us, always with the same questions,
the same innuendos; and we kept on giving them the same
answers, very patiently. Whalen Borg, to my surprise, didn't
show up again—and that alarmed me more than the rest of it.
It was a dead certainty—that he was watching, planning, waiting. Of course, we kept on shouting to the media about our
stolen submarine, but I knew Borg didn't believe that it was
stolen, though the rest of them swallowed the story, hook, line
and sinker.

Then suddenly all the fuss died away. The party noisemakers
found new issues to panic their constituents. The media found
new targets to attack. And I redoubled our precautions.

Franz Andradi came back from his vacation a few days later.
He checked in at the office, and it was obvious that Saul's
disappearance had been no surprise to him; but we didn't want
to start questioning him, not then. The admiral had sponsored
his parents years before when they had emigrated, and he and
the Endicotts had been close friends ever since. Andradi was
dark and lithe and wild, looking more like a Hungarian hussar

than a nuclear engineer, and where the ladies were concerned he made the most of it. But generally men liked him; he played fair. We had hired him with only his M.S., and he had worked for us for a little more than a year, mostly with Saul but sometimes on more conventional projects.

It wasn't until all three of us were in Laure's car on the way to lunch that Franz began to talk about it. Saul had tipped him off, had told him to get out of town and stay out until the flap subsided. He promised him that, yes indeed, there was going to be a flap—a simply lovely flap—and that when Franz heard about it he'd know exactly what had happened, even if he didn't understand exactly how. Franz had trusted Saul implicitly, guessing that whatever he was planning was in the best interest of us all. Now Franz looked at Laure apologetically to see if she was offended at having been left out of it.

She wasn't. She simply nodded. "And what *did* happen, Franz? What, exactly, did Saul's invention do?"

"I wouldn't know. I'm a nuclear engineer—not a theoretical physicist," he answered; and I saw that now his jauntiness had vanished, and he was deadly serious. "Even if I were, I probably wouldn't understand it, Mrs. Endicott. He told me that it was a drive—and, knowing Saul, I'm sure that's what it is. But I've never seen it driving anything. It occupies a space only about five feet by three by maybe two, and it can swallow all the energy the ship's nukepak puts out without even warming up. Once or twice Saul let me watch it when he turned it on— watch the instruments measuring its appetite. The readings were unbelievable. Then he always turned it off—'Before it scares you,' he said. That's about all I can tell you at firsthand. He wouldn't tell me any more—all he needed me for was for modifications to the nukepak and its controls. The last time we talked about it, he twiddled that absurd moustache of his and reached up and tweaked my ear, and said, 'Franz, laddie by and by you'll find out a lot more. Just be sure you're back right after the flap's over, in time for Laure's birthday. Tell her you are invited to her party—that *I* invited you—and have a dozen of her drinks for me.' Then he went off, chuckling to himself and whistling *'Marlborough s'en va t'en guerre.'*"

"Is that all he ever told you?" I asked.

"Not quite, Geoff," he answered, almost reluctantly. "It's . . . well, it's hard for me to believe it even now. What he said— as nearly as I can remember—was, 'Franz, this is the most efficient, most powerful drive anyone ever made. There's just one trouble with it. It can't be used in ordinary space, in space-as-we-know-it. But in its own space—ha! That's a white horse of a different color. Why, in such a space it'd be swift as thought!' I answered him with some wisecrack about how much did he intend to speed up his stupid submarine anyway? Then he raised a hand to heaven and swore he'd never tell me because I was jealous of his magnificent moustache." Franz stroked his own coal-black redundancy, grinning a little ruefully. "And all the time I thought he was just kidding me?" He paused. "Okay," he said, "just how did *Cupid's Arrow* disappear? Did it get shifted out of phase with here and now? Did it get thrown into a science-fiction universe? Whatever did Saul do with it?"

We told him exactly what Dan and Rhoda had told us, and he asked us to repeat it.

Then the three of us were silent for half a mile, all of us thinking the same thoughts. Laure and I had learned no more than we'd already guessed, but now we *knew*. What *had* really happened? And where were Saul and his Lillian and his daughter now?

"Saul used words very strangely sometimes," Laure said finally, "but he wasn't one to waste them. His mentioning my birthday and my party couldn't have been accidental." She frowned. "Franz, my birthday's only three days off, and I want you to fly down and spend those days with that girl of yours at Stanford, the one who's silly enough to take you seriously. It'll seem more plausible, and you can still be back in plenty of time."

"And Franz," I added, "watch out for dark alleys and strange women."

He grinned. "Don't worry, Geoff. Dark alleys don't appeal to me, and the women I already know aren't strange at all."

3

Laure Endicott's birthday parties had started while the admiral was still living, and they had always been small family affairs—Janet and I; Saul and his Polly Esther and, later, Lillian; Rhoda and her husband until he died, and finally Rhoda and Dan Kellett. Then, of course, there was always Mrs. Rasmussen, who'd been with the Endicott's for twenty or more years, and who was family as much as anyone. It was she who served the dinner, which was invariably a triumph, sometimes calling in her daughter to assist her, but more often than not doing it all alone.

She had been very fond of Saul and of his Polly Esther, and at first the shock of his disappearance had depressed her, but she was cheerful now, and the party, which could have turned into the sadder sort of wake, became a celebration. But then she knew something we didn't know.

We found out right after dinner, after Laure had blown out the candles and the cake had been cut and served. First knocking on the door, which got our attention instantly because it was something she didn't have to do, Mrs. Rasmussen came back into the dining room, and this time she was not alone. With her there was a Boy Scout, a very young one in full uniform, neat and clean and freshly pressed, his blond hair falling down over his forehead. He was carrying a flat package wrapped in fancy paper, with a big ornate bow at either end, and he was obviously embarrassed. Seeing us there, he hesitated, blushing, shuffling his feet.

"You know my grandson, Keithy," Mrs. Rasmussen spoke with a lilting Danish accent. "He's got a message for you, Mrs. Endicott." She urged him forward. "And doesn't he look nice? Just like in Normal Rockwell's pictures. And look at those merit badges—and him only into scouting for a year already!

17

Now come on, Keithy, you keep your promise."

Keithy blushed even redder than before. Then, squaring his shoulders, his eyes closed tight, he sang, *"Happy Birthday to you! Happy Birthday to you! Happy Birthday, dear Auntie, Happy Birthday to you!"*

He opened his eyes again, and looked at Laure apprehensively. "That 'Auntie' wasn't mine, Mrs. Endicott," he blurted. "That was Uncle Saul's! He told me to sing it just like that, and then to give you this." He came forward, holding out the package. "He made me promise I'd never tell about it, not to anybody, and I promised him, scout's honor!"

Smiling, Laure took the package. "Thank you, Keith. Nobody ever called me Auntie except Mr. Gilpin, so you did exactly right. Would you like a piece of birthday cake?"

She placed a generous slice on a cake plate. "Sit here next to me," she said.

"I'm sorry, Mrs. Endicott," his grandmother put in. "That wasn't the way Mr. Gilpin wanted it. He said Keithy could have a great big slice of cake, just like the one you cut, but he was to have it with me in the kitchen, because what's in that package is a big secret. Isn't that right, Keithy?"

"Yes, ma'am, that's what he said, and I won't tell anybody that, either. Happy Birthday, Mrs. Endicott."

Laure thanked him once again, and no one said a word until the door had closed behind them. In a whisper, Franz Andradi said, "I hope your present's what I think it is!"

Carefully, patiently, Laure took out an envelope half hidden by a bow. She opened it. She took out an enormous birthday card. There was a folded letter in it, but first she showed the card to all of us, a horribly sentimental thing featuring pink bunnies peeking out from behind enormous mushrooms. When we had all had a chance to smile over it, she unfolded the letter.

Mi chère Matante (she read aloud),

Didn't know I could speak Liègeois, now did you? Admit it! Admit you didn't know! Nor did any of those other nice people at your table. Well, there's a whole lot they don't know about their Uncle Saul—not *your* uncle, Auntie Laure. And anyhow, you're probably all sitting there mad at me because I stole your little submarine, and you're wondering what's become of me and Lillian and Polly Esther. Well, I'm sure we're going to be all right because I've made all sorts of preparations for a long, long journey. And don't you ladies sit there worrying about Polly Esther, because her boyfriend, a nice sort of engineering character from Cal. Tech., is with us, and now that I'm the captain of the ship, I'll marry them myself.

I'm guilty. I did steal *Cupid's Arrow.* But dear Aunt Laure, like a good pack rat I've left you something in place of it. Can you guess? Of course you can't, though I suppose Franz has been doing his damnedest.

What have I left you?

Madame, I have left you a hot potato.

I have left you a ticket to the stars.

And to you, and you, and you, and you and you, and you too, I leave

> My love,
> Saul Gilpin
> Captain, Starship
> *Cupid's Arrow*

PS: You now have full instructions, in words and drawings any intelligent child can understand, as to how to build it. If you follow them, you will find out what it is. It will not shift you into another universe, because God made only this one (or so He told me). But He made it with an infinite number of states or aspects. Into one of these my device will plunge you. The silly rules of physics as we know them will not apply to you. When the device is in its drive modes—it has others—you will not have to suffer the torments of acceleration. You will not, in your journeyings, have to wait on sluggard light.

> God love you, gentles all!
> (signed again) Gentle Saul

PPS: Now don't forget—I want you to start building right away, before the IPP devours you. However, to make that a bit less likely, I have already built you one extra drive, complete with its computers and controls. Follow directions and your starship will be set to go.

And, dear hearts, *keep* it that way. Provision it. Put aboard everything I've thought of and anything else you can find room for. You may have to take off as fast as I did.

Laure put the letter down. What does one say when a door too vast, a door always safely welded shut, is suddenly thrown wide to show the absolutely unbelievable? In a very low voice, finally, she spoke. "If what Saul tells us here is true, and I'm sure it is, perhaps his hot potato will prove too hot to handle. Only science-fiction writers, only a very few far-out scientists, have dared to dream of starflight as actually attainable, and even they have thought in terms of decades, of centuries, for research, of uncounted billions for development. Now suddenly *we* are given it—simple, cheap, instantly available. Our world's a bomb—a bomb with as many fuses as there are crazy little nations, as many as our savage dictators, our corrupt politicians, our power-hungry plotters, manipulators, terrorists! How would these people see our starship? As a weapon only, a secret to be seized at any cost. But there'd be many, many others who'd look on us as saviors, helping them escape the dread they live with to face less certain perils. Very well, what shall we do with it?"

"My God!" Dan said, more to himself than to the rest of us. "My God! Brought to us by a Boy Scout!"

"There's one thing Saul didn't mention," Franz put in. "Just *where's* that extra drive he said he's made?"

Laure smiled at him. "Perhaps another Boy Scout will come along with it."

She undid the package, rolled its ribbon neatly, took out three fat manila envelopes. One was addressed to her, one to Franz, and one to me.

"What shall we do with it?" she asked again.

I thought of what would happen if it fell into the hands of Good Ol' Breck and those even darker figures who pulled his strings, or of the grim old men inside the Kremlin.

Everyone, I think, spoke at once, saying the same thing in different ways; and Laure listened till we had finished.

"We are agreed, then? *They* mustn't have it?"

I spoke for all of us. "We're all agreed. Nothing we've learned tonight will be told to anyone not now in this room."

Coolly, penetratingly, Laure regarded all their faces. "I'm

satisfied of that. But still we must decide what use we'll make of it. Let's all consider it, knowing that we will have to plan swiftly, and act more swiftly still." Astoundingly, she smiled. "And let us pray that what we do is right. And let us pray for Saul and Lillian, and Polly Esther and her lad, whoever he may be, and for *Cupid's Arrow*. And now—let's have some birthday cake. Then we'll have coffee and liqueurs."

Thus she shunted us back into reality—a reality that now seemed all the more unreal, with its birthday icing of affection and friendship and festivity. We ate our cake, and sipped our demitasses and savored our liqueurs, realizing that what had overwhelmed us was much too dangerous—yes, and much too sacred—to be discussed even among ourselves, not then. Only Franz had been unable to conform. He picked up his liqueur and, muttering an apology, retreated to a corner of the room to open his envelope. I could see him from my place at the table, the changing expression on his face showing amazement, disbelief, grudging acceptance, puzzled annoyance, wonderment. He was oblivious to everything and everyone around him. Once in a while, he would make small grumbling noises, or gasp in astonishment.

The rest of us went on with our charade for half an hour, an hour, until the time came to break up the party. Dan and Rhoda were the first to leave, and Laure walked them to the door. I could tell that Janet was just waiting for me to give the word, but before I could, Laure asked her if she'd mind going to the kitchen and saying a word or two to Mrs. Rasmussen and Keithy. "They're very fond of you," she told her, smiling.

Then, with Janet gone, she turned to me. "Geoffrey, we're going to have to act as rapidly as possible. I mean decisions." She called to Franz, jarring him out of his other-world of physics. "Franz, how does it look to you? Have you any idea how it works?"

Franz came over to sit down next to us. "How does it work? Mrs. Endicott, I have *no* idea. If I hadn't seen Saul's tests and heard how *Cupid's Arrow* dissolved before God and everyone—well, I would've said Saul had flipped, that he simply had concocted a topologist's nightmare of a nothing-gadget. It has metal elements; it has ceramic elements; it has what look like massive, twisted monofilaments going nowhere; it seems to have no moving parts, though there are some that look as thought they *could* move if they wanted to. Yet everything in

it is made of common stuff, stuff easily found and easily fabricated. It has me stumped. I have no takeoff point. *None*. But
Saul is right. Each part, if it's subcontracted, looks as if it
could be part of almost anything—a paper mill, a cotton gin,
you name it. And every unit, following his directions, shouldn't
cost more than in the low six figures. That's only a quick guess,
of course, but I'd bet I'm not too far off. The computer equipment would be extra."

"Who do you think should get it?" Laure asked, addressing
both of us.

"We should," I told her. "But how could we protect it?"

"The whole world should," Franz said. "That's the safest
way."

"You're both right," she answered. "We ought to have it
because Saul produced it for us, but there would be no way
for us to keep it secret, even if we died trying—which I suspect
we would. And the whole world should have it, because the
whole world needs it desperately, and we could sell it to them—
except that we'd not be allowed to. Therefore there's only one
thing we *can* do—" She broke off, questioning us with her
eyes. "We can give it to the world, for free, but not until we
ourselves have built one, and tested it, and can safely say, 'This
is our gift to you. It will take you to new worlds. It will dash
you into undreamed-of dangers. But it will never injure you
itself.' Perhaps we can keep it secret long enough for that."

I nodded. She was right. I could see that Franz was also in
agreement. He said, "Yes. If you were to publish it—or even
try to publish it—just as it stands, you'd be destroyed, and
Lord only knows what'd become of it."

Laure reached out to us. She put one hand over one of mine,
and one on his. "Our time is short. The election is only two
months off, and it will give them both Houses of the Congress.
Their power will be absolute, and it'll be too late for us. Tomorrow I'll announce that I am giving up competing where
major vessels are concerned, that Underseas is going to stick
to small special-purpose craft. I'll tell the media I know when
I'm licked. I'll even hint that eventually I may sell out completely. It'll be plausible—I'll really scream my outrage at
what's been done to us. It'll be a cover-up for new activities
and changes around the yard. The first order of business, naturally, will be to find that drive and get it installed aboard either
Owl or *Pussycat*. That'll be pretty much up to Franz. But he's

also going to have to recruit one or two helpers who won't be frightened by the thought of starships. We'll need steady, solid men—and women—but with imagination, the kind of people who'd have jumped at the chance to sail to the Indies with Columbus, or round the world with Drake, or down into the sea's dark depths with Captain Nemo. You'll find lots of them who are already interested—members of the L-5 Society, for example. I doubt if we'll ever be able to set up actual manufacturing ourselves, but if there's time, we'll try. But we're going to be busy, busy, busy from now on."

4

WE TOOK FRANZ ANDRADI home with us, more so that he and I could have a chance to talk than anything else. I could see that he wasn't quite his usual effervescent self, and when we'd settled down over a round of drinks it all came spilling out. Hadn't Saul been taking a hell of a chance, making all those copies and passing them around like that? And where the hell *had* he hidden the extra drive? And now that we'd had a chance to think about it, weren't we really taking on a terrible responsibility, making the decision to turn the human race loose on the Galaxy—to say nothing of the dangers to the race itself?

"Saul," I told him, "isn't an undercover, Frederick Forsyth type. Though he's supposed to have had a high clearance somewhere along the line, he isn't even what you could call a security type. He's eccentric, to put it mildly. But we must admit he's not done too badly up to now. Would you have thought up that pretty little caper with the Boy Scout? Would I? We'll protect our copies. Perhaps Laure's and mine can be reduced to microdots, but you'll need yours to work with. We'll see tomorrow. Anyhow—" I grinned as cheerfully as I could, "— we still aren't helpless. The Big Purge won't come till the next election. There's only one thing that really worries me—"

Then I told him about Whalen Borg. "Right now, we don't really know how much clout he has, or what facilities. I'm going to see what I can learn from Garvey, in NavIntel—after all, he just about owes the admiral his career."

Janet, tired now, made us another round and said good night, telling me not to be too long.

"And what about the destiny of the human race?" Franz asked. "Are we the people to decide?" He grinned, twisting his moustache savagely. "Naturally, *I'm* sure we are but some folks might wonder."

"What has the race done to its destiny already?" I asked. "Breeding itself out of existence, eating itself out of existence, bleeding the precious earth that nourished it, burning up irreplaceable metals, minerals, petrochemicals, fouling the air, fouling the lakes and seas? And if we don't make the decision, now that we have the power, who *will?* Good Ol' Breck and his puppeteers? The executioners in the Kremlin? Some hideous murdering little dictator in what Eleanor Roosevelt would have called an *emerging* country, sucking up to both sides for weaponry?"

"'Ear! 'Ear!" Franz cried, exuberant again.

"And as for the perils of the planets, and the dangers of vasty space—well, they shouldn't deter us any more than the dangers of the deep deterred those Chinese navigators who crossed over to the coast of South America, or the Vikings who made their icy way to Vinland, or St. Brendan in his boat of skins. They, too, faced the unknown—unknown lands, unknown seas and spaces, unknown beings, unknown diseases. And they didn't have instant computer analysis of any and every antagonistic chemical and hostile organism. Nor did they have computer-enhanced syntheses of almost instant agents to counter any one of them. Back in the eighties, I'd have said *no* myself. But not now. The human race has the right to risk its lives, the right to venture freely, the right to escape the suicide of the world!"

"You should've been half-Magyar, just like me!" cried Franz admiringly. "I drink to you. Perhaps we can make you an honorary one."

"That would be nice," I told him; and a few minutes later I saw him off to bed, thinking that at least I had been able to cheer *him* up a little bit.

I myself was by no means as certain as I had sounded. I sat down and poured myself a double brandy. I had been Navy all my adult life—never doubting where my duty lay. And yet the Constitution of the United States—that Constitution I had sworn to defend against all enemies domestic and foreign—was already almost a dead letter; after the next election it would have no more weight or substance than a pricked balloon. And yet—I sat there, wondering how many Reichswehr officers had thought such thoughts when Hitler first took power, how many Austrian officers had thought them at the *Anschluss*. I picked up the envelope Saul had marked for me.

At the very top was a letter addressed, in Saul's erratic hand, to *Commodore Cormac*. I opened it.

Dear Commodore, I know you're not a commodore, and *you* know you're not a commodore, because the Navy hasn't had the sense to retain that splendid, picturesque, historic rank. But I will confer the title on you because I love you (fraternally, in case some nasty minded busybody should see this letter).

Very well, beloved brother, if you're doing what I strongly suspect you are, wrestling with your commodorish (commodorian?) conscience, let Gentle Saul offer you good advice:

Don't.

Geoff, I have made enough copies of my work to ensure that it will eventually be disseminated to the entire world whether Laure publishes or not. So giving a set to You-know-who would only do our poor old world much harm. All *they* will see in my device will be a superweapon, and if they had the wit and will and decency to use it decisively to set up a civilized world order—if, instead of Good Ol' Breck, their leader were Winston Churchill or even Napoleon Bonaparte—then I myself would give it to them with my blessings.

But, Geoff, they aren't. It would be the "secret of the atom bomb" all over again—only how much worse?

I know what Franz believes. I'm sure that Auntie Laure agrees with him and me. And I'm betting that you will, too. So here's your set of plans for Gilpin's Galactic Star-Drive.

Lovingly,
Saul

PS: I've sold Franz my old Dodge van, but he doesn't know it yet. It's in its usual spot back of the machine shop, where you untidy people keep things like broken-down forklifts. The papers are all dated six weeks ago, and he's just been too busy to change the registration, in case anybody asks. I told Keithy to leave them with Mrs. Rasmussen—also the keys.

I frowned, puzzled. Saul was bound to do things in a Saulish way, but—

Then, abruptly, I understood, and I knew where we would find the extra drive Saul had made for us.

I put Saul's papers back into their envelope—I wouldn't have understood them anyway—and for another half-hour I sat there weighing and balancing the odds. Even if we could keep it secret, the elections would be our absolute cutoff date, with perhaps a breathless week or two afterward—the time the IPP might need to make sure all heads had rolled. Meanwhile, we still could count on friends—patriotic and powerful friends—both in the Pentagon and in the Congress. We probably could still count, if not on the friendship, at least on the dispassionate honesty of some of the high courts. If our luck held.

When Janet, who had been wakeful waiting for me, came in and told me that I was much too tired to think, I kissed her and let her lead me off to bed; and, when I tried to tell her what was in my mind, she shushed me with a finger on my lips, and smiled, and I realized that she knew as well as I. Just before she turned out the light, she gave me an envelope and two keys on a ring. "From Mrs. Rasmussen," she told me. "She seemed to think you'd be expecting them."

I drove Franz down to the yard after an early breakfast during which I broke the news to him about the van. It was a lovely day, cool and clear, unsullied by smog and with the fresh smell of the sea in the air. On the way to the parking lot, we glanced at *Owl* and *Pussycat,* now almost ready for their sea-trials, moored securely to their pier with only the eerie space where *Cupid's Arrow* had once been between them. All three had been designed for maritime archaeology and salvage, for not-too-deep exploration, for search and rescue, but though basically they were sister-ships, each had her minor variations. *Owl* was conspicuous for her manipulators—great lobster claw-like servos with which she could cut into steel deck-plating or tear an ancient oaken hull apart to pilfer a single coin from whatever treasure it contained. They fascinated Dan Kellett, who several times had asked permission to try them out, and had always come ashore grinning happily and saying they made him feel like a super sea monster. *Owl* also had pressure hatches which could give birth to armored divers and draw them in again.

With more observation ports in her ship-wide control tower than either of her sisters, she was a many-eyed creature which could see everything—around, before, behind.

Now I saw her, not on the ocean floor, but on the strange surface of an unknown world, extruding instruments to test its atmosphere, fingers to seize its life forms for examination— those that didn't seem too likely to seize back—and finally, men to prove its hospitality or enmity. I saw her swimming, swift and solitary, in deep space, the stars instead of starfish in her eyes.

That was when I first understood that, inevitably, some of us were going to become astronauts—true *astronauts*. To Franz I said, "We're going to have to start picking crews—one to start with. Probably for *Owl*."

"*Owl* looks like the better bet," he answered; and I knew that the same thoughts had been running through his mind. "I'd say Tammy Uemura for a starter, definitely. I've been drinking with him and playing go and chess with him for a year, so I know how he thinks—and his wife, too, which is something else to think about. Then there's Jamie Macartney, but we'd have to get him back from Ireland. He's as solid as Tammy, and he's a genius at planning for the unexpected."

"Which is something we're really liable to need."

"Like never before!"

As I did every morning, I drove slowly through the yard. Saul's old Dodge was parked in the messy lot behind the machine shop, as he said it would be, between a disabled pickup and a rig I didn't even recognize. When it was new, Saul had had it gaily painted with curlicues and diddlies. Now it was ancient and dusty and scarred with souvenirs of his dreadful driving. There were two ragged stickers on the rear bumper:
EAT AMERICAN LAMB—TWENTY MILLION COYOTES CAN'T BE WRONG
and

LEMMINGS OF THE WORLD—U
N
I
T
E
!

"There's your new car," I told Franz. "After a bit, why don't you wander down this way, look things over at the shop, and then casually take possession?" I handed over the papers and the keys. "If, as I suspect, it's full of all sorts of interesting gadgets, just drive it over to the warehouse loading bay. I'll join you there."

At the office, we told Laure about it, then waited half an hour. Finally, Franz went off, stopping to board both *Owl* and *Pussycat* for his regular nukepak inspections on the way, then taking a look-see through the shop. We saw him get into the van and, with what seemed to be a lot of backfiring and smog-making, started what remained of its engine. He waved cheerfully to a couple of the hired hands as he backed it jerkily off the lot and headed for the warehouse.

I met him there, and waited while he let the engine gasp itself to death. The warehousemen were all inside the building, and no other vehicles were in the bay.

"Well?" I said.

He was wrestling his moustache in his excitement. "It's full of stuff!" He pointed back over his shoulder. "Cartons. One of 'em says its a Sears-Roebuck freezer, but I don't believe it—it's just about the right size and shape for Saul's drive. Then there are three or four more, one squarish and the rest wide and flat or flat and long. What do you want done with 'em?"

"Let's get them aboard *Owl* as soon as possible. Is there anything more ready to load on her today?"

"There's always something. Shall I ask the warehouse foreman?"

"Do that, Franz. I think there's still some of her galley equipment to go aboard, so I guess the freezer carton will be especially plausible. Get two or three of the men to help you move it, and if they get curious tell them some damn fool of a truck driver dumped it at the office. I'll join you on *Owl* when the job's been done."

"Where on *Owl* do you want it?"

"In the galley. Obviously. Besides, it's just forward of the engine room and under the command center."

I walked back to the office as casually as I could, and presently I heard Saul's van snorting and farting its way out to the pier.

We watched the unloading with a little apprehension, Laure and I, wishing the warehousemen hadn't had to be brought in, wondering if any of the cartons would treacherously break open, and congratulating ourselves that nothing, not even the freezer carton, turned out to be too heavy to move by muscle power and a large dolly. It took only twenty minutes—very long ones—after which Franz locked up *Owl* and drove the men back to their jobs.

Presently he joined us, and he and I walked back to *Owl*—walked when what we wanted to do was cover the distance in one leap. Laure, smiling, had shaken her head at our suggestion that she come with us. "It'd be too conspicuous after all the activity," she said. "Besides, I can wait. Women are so much more patient."

We boarded *Owl*, locking the entry hatch behind us. We went down to the galley. Franz had left the lights on, and there the cartons were.

"Which one first, Commander?"

"The freezer," I replied.

It looked new, as though it never had been opened—and for a moment I wondered whether Saul was playing a gigantic practical joke on us. I watched Franz taking out the heavy staples with a pry-bar, ripping the thick cardboard open.

It was not a freezer. It was exactly what Saul had said it would be—about five feet by three by two, fabricated of dull gray metal, with eight massive terminals and a score of smaller ones glaring from a deep recess along its top.

"That's *it!*" Franz cried.

"And what's *that?*" I pointed to one of Saul's big manila envelopes scotch-taped beside the terminals.

Franz pulled it off, took out a thirty-page computer printout. I read over his shoulder:

OWNER'S MANUAL
*Instructions for the Simple Installation
and Everyday Operation of Your New
Gilpin Star-Drive*

Then,
Dear Consumer (it began),
You are now the fortunate possessor of a genuine Gilpin Star-Drive. In installing and operating it you must observe certain precautions:
1. You must *not* install it in any vessel not designed expressly for extended undersea operation—motor cruis-

ers, fishing trawlers, campers, destroyers, or whatever.
The results would be disastrous.
2. Because of Mr. Gilpin's unique abilities, you must
follow his instructions *to the letter*. (If you fail to understand any of the terms he uses, look them up in a good
dictionary.)

Franz grinned at me. "He isn't giving us too much credit
for intelligence."

"He's crediting us with a Gilpinesque sense of humor. Let's
keep going—a few more insults aren't going to hurt us."

3. Please understand that Mr. Saul Gilpin, as a mere
child, learned to speak (and to think in) the Hopi language
before he even began to prattle English. That is why no
one else can understand his view of the Universe and of
the Natural Laws said to govern it. Therefore:
4. You must NEVER attempt to repair or *in any way*
adjust your Gilpin Star-Drive. It is warranteed *never* to
require repair or adjustment, and is so perfectly designed
that it can readily be installed with a few simple tools
by any home handyman or nuclear engineer—

"Ouch!" said Franz.
"Hush! There's more to come."

These features have been adhered to throughout, so that
anyone who has ever run an outboard motorboat can
supervise its practical operation. (Former naval officers,
however, are warned that they should read this handbook
with special care. The Navy way so often just isn't the
right way.)

"Shall I say *ouch* for you?" offered Franz.
"You shall not. Saul may have a point there. But before we
dig any further into Saul's verbosities, let's sit down."
We pulled two chairs up to a galley table and went through
the rest of Saul's Owner's Manual hastily. He had thought
everything out clearly, and beautifully. The first thing we learned
was that the other three cartons, completely forgotten in our
excitement, contained the computer elements he had designed

to mate into the ship's ordinary computer system, extending many of its functions and performing others it never could perform. He also pointed out that, because computers were by no means as perfect as Gilpin Star-Drives, he was providing us with a superfluity of spares just in case.

Finally we came to the section on actual operation, light-heartedly headed: *AND AWAY WE GO!*

1. The Gilpin Star-Drive transfers your vessel and all it may contain (including you) into another aspect of our Universe. It will appear to you, not that the normal Universe has ceased to exist, but that it has died suddenly and that you are now seeing, all around you, its very tenuous ghost. There will be no real light as we know it, but you will see the ever-present ghosts of sunlight (when you're close enough), of moonlight, of starlight, of every nebula and galaxy. You will be in a ghost-universe. (The Hopi, God bless them, would understand. How else do you think kachinas travel?)

2. In this ghost-universe, where you will seem to be the only real and living things, there will be no gravity as we know it, but there will be the ghost of gravity, and it is this ghost that your Gilpin Star-Drive and its computer will sense even when you cannot, so that you may traverse the ghost-distances between star and star.

3. *Attendez, mes enfants!* Distance is not a function of "empty space," for if there were such a thing as truly *empty* space, it would be non-dimensional. No, distance is a function of the forces of which space is woven. In Gilpin's Space, these forces are mere ghosts. In its drive mode, your space-driver can and will perceive these ghosts and respond to them, so that you will never have to run the risk of transferring into normal space at any dangerous speed.

4. Your Gilpin Space-Drive's several modes are:

  a. Primary warm-up. (This is the mode Franz has witnessed.)

  b. Idling.

  c. Transfer, which is almost instantaneous.

  d. Drive: forward, left, right, "up" and "down," and what for lack of a better term we can call braking or reverse. When the ghost-forces do not dictate otherwise, you will have full control over your vessel's speed. Gravity, *in* your vessel, will remain at one-half Earth-normal at all times (a service no other star-drive can provide).

  e. Retransfer mode, which throws your vessel back into normal space.

Ashamed at keeping Laure waiting, we leafed through the rest of it: detailed instructions for installing the drive and its computers—the drive in a compartment somebody had thoughtfully engineered into the forward bulkhead of the ship's engine room; the computers in the control center, where there was just enough room for them.

Finally, I put it all back in its envelope. "Let's go back and show it to the Boss Lady," I said. "If she's mad at us, I don't blame her."

"I have the damnedest feeling," Franz answered as he locked up *Owl* behind us, "that none of us is going to waste any time getting mad at one another. Tammy Uemura and I can get that drive in and fastened down in half a day, I *think,* and I'll bet the computers won't be more difficult. We'd better fly Macartney over."

My mind threw questions at me as we walked. What preparations do you make for a sudden star flight? How do you provision your ship? What about simple things—like nuts and bolts? What about weapons? I thought of all the lurid covers on years of science-fiction magazines and paperbacks. What about stored information—science and technology, music and art and literature, all inherited treasures of our past?

I said, "We'll get Macartney. I'll phone Ireland and tell him he's being promoted because Laure's changing company policy, and to get his tail over here as fast as possible."

Then I began to wonder how big a crew we'd really need. Though *Owl* and *Pussycat* and *Cupid's Arrow* could each sleep fourteen or more comfortably, Saul hadn't hesitated to put to sea—or put to space—with, unless he had left some out in the telling, a complement of only four.

When we got back to the office, Laure had scarcely missed us.

"We're getting Saul's material ready for publication," she told us. "Some of it's going to be on paper, but most of it'll be computerized—sent out on satellite autofax. And we're going to make sure of total international news coverage. Trying to stop it is going to be like trying to kill dandelions or starlings. I'm pretty sure the way I've set it up is foolproof, and anyway, Saul says he's made enough copies to make sure it'll come out no matter what."

"I know," I said, and wondered for a second whether he'd told us that just to make sure none of us would ever rat out to the IPP.

Then I told her about the equipment Saul had given us, and what Franz had said about getting it installed.

Laure gave it thirty seconds' thought. "Very well, Franz can get hold of Tammy Uemura, and you two can brief him. Then they can set to work. As soon as all that stuff's out of *Owl*'s galley and installed, we can finish up what's to be done on both *Owl* and *Pussycat*. There's still quite a bit to be loaded before their final trials, and we will have to get Macartney over right away. Don't forget—it's not just a matter of setting ourselves up with our private lifeboat..."

No one commented. We all knew that the term was apt.

"... We'll also have to get things started so that any general exploitation of Saul's material will be as simple and certain as possible. He's actually included a list of firms that built the individual pieces of the drive to his instructions, and another list of the cover descriptions—very ingenious ones—he used so that they'd not suspect what they were making. There's nothing more believable than the rich, oddball inventor of a perpetual motion machine! And once the cat is out of the bag, *any* information is going to be a help to star-drive builders. In the meantime, we'll give it out that something's wrong with *Owl*'s power plant—that'll explain Franz and his friends' backing and forthing. What are you going to do, Geoff?"

I told her I was going to get in touch with one or two Navy friends, like Garvey, to get a line on what Borg might be up to, and, in a pinch, see what help we might expect.

What the impact of instantly available star-drives on the world would be was simply mind-boggling, but that was not central to my worries. First, we had to get our own escape vehicle ready against the odds. How much might Whalen Borg suspect? How much might he already have found out? Yes, we could count on Franz, on Tammy Uemura, on Macartney and Dan Kellett, on Janet, and of course on Rhoda—unless a cunning enemy found points of vulnerability. But how could we be sure of other wives and other girlfriends, of bosom friends and beloved relatives? Just the fear of a star voyage might be enough to purchase our betrayal, let alone the rewards the betrayer could expect from the Individualist People's Party.

I sought out Dan, and gave him the whole picture; and he—bless him! gave me common sense. "Commander," he said, "just leave the local security end up to me. You're going to have enough to do, what with planning and coordinating—and practicing how to be a spaceship skipper."

5

I DON'T KNOW how Franz broke the news to Tammy Uemura, but he told me later that they were at work on *Owl* within an hour. They let the word get out that she'd been having trouble with her nukepak, so no one asked questions when the preparatory work aboard her was suspended. I myself took Dan's advice. I knew how to get through to Garvey and one or two others who were sure, for the time being, at least, to have protected phones; and the office phone of a retired CPO, Paddy Garrison, an old friend of the admiral's now happily running a raunchy bar, gave me just what I wanted. He and I had four or five drinks together; then he went out to keep an eye on his topless-bottomless hired help. I made my calls collect, knowing that the phone company's records would be blank where Garvey's number was concerned.

"It's about the monster," I told him. "He's surfaced, and he's zeroing in on Laure."

"No surprise," he answered. "I read the papers. That sub of yours disappearing was made to order for that bastard. He's been looking for any way to get back at the admiral—you know it; I know it. Okay, I'll tell you what I can . . ."

He made it short and simple. Whalen Borg was very close to the top echelon of the IPP—but his position was precarious. Two men were struggling for second-place supremacy in the party: "Ham" Smithfield, who was Good Ol' Breck's Secretary of Defense, and Mort Marrone, who wanted to be. Smithfield had been Breck's buddy since the beginning, but for an IPP honcho he was cautious and pretty colorless, and lately Marrone, who headed a barely legal outfit called Individual Activists—funny uniforms and all—had been coming up fast. The word was out that before long there'd be a showdown. "And when that happens," Garvey told me, "chances are the loser's going down the drain like Herr Roehm—you've heard of him? Anyhow, Borg is Marrone's boy, and he's been promised— among other things—that if his boss gets Defense he'll be back in uniform with all honors and his fourth stripe at least. At *least*, Geoff. Just what this Navy needs."

"*Jesus!*" I said.

"Exactly. For now, and as long as this Marrone-Smithfield thing is up for grabs, he'll probably be on sort of a tight leash— if he tries anything too raw, it'll be on his own hook. But if Smithfield tumbles, that'll be a different matter. Some other big wheels—Interior, for one, and the Attorney General—are going to tumble with him, and then Marrone and his faction will be in with all four feet. They won't even wait till the elections before they start. There'll be nothing left holding Borg. And I mean *nothing*."

"You'll let us know at the first rumble?"

"At the first whisper," he promised me; and I thanked him and hung up, praying that "Ham" Smithfield would live and prosper and confound his enemies—at least his enemies in the IPP.

After that, I called one or two other old friends, and heard pretty much the same story. Then I drove back to the yard, and told Laure and Dan and Rhoda what I'd learned. "At least we may have a little warning if and when."

Laure smiled. "Geoff, it's good to know, but we can't count on it. Let's just pretend we don't have *any* friends, and keep things rolling as fast as possible. Then, if Borg strikes suddenly and we're warned in time, fine—and if not, well, we won't feel our legs have been kicked out from under us."

"Yes, Auntie Laure." I laughed and so did she. "Sorry you caught me whistling in the dark."

The next few days were busy ones—busy without a letup, and strangely schizoid. We knew—we felt it in our bones—that we were going to have a starship, that the fetters which had for so long bound man to Earth would at last be broken. But still it all seemed utterly unreal, like the first terrible hours of an unexpected war. That evening, at Laure's place, we again held council, and it was decided that first, *Pussycat* be prepared for sea as fast and inconspicuously as possible; second, that we pick a crew for her—a crew to whom we would tell nothing, not right now, but one that at least might be a good bet to pick up where we'd left off if, somehow, Borg did stop us or if we were forced to flee prematurely to the stars in *Owl*. Her captain had already been selected—Steve Placek, a hell of a good man, now several years with the firm. Names were suggested and considered, one or two of Dan's boys, one or two engineers, a computer specialist, a couple of college friends of Franz's who were deeply into the space thing. We didn't go so far as to choose them then, but we felt that we were getting some-where; and we did decide—or at least Laure decided—that *Pussycat* would be put to sea at least a day or two before the work on *Owl* was finished.

"Then," she said, "if she gets back while *Owl* is gone, she can take *Owl*'s mooring, and anyone sneaking around will be hard put to tell which is which unless he's familiar with both of them. A little confusion never hurt anyone."

Next day Jamie Macartney arrived, a short, freckled, de-ceptively tubby Scot of the type you sometimes see beating the devil out of a great drum in a Highland band, and Laure and I met him at the airport. "Of course, I heard about poor old Saul vanishing," he said. "You don't mind if I say I don't believe a word of it? I suppose the man's invented something horrifying. Is it a time-machine? No? Well, how about a matter synthesizer—you know, free roasts of beef out of the waste-compactor? Shall I go on?"

"None of those," Laure told him, "but it's just as startling."

"So that's why I'm over here so suddenly?"

"Right on, Jamie," I said. "Saul has indeed invented some-thing. He's given us a starship, using a drive no one else in the world can understand, and we're hustling like the devil to keep our Darth Vaders from getting hold of it."

"And succeeding, I expect," Macartney didn't bat an eye. "Well, if it's astronauts you want—First Contact, Earthman's Burden types—I'm your man, and I've a wife, a teenage boy, two girls, and two fat British cats, all as mad as I am. When do we start? I suppose you realize that star travel has to be a family affair? Can't start civilization with a crew of—forgive my saying so—San Francisco lads. No offense intended."

"Nor taken," I replied, laughing. "But Jamie, please try to understand—we're *serious*."

"My God, man! So am *I*."

That kind of vote of confidence does something for one. I told him what I could, and after we had dropped his luggage at Laure's apartment, he insisted on going directly to the yard, where it took him only minutes to bid us farewell and join Franz and Tammy in *Owl*'s innards.

We went directly to the office, where we found Rhoda hard at work on the preparatory program. Saul had outlined—what to publish, when to publish, where to keep it hidden till it was time to publish. Saul had even left orders, under his perpetual-motion-inventor cover name, for the drive components for *Pussycat*, which was nice to know because by this time we were all convinced she'd need them.

We worked. We chose the crew for *Pussycat*, bearing in mind not only their ability, but also the strong possibility that they, too, would become astronauts—and that they might be subjected to threats and temptations and even direct peril from the IPP. Star flight was a subject that still seemed totally unreal to me; I had to tell myself that it could quite safely remain unreal until the drive now being installed in *Owl* had been tried out. It was Macartney who wisely pointed out that, given everything Saul had promised us, there was no reason why we had to abandon Earth completely—at least the first time out. We could return. From Gilpin's Space, we could set *Owl* down anywhere, on land or sea. If there were supplies we thought it would be indiscreet to buy openly in the United States, he could arrange to purchase them in the U.K. or Ireland. He and his brother, Alec, owned a ketch together, a forty-footer, and we could rendezvous at sea and transfer everything. He grinned. "When you pick up my family and me," he said.

And that brought up another question. A nukepak doesn't last forever. At sea, it's good for perhaps three years of more or less steady cruising, but we had yet to discover how long it might last in space. It would be neccessary either to carry one or two spares aboard, or else have them stashed away where we could return and pick them up without anyone being the wiser. Saul had assured us that there was no way the powers that be could detect us once we were in Gilpin's Space, but what would they be able to do a year from now, or three, or five—after the whole world had his plans?

We worked, and the days flew by. By the afternoon of the third, Franz reported jubilantly that he and Tammy and Macartney had completed the installation of *Owl*'s drive and computer complex. It's a poor engineer who can't handle his own tools, and they had been able to do all the work themselves, not needing to call in outside help. I went aboard. The drive was completely out of sight in its compartment off the power area. The new computers were installed, two extra seats in front of them, next to the ship's basic computer in the control area. Their several screens were dark, their displays dull and dead. But Tammy and Macartney were waiting there eagerly. I saw that Saul's assembly manual, now well thumbed, was much in evidence.

Franz pointed proudly to one panel of displays. "It tells us how far we are from any object we designate in normal space— any object we're headed for, any on which we might be planning to set down, or any that might be heading toward us." He turned it on, and the displays glowed: *0, 0, 0, 0.* "Right now, it's concerned only with the set-down part. We're down, and it tells us so. Would you believe that the topmost line reads in centimeters, the next in meters, and the one below that in kilometers?"

"And those bottom three?" I asked.

"The first two—" He paused for effect. "—the first two, Commander, read in light-minutes and light-years, and the third—well, I don't yet know *what* it reads in. All I know is that Saul has it labeled *For Extra-Galactic Use Only.*" He saw the look on my face. "There's more coming," he told me gleefully, as another display lit up. "That one tells us our acceleration in G's—Saul says in pseudo-G's because there's only the ghost of gravity in Gilpin's Space; and the one next to it informs us how fast we're going at any given instant. It has six different readout values, corresponding, so Saul says, to those on the distance readouts. We gather that there's just no limit to how fast we can go, except that when we get too close to objects in normal space, the drive and its field take over, and we are decelerated automatically."

He showed me the drive controls, and even though I had read what Saul had to say, I still was astounded at their simplicity. UP—DOWN. FORWARD—REVERSE. LEFT—RIGHT. "Those are just the manual ones," Franz said. "You set the incrementals on the computer or, if you forget to, it'll do it for you, keeping within safe limits. You set the modes manually, too. Look: OFF. ON. IDLE. And GILPIN'S SPACE. That's the spooky one. When you touch down, you reverse the procedure, but you have to be down to do it. It won't work when you're moving. Well, shall I turn it on?"

"You mean *now?*"

They all laughed. "Yes, indeed," Macartney answered, "we've had it on three times already without going anywhere, just like warming up your engine in the morning. But watch the power it gobbles. You'll be impressed."

Franz turned it on. Nothing happened. There was not a quiver, not a sound. But the dials that told us what power the nukepak was turning out swung over till they hit their pins, and stayed there.

"My God Almighty, where's it *going?*"

"We think it's flowing into Gilpin's Space," said Tammy, "and it sort of scares me to think that if Franz throws that next switch we'll be flowing with it. You never can tell about these mad Magyars."

6

LATER THAT DAY, I sent Dan over for a demonstration, but both Laure and Rhoda said they'd wait, Laure having pointed out that we'd be sensible to avoid anything that looked like a special Ladies' Day aboard *Owl*, especially after having publicized the ship's alleged nukepak troubles. But she ordered *Pussycat* to be ready to put to sea for her tests, fully provisioned, within forty-eight hours, and had Rhoda notify the friendlier members of the media. "We'll emphasize *Pussycat*'s research and recovery functions," she declared, "and let them know again how the conglomerates stole *Cupid's Arrow* because they thought we'd made a major breakthrough in drive design. We'll let a few reporters come aboard, just to show them that even though our vessels are superior there's nothing worth stealing a whole ship for."

"And *Owl?*" I asked.

"*Owl* will be off-limits, naturally. After nukepak troubles, any ship is. We'll tell them we still don't have it completely ironed out."

"We're damn lucky," I told her, "that the conglomerates pulled the Coast Guard's fangs where it comes to inspecting merchant vessels. If this had happened back in the seventies or eighties, we'd have them swarming over us. Then where would we be?"

She patted my hand maternally. "Not in Gilpin's Space, Geoff, not anywhere near it. As matters stand, maybe we can do most of our loading and provisioning without exciting too much undue interest. I hope we can. Let's get together again this evening and see what sort of lists everyone comes up with. I've thought of food and water and star charts, weapons, medicines—that's going to be your Janet's department, isn't it?— whatever lab equipment you can think of, a basic scientific and cultural library, not just computerized but also books, and music and—oh, one could go on forever, couldn't one?"

I reminded her of what Macartney had said about our not being cut off from Earth entirely.

"Perhaps that's true," she answered. "But it may not be. You may be able to scuttle back to Earth as easily and as often as you want, but let's not rely on it. The first thing the IPP's going to do—and the Russians, too—is try to develop a Gilpin's drive detector. Wait and see. Let's make *Owl* as self-sufficient as we can."

Everything went well—perhaps, I thought, a bit too well. One of Dan's boys found a bug newly installed on one of the warehouse phones; it was where it could easily have been placed by any one of a hundred deliverymen. Besides that, several of us had the feeling that occasionally somebody'd been tailing us, but we never caught them at it, and were never sure. In any case, none of it really smelled like Whalen Borg.

Then, the day before *Pussycat*'s maiden voyage, Dan told me that Rhoda's brother was back pestering her.

"Mooching again?" I asked.

"No, and that's what sort of worries me. He seems pretty flush—new clothes, flashy new car, so she tells me—and he swears all he wants to do is kiss and make up. 'Let's take in a show like when we were kids,' all that sort of thing. That's not like Arley. Now his latest notion is he wants Rhoda to go to some kind of birthday party he's cooking up for Grandma, and I've been trying to talk her out of it. The old gal lives a hundred miles away—a retirement community near that Salt-marsh development, which means Rhoda'd probably have to stay the night. Do you suppose Borg's people and the IPP could be pulling Arley's strings?"

I didn't think it likely. Arley was certainly a punk, but he rated zero for reliability and I'd never have put him down as a hit-man type. "It seems to me, Dan, that they could think up half a hundred better ways to go about it."

"I hope you're right, Commander. I've been doing everything I can to make sure Borg's people don't get to her, either through Arley or any other way. I—I guess you know I've moved in with her?" To my surprise, he blushed beet-red, something I didn't know ex-Marines could do. "I—I guess we'd better not say anything—that is, I mean, to Mrs. Endicott?"

"Our Mrs. Endicott," I told him, "is a very sophisticated,

very kindly, very compassionate person. The fact that she is older than you or me doesn't mean she doesn't know that men and women who love each other frequently sleep together. I'm sure her only reaction would be to wish you well, and perhaps hint gently that she'd be generous with a wedding present. As to the Arley business, why don't you drive her to her grandmother's, stay the night in a motel, and bring her back the next day? If she won't hold still for that, you can follow her and keep an eye on things from behind the bushes. If I can't come with you, you can take one of the company cars and any of the boys you can trust with something all that personal."

"Well, first I'll try again to talk her out of it. She knows that anybody might have enough on Arley, what with his drugs and dirty little deals, to foreclose on his soul anytime they want to, but she still says he never, never, *never* would hurt *her.*"

"What day's this birthday party scheduled for?"

"Saturday—next Saturday, that is."

"Well, that gives us at least a little time to think about it. Today's only Tuesday, and *Pussycat*'s first run starts tomorrow. We're planning to have her back by Friday, and as of now Friday night's set for *Owl*'s first flight. I suppose flight *is* the right word?"

A chill went through me at all the word's implications; and little problems like Rhoda's brother Arley suddenly seemed utterly insignificant by comparison.

They shouldn't have. I should have remembered that there are two ways to procure effective service even from men as chickenshit as Arley. One is by offering huge rewards. The other is by instilling sheer terror. Whalen Borg knew how to use both.

Pussycat put to sea on the Wednesday morning, seen off by a few friendly media people, a few not so friendly, and the wives and girlfriends of her small crew. As we expected with Steve Placek in command, all went well. She performed beautifully, on the surface and submerged, attained speeds a bit higher than expected, and set a record for the efficient use of power. Steve's reports came right on schedule; and on Thursday afternoon he topped them off by locating and identifying, at a depth of half a mile, the wreck of a paddlewheel steamer, *Narwhal,* which had gone down in the 1860s and was reputed to have carried a probably mythical vast sum in minted gold. It was beautiful publicity, and a personal triumph for him, for he had been digging into the old records for years to get a line on where she lay. We, of course, were pleased, but we weren't excited. A living starship fired our imaginations—yes, and our fears— far more than any long-dead vessel, regardless of her treasure trove.

Supplies—everything we could think of—were now being delivered constantly to *Owl*; and we announced that, after *Pussycat*'s return and *Owl*'s own shakedown cruise, we were planning to send both ships out on a major salvage expedition— destination undisclosed, but very far away. That way, a lot could be loaded openly which might otherwise have been questioned. There were a lot of things, too, that we sneaked aboard, either personally or in closed cartons: Franz Andradi's Celestron telescope (because we simply didn't want anyone even to think of stars where *Owl* was concerned), and far more of a reference library than a ship of her size usually carries, and even a partially dismantled light four-wheel-drive vehicle. Laure paid for all of it, using her personal funds where that was preferable; yard money where it didn't matter. Macartney had reserved air passage back to Ireland for Saturday, as soon after the tryout as possible, and we had worked up a list of stuff to be procured overseas, which he'd already sent on to his brother: scientific instruments, more medical supplies, communications equipment useful only on dry land, cold weather clothing, and a miscellany of other things which would have seemed wildly improbably as equipment for any submarine.

"We can do it," he told us. "Alec's an accomplished scrounger. But there's one thing we'll have to remember. According to your friend Gentle Saul, there can be no communication with you once you're in Gilpin's Space. We'll have to wait till you're down. So we'd better set up our rendezvous where you can easily find us, and also where our lying off the coast for days will seem quite natural—somewhere, I'd say, where the fishing's good. Luckily, at this time of year, we probably won't have to worry where weather is concerned. With my wife and kids aboard, to say nothing of the cats, it'll look like a nice, lazy family party, in case anybody gets curious. Anyhow, Alec knows just about all the officialdom in those parts. Even when he comes back to port without us, he'll be believed when he tells everyone that we cruised down to Skerrytown and he dropped us all off there because you were transferring me to the States and it's closer to the airports."

Early Friday morning, right on schedule, *Pussycat* was back at her moorings, and Steve Placek, proud as punch, was showing the media folk pictures of what remained of *Narwhal's* hull and engines, and being photographed holding her bronze nameplate. (Next day, one of the IPP papers actually printed an editorial saying that petty salvage was a proper activity for wildcat enterprise to busy itself with, and that Mrs. Endicott was, for the first time in years, showing good sense and recognizing the hard technological and economic realities of the times.) Mrs. Endicott and I took Placek and his engineer to lunch, and promised them—feeling guilty because the promise might very well prove false—that the yard would throw a proper party to celebrate their achievement as soon as possible, but that we couldn't right away because I was going to take *Owl* out for her initial trials that evening. I explained that we had to be sure of her nukepak, and that we also wanted to check out her diving capabilities. It was a good time to do it because the workweek was over, and our being away wouldn't leave anybody idle.

After lunch, we drove back to the yard: Placek and the engineer to do their final checkup on *Pussycat,* Laure to her office, and I to join Franz and Tammy aboard *Owl,* where at least we could find enough to keep us busy and make the waiting until late afternoon less unbearable. I had decided not to start out till five or six at least, and of course not to dive until we were well out at sea. I wanted to be sure that, even when the time came to go into Gilpin's Space, even if first we had to dive and surface a dozen times, we would not be observed. Saul had made it clear that, though the shift could be made while we were on the surface of the sea, trying it submerged might be perilous. "Let's pray for fog," I said, "and for some nice dark clouds against the moon. I don't want a pretty little Coast Guard cutter seeing what Dan and Rhoda saw, and maybe even getting a photograph. I don't even want any crazy fisherman yelling he's seen the ghost of a submersible Flying Dutchman."

Against our urgings—for who had better right than she?— Laure refused to go. No, she had said, if she were seen it would be too much of a break with the established order, too conspicuous. Dan, too, when I came ashore to see if he was ready, had said he couldn't—there was no way he could leave Rhoda with the question of that damn party still unresolved.

"We can come later, Geoff," Laure said, seeing my disappointment. "Dan has to do what he thinks is right, and so do I." She smiled wonderfully. "But there's someone else who really wants to go."

"Who?" I asked.

"Go back to *Owl* and you'll find out. Somebody sneaked aboard while you were walking over. Franz phoned to tell me, but he made me promise not to tell."

I hurried back, trying all the way to guess. Was it Steve Placek, hungry for more adventure? Or some loyal employee bent on being of service? Or even Mrs. Rasmussen's Boy Scout grandson?

But it was none of them. It was, as I should have suspected, my Janet.

"You," I told her, "are supposed to be ashore practicing medicine."

She stood there in the galley, with Franz and Tammy pretending to protect her from my wrath, and laughed at me, and said, "Geoffrey Cormac, did you think for one moment that I'd let you go kiting off to strange planets and strange stars without me? I've read science-fiction magazines. I know what kind of females they have out there. So—"

"So-o?" I said.

"So I'm your ship's doctor, your ship's cook, and the official guardian of your morals if you decide to land on another world."

7

THERE WAS SOME overcast when we set out, a fresh wind from
the sea, and a very mild chop. As we pulled out into the channel,
a small Coast Guard cutter started tagging along, tactfully keeping half a mile or more behind, but still obviously following
us. We didn't watch her; there would've been no point to it—
and besides, we were too busy checking on *Owl*'s performance.
It took us three quarters of an hour to get to where I had planned
our first diving test. I saw a fog bank in the distance, and the
wind was right. I took *Owl* down, forcing myself through all
the prescribed routines to determine her behavior and seawor-
thiness submerged. It was perfect. After about twenty minutes,
we went up again and, breaking water, saw that the cutter was
still circling around, a little aimlessly, now perhaps three miles
away.

Both *Owl* and *Pussycat* had been designed for maximum
visibility down deep; their viewports would have been impossible fifteen or ten or even five years before because the technology for the perfect clarity, the immense strength, and
insensitivity to temperature changes simply hadn't existed.
Franz, who had gone through a phase of being an antique
railroad nut, had dubbed our control tower "the caboose." We
had a clear view forward and aft and to either side. It was
actually frightening until you got used to it, for duroquartz is
virtually invisible—you could hardly believe in its existence,
or that behind it you were safe from the tremendous pressures
doing their best to crush it and destroy you.

We dived six more times before we saw that the cutter had
given us up as a bad job, and was just slipping out of sight
around a distant headland. Night had fallen, but the moon was
up, almost at its full. The wind had freshened, and the fog
bank was almost over us.

I took her down once more, just for luck; and when we surfaced ten minutes later the thick fog, whitened by moonlight, held us in its arms.

We all looked at each other in utter silence—until I realized that it was now up to me to take that first step into the unknown, the impossible, the still-not-quite-believed.

"Well," I said, "let's get things started."

Franz sat down, taking a seat to the left of the computer console, where he had access to all the power controls. Feeling thoroughly unreal, even though we had rehearsed the procedure half a hundred times during the past three days, I sat down in the chair to his right—the navigational controls in front of me.

I watched Franz's fingers move; and the console told us that *Owl*'s conventional drive was off. They moved again, and the dials that told of the vast flow of energy in Saul's drive swung over steadily until they hit their pins.

Franz turned, pale as a ghost. "Ready, Commander?"

I nodded, not trusting myself to speak, and Franz touched the control labeled GILPIN'S SPACE.

For an instant, nothing seemed to happen. Then, so suddenly that it took me a moment to become fully aware of it, I felt as though I had been lifted in my seat—and I recalled Saul telling us that we would have half Earth-gravity.

Then, simultaneously, every light went out, the glowing computer displays dimmed, and a voice filled the room. We all recognized it immediately.

"This is a recording," it announced. "Have no fear! You are listening to the voice of your old friend, Soft-Hearted Saul, the Spaceman's Friend. Welcome to Gilpin's Space, which you—the as-yet-favored few—now share with me; my dear daughter, Polly Esther; her husband, Marco Guglielmi; two other very devoted couples whom we picked up on our way; and my own lovely wife, Lillian—to say nothing of myriads of weird alien creatures whom you do not yet know exist, but whose whispers we believe we may have heard. Well, we can all worry about *them* later. Now, for your welcome, I have arranged, as you have seen, for the lights to be turned out. That is so that you can go to your viewports and look out for the first time upon Gilpin's Space and all its wonders. I will say no more until you have had a chance to do so."

Janet laughed a little hysterically. If a man can chuckle

hysterically, that's what Franz did. Tammy Uemura uttered an expletive in Japanese.

Macartney was the calmest of us all. "Ah!" he remarked. "The man's just trying to make us feel at home. Let's take a look and see all that's so wonderful about it."

We moved up to the enormous viewports. We saw the sea. We saw the world. We saw the moon and stars. We saw the Universe. But this was not the Universe that we had known. This was its ghost—transparent, tenuous as a forgotten dream, but real, real, *real* with a reality none of us had seen before. In part at least, this was due to its clarity, every minute detail of every ghostly wavelet shown as though drawn in infinite microscopic detail by some supernatural Leonardo, every far ghostly star with its infinitesimal nimbus—of light? No, of light's ghosts. There were no colors there, only their memories, as though the entire spectrum had been reduced to specters scarcely seen but movingly remembered.

We stared, saying nothing. This was the Universe through which we'd move, the Universe that bridged the distances between the stars.

Overhead, the moon's thin spirit sailed the skies; and abruptly I realized the fog was gone, that fogs must be too wraithlike to have ghosts.

The light came on. "Thank you, ladies and gentlemen," Saul's voice said. "God bless you all."

"Let's go," said Macartney soberly; and that seemed to cover everything.

Franz and I took our seats again, now fully conscious of our much lighter weight.

"Watch at the ports," I told the others. "Tell me what you see."

Slowly, I moved the control that said UP, and felt nothing. Franz and I looked at each other. Then we looked at the display that read in meters: 243, it read.

"We've risen!" Janet cried out excitedly. "We . . . we're *flying*. We're above the sea!"

"Let's take her up to a thousand," I said to Franz, and he nodded.

A few seconds later, the display read 1003.

I tried the control that said FORWARD, and Tammy and Janet both reported that we were underway.

After that—well, for half an hour or so we were like a

young man trying out his first new car, seeing what it would do, putting it through its paces. Twice we touched down again on the surface of the sea. Once, at almost ten thousand meters, the computer seemed to slow us momentarily and we saw the ghost of what must have been a supersonic jet against the sky. I ordered the lights turned down again so we could see Gilpin's Space more clearly, and we headed south, following the eerie tracery of the coast against the even fainter ectoplasm of the sea. We looked down at what, in our segment of the Universe, was Mexico. Sharply, we turned north. The Rockies were like point lace under us. Our rates of acceleration and deceleration were absolutely unbelievable. So was the fact that we experienced none of their effects. Indeed, had it not been for our viewports and the glowing displays in front of us, we never would have known that we moved.

The realization hit us suddenly and simultaneously. What Saul Gilpin had given us was *real*. It was the ultimate in magic carpets. We could cross a continent in minutes—when we had scarcely *started* to accelerate. A mighty ocean was a frog-jump for us, nothing more. The great Earth itself was a mere pebble, to be glanced at and left behind. We were absolutely drunk with it, with the knowledge that now nothing, *nothing* stood between us and the beckoning stars, the calling galaxies.

Macartney went into the galley, Janet following him, and returned a moment later with five glasses and a bottle of fine brandy. "One round," he said triumphantly. "One only! We need no more."

Janet filled the glasses, and—one sip at a time—we toasted Saul, then *Owl*, then Gilpin's Space. Laughing, we toasted extraterrestrials everywhere. Finally, "To far journeys!" proposed Franz soberly; and "To new worlds, new homes!" I added, remembering what our purpose was.

I set *Owl* down again somewhere in the South Atlantic, just long enough to contact Dan, still on duty at the yard, by satellite phone.

"Well, *that's* a relief!" he said. "We were beginning to think *Owl* went down and didn't come back up."

"No, everything's all right," I told him, striving to keep my own excitement out of my voice, even though of course the call was scrambled. "*Owl*'s performance has been beyond all expectations—better than *Pussycat*'s, Dan, so much better that we've decided to keep on with the tests we'd planned for later."

"That means you'll be home late?"

"Right. How much later, I don't know yet. From the looks of things, I'd say—hell, it's just a guess, maybe twenty-four hours."

"Well, we won't keep dinner for you, but there'll be a welcoming committee. I'll get on the horn to Mrs. Endicott and let her know. I just wish I were with you people now, that's all."

He didn't try to talk us out of it, so I knew that Laure had left no instructions for us to hurry back. Anyhow, at that stage it would've been like trying to talk De Quincey out of an opium dream.

I broke off, and threw *Owl* back into Gilpin's Space as fast as possible.

"Let's shoot for the Moon," I said.

Nobody argued, so I took her up again—and the trip took us exactly twenty-seven minutes, including acceleration and deceleration, and these were automatic, by the book. The dead Moon's ghost was even stranger than the living Earth's, pallid and—even though in Gilpin's Space you always had the feeling that there was no true light—curiously translucent.

We circled slowly, gawking like tourists at that mysterious moonscape, filled with wonder but bored nonetheless because in the living Universe it was already dead. We looked at it, while eating sandwiches and drinking coffee.

And then—

Then we set out on tour of the solar system, the inner planets first, then the great outer giants, and finally, frozen Pluto— and they all were ghosts, insubstantial, nebulous. Even the great, glorious Sun, that roaring furnace which had fueled our lives, no longer warmed us. In Gilpin's Space, even though we could see hints of the turmoil in its corona, it was only a greater ghost among the lesser ones. And yet always, always there were those hints of colors that were not there, infinitely elusive, infinitely tantalizing.

Four times we set *Owl* down, *very* carefully, on alien soil. Twice on Mars—who could resist doing that?—where for a quarter-hour or so we shifted into normal space to look at Olympus Mons and the Valles Marineris, and again for a few minutes on a moon of Saturn's, then a moon of Jupiter's— mostly, I think, to remind ourselves that normal space still existed.

For Gilpin's Space was even stranger than we had first perceived. No matter what speed we had attained, we had observed no change in its persistent pseudolight.

Franz first commented on this. "So far, there seems to be no limit to our velocity. Our acceleration rate hasn't even started to level off. Of course, the distances we've covered are no great shakes astronomically, but still I'd have expected some spectroscopic evidence of motion."

"What makes you think *anything* in Gilpin's Space yields spectroscopic evidence?" said Tammy Uemura. "That's just not real light out there."

"Then what am I seeing with my eyes?" demanded Franz.

"Spooks," Tammy answered. "Remember all those UFO reports—impossible acceleration, impossibly quick turns, instant appearances and disappearances? That's us. In this phase, or aspect, or whatever you want to call it, of the Universe, *we're* not real. If Gilpin's Space has its own conscious entities, we must be spooks to them. That's why we seem to be exempt from the laws of physics—just as ghosts are, and always have been, in our own non-Gilpin Space."

"My best friend," laughed Franz, "and I never guessed he was an eminent authority on the physics of the supernatural!"

"I'm not." Tammy bowed, looking very well satisfied with himself. "I am a modest man. I would refrain from displaying my own erudition, especially to Westerners. The authority was my Uncle Hiroshi. He was a Buddhist priest, a very learned man who wrote all sorts of abstruse books. He knew all about ghosts and their doings, and he passed a little of his knowledge on to me. It's all very simple if you understand it. Needless to say, *I* don't."

"Well, I daresay it's as good an explanation as any we're likely to come up with," said Macartney wryly. "My question is a bit more practical. Geoff, where do we go from here?"

There was one answer to that, and one only. "Out!" I answered, pointing to the vast vault of heaven, so faint, so finely etched, so crystal clear. "Out there! We *can't* go straight back now. Let's aim her at a star—Alpha Centauri A, for my money—and see how fast she'll *really* go." I looked at each of them, and saw the same expression on each face: that terrible, lovely eagerness which sparks all adventures into the unknown. "I see," I said, "that we're agreed."

There was no discussion. Carefully, I turned *Owl* so that

the three suns of the Alpha Centauri system—or their ghosts—lay dead ahead. I asked Franz and Macartney to check the star charts to make doubly sure, and to zero in on Alpha Centauri A as closely as the computer would permit. We started to accelerate.

We watched the readout as its numbers climbed. For a half-hour we watched it. We also watched those unbelievable displays that gave us our distance from the object we were aiming at and the rate at which we were approaching it. We did not find out then what our maximum acceleration and speed might be—frankly, because I was afraid to. It is hard for anyone accustomed to Earth speeds to adjust to traveling at velocities of millions of kilometers a second. After that half-hour, when I realized that even at the speed we had attained, we would reach our destination *in less than seven hours*, I cut back to where our speed was constant and we were accelerating no longer.

"We'll get there soon enough," I said. "Dammit, it'd be presumptuous of us to rush at man's first new star!"

"Damned presumptuous!" said Macartney. "We don't want everybody saying that Earthmen haven't decent manners, do we now?"

Everyone agreed that we did not. We were all wildly excited, afire in our elation, and not quite in our right minds—whatever that may mean. What did we do? We ate our dinner. Franz and Janet and Tammy got it ready, and it was a banquet. Everything tasted better than it ever had before. The white wine was superb; the red, superlative.

And we talked. We talked about Man's future in space, about the infinite possibilities of First Encounters with other sentient beings, about what every well-equipped spaceship needed. We had no doubts about the future then—how could we, with Alpha Centauri A so near, so very near? And with all the rest of the Universe opening its arms to us? Besides, we had made a discovery that had excited us even more—that as soon as we ceased to accelerate, the power drain to the drive dropped to a small fraction of what it had been, apparently just enough to keep us in Gilpin's Space. We knew now that on one nukepak we could probably stay in space almost indefinitely, especially when the problems of air renewal and water recycling had been solved more than a decade before, when subs were still not too vulnerable to use in war and there was a premium on the ability to run submerged forever and amen.

On and on we hurtled, and our speed did not slacken. Earlier we would have worried; now we knew that there seemed to be no limit to our acceleration rate and there would be none to the rate with which we were decelerated when the drive-computer complex decided the time had come. Then finally, after six and a half hours, our speed began to drop; the acceleration display, instead of reading zero, started showing minus quantities; and we saw that the still-incredible distance separating us from our goal was diminishing. It was uncanny. It was like participating in the illusion of a telehologram. We felt nothing. We were part of the unreality.

The thought did not sober us. We were triumphant, and reveling in our triumph.

Then, at long last, the ghost-point that was our star became an infinitesimal disc, but still a ghost, still as faint, yet as sharply scribed, and as utterly clear as all else in Gilpin's Space.

It grew, and we watched it grow. We watched it—that star so much like our own sun—until it subtended as much of its own sky as our sun did from Earth. At that point, I slowed *Owl*'s speed to zero, and we hung there, staring at our great cold goblin star. I was tempted—we all were—to shift into normal space just for a second. We resisted the temptation, knowing that if we came to no harm from radiant energy, we'd then go on, searching for planets almost certainly not there, not in a three-star system, and perhaps taking more time to visit Alpha Centauri A's companions. We made one powered orbit, simply as a symbolic gesture.

Then, "Franz," I said, "let's tell the computer to take us home."

He touched the necessary keys, watching the displays as they reported our new course, our renewed acceleration. He grinned at all of us.

"What was that funny word you used?' he asked.

"Home?" I answered—and then I caught his meaning, knowing that no matter what occurred, Earth could no longer be our home or *Owl*'s home port, that maybe in the future we would be able to come back openly—but that that future was bound to be uncertain and perilous and far away.

Then we did sober up. We were still triumphant, but now there was more to it than simple euphoria. There was determination.

On the return, we took turns napping. We ate again, as humans must eat to keep the fires fueled. And we kept busy, exultantly.

We set *Owl* down in the Pacific within a mile of where we'd taken off, and even though there was a rain and nothing whatever in sight, I submerged immediately, not surfacing again until we were just about to enter port. Then I radioed ahead that we'd returned, and that *Owl* had behaved perfectly; and Dan's voice, strangely agitated, told me to for Christ's sake hurry up. I knew better than to question him.

When we pulled up to our dock and moored once again behind *Pussycat,* we had been gone twenty-three hours and fourteen minutes, having performed a voyage longer than all the sea voyages of man's long history, *all of them together.*

8

THE DOCK WAS brightly lighted, and we could see that people were waiting for us there: Laure, of course, and Dan and Sousa, and Whittington—another old reliable—standing at the door of a company car. As soon as the short gangplank was in place, they came aboard, but their faces showed none of the excited anticipation we'd naturally expected. For the first time since I had known her, Laure looked frightened, and Dan's face was taut and grim.

Once I had a long talk with a friend who was deeply into mysticism, and listened to him describe an out-of-the-body experience he'd sworn he had. He found himself projected into realms of seeing and knowing more wonderful than he ever could have dreamed, with no desire ever to return—and then, suddenly, something had told him very firmly *No!,* and he had been snapped back into the dull body he had left behind, in one dreadful instant and irresistibly.

I looked at Laure and Dan and, like my mystic friend, I was instantly and painfully brought back to Earth, a cruel Earth, an Earth only too, too real.

"What's happened?" I exclaimed.

Dan choked, then got the words out. "Rhoda—Rhoda's gone."

"It was her brother," Laure said. "Arley. She told Dan that the birthday party was going to start early, and that she'd stay with her grandmother tonight. She said Dan could come for her tomorrow morning, and he was *not* to follow her."

"I shouldn't have fallen for it. I *should've* tailed her. But it wasn't until half an hour ago that I began to wonder whether she'd got there safely." Dan's angry voice was gaining strength. "I phoned the old lady, and she said, yes indeed, Rhoda and Arley had arrived; and she started to tell me about all the presents they had brought, and the cake, and the catered dinner. I tried to cut her off, but she kept on reciting until I really busted in on her: Was Rhoda *there?* Was Rhoda okay? Then she started crying and getting damn near hysterical. No, Rhoda *wasn't* there. Right after supper, she'd started getting faint, said her eyes were playing tricks on her—and wasn't it just like that silly girl to spoil *her* birthday party by getting herself sick? Drinking all that liquor and eating all that cake and—believe me, I had to yell like hell just to get her to tell me that Arley had driven off with her, she thought to find a doctor, or the emergency hospital or something."

Rhoda's symptoms sounded like those brought on by one well-known nasty substance from the increasingly sophisticated pharmacopoeia of coercion—a preparation usually given orally and followed by an even nastier shot. I said so, and Laure nodded. "If something isn't done," she said, "and very, very soon, Rhoda's going to tell everything she knows. It won't be her fault. She won't be able to help herself. But what can we do?"

"Depends on where they've taken her," Dan growled. "If it's to Arley's place, maybe we've got a chance. I looked through Rhoda's desk and found his phone number, a new one, and then ran down his address. He's got himself a condo maybe twenty miles away, between here and Grandma's place."

"It seems to me," I said, "that at this stage of the game they'd almost certainly take her there. If anything went wrong, it'd be just about impossible to nail them for kidnapping—not at her brother's place after her going to a birthday party with him. Anyhow, it's the only lead we have, and how we use it is strictly up to us. It'd be no use going to the law—none at all."

I thought of the glorious ghost of Alpha Centauri A in Gilpin's Space, of the journey we'd just made, of the welcoming Universe—and of the people who'd move instantly to deny it to us.

"Then it's up to us to act," Laure said very quietly.

"Exactly," I replied. "Dan, which of your boys can you *really* trust—I mean who you'd tell the whole story to if you had to?"

"Sousa," he answered, "definitely. And Whittington."

"Very well, then. It'll be you and me and the two of them. Macartney has to catch his plane, and Franz and Tammy still

have a lot of buttoning up to do on *Owl*. Stun-guns and laser
pistols. Oh yes, and a couple of air pistols with veterinary
tranquilizer darts. We'll damn well have to manage the whole
business silently. Let's hit the road. Laure, we'll be in touch.
We'll let you know immediately whichever way it goes. We'll
take two cars. Sousa and Whittington can tail us. And Janet,
I guess maybe you'd better come with Dan and me. Rhoda's
going to need more than just tender loving care, even if we
get there before they have a chance to pump that shot into her."

We picked up the second car, and were on our way, driving
as inconspicuously as we could. Low limits impose a terrible
impatience when the need for speed is genuine and you're
praying you won't be too late; and twenty miles to Arley's
place stretched out like twenty light-years, over the bridge, into
the city with its damn traffic lights, onto the freeway once
again, Sousa's car now in the lead because he'd located the
address on his street map.

We didn't talk much. There were no plans we could make
until we saw what was waiting for us. Dan had already prepared
Sousa, telling him that Rhoda had been snatched, that it all
had to do with *Cupid's Arrow* disappearing, and that there was
a lot more to it we'd let him in on later.

The condo development sprawled in and down a hillside,
and luckily it wasn't one of the high-security outfits—com-
munal swimming pool with a small recreation hall nearby,
maybe a once-an-hour patrolman after midnight, every unit the
twin or exact mirror image of its neighbor, two stories, entrance
next to the double garage—all very standard. We split up before
entering the development, not wanting to look like a convoy,
and drove into the circle where Arley lived from different
directions. Arley's place, No. 177, showed no porch light, but
the upstairs windows were lighted dimly; its two siblings at
either side were completely dark, which of course could have
meant simply that their denizens were glued to the boob tube.
However, Arley's garage was open, and there was a car in it.
Sousa had parked almost in front of it, and we rolled to a halt
across the street. "If that car's Arley's," I said to Janet, "maybe
we're in luck. It looks as if the bastard left a space for his little
friends. He can't have arrived more than a few minutes ago,
and the odds are they'd want to be damned sure he had her
before showing up."

Dan and I got out, leaving Janet at the wheel, with the radio

turned low to a good-music FM station. Sousa and Whittington
joined us. "Yeah, it's Arley's machomobile," Dan told us.
"Let's go on in through the garage like we were his buddies."

We entered, and Dan knocked casually on the door that led
inside. We heard footsteps. Finally, a man's voice, a rasping
tenor, said something about, "Hold your water. I'll have it open
in a min—"

A lock clicked. The knob turned. The door began to open—
and Dan, using all his weight, burst through it, carrying Arley
backward in his charge. When we came after him, his hands
were round Arley's throat, thumbs crushing at his windpipe,
and Rhoda's fish-pale, overweight brother was acting as if he
were about to have a heart attack.

Dan didn't say a word. Finally, he flung Arley to us like a
sack of straw. Sousa grabbed him, twisting an arm behind his
back. Arley was choking, gasping, trying to mouth something;
and Sousa, applying more leverage to his arm, told him to shut
up. Dan had dashed on ahead, and I closed the door, deadbolted
it, and told Whittington to cover us in case Arley's guests
showed up.

We found Rhoda on a long sofa in the living room, sitting
upright, arms hanging at her sides, legs rigidly straight in front
of her, her features strangely loose, the pupils of her staring
eyes dilated like some night creature's. There was a cassette
recorder, which Arley had left running. I switched it to rewind,
let it run until it stopped, and confiscated the cassette.

Dan was kneeling next to her, holding one of her hands in
his, trying with his voice and with his love to elicit some sign
of recognition, some response. Distraught, he turned to me.
"Commander, oughtn't we get her out of here? Maybe to Janet
in the car?"

"Not yet," I told him. "They could show up at any moment,
and we'll be a whole lot better off if we can put them out of
commission for a few hours—which we can." I went over to
where Sousa was holding Arley, and started going through his
pockets. Arley didn't like it, and began to squirm. Sousa slapped
him in the chops, hard. I found what I was looking for—a
drugstore pill bottle—and held it up for Dan to see.

"We're in luck," I said. "Look at this! Arley's name; the
doctor's name, Dr. Vlachik—everything. The damned fool!"
I put it in my own pocket. "And it's exactly what I thought it
would be—the softener-up. The shot's the next step—after

that, they blab everything they know. They wouldn't trust this slob with *that.*" I turned back to Rhoda's brother. "Okay, when'll they be here?"

He shook his head. His bruised throat croaked that he didn't know. Sousa went to work again, and Arley folded. "R-right a-away," he muttered.

"Well, we'd better organize the reception committee. Dan, how'd you like to hide behind Arley's car, where you can get a clear field of fire? Chances are there won't be more than two or three. They ought to be duck soup for your stun-gun. When they knock on the door, I'll open it myself, so watch out you don't get me. Also, we'd best locate the switch for the garage door. We'll want it closed the minute they're taken care of."

Dan stood up, reluctant to leave Rhoda, but recognizing the necessity. Leaning forward, he kissed her, and ever so slightly she smiled. Whittington unlocked the door, took a quick look out. The coast was clear. A moment later, Dan was gone and the door was locked again.

We did not have long to wait—six minutes by my watch. We heard the car drive in. We heard its engine die. We heard its doors open, and voices just outside. Then, in swiftly measured cadence, three times, the low, dull *poof* a stun-gun makes. Dan had done a good job. When I threw the door open, they were still falling. He had shot each of them neatly in the back of the neck, a spot made to order for the stun-gun—it guarantees at least two hours of sack time for the target.

The garage door came down, and Whittington and I went into the garage and started hauling in bodies. Two of them were run-of-the-rattrap goons, beefy, ham-fisted. The third was thin and spidery, with that tense, haggard look so many addicts get, and when we searched him he turned out to be Dr. Vlachik. Dan found his hypodermic, all nicely loaded, opened his shirt, and gave him a shot under the skin of his abdomen. "That'll give the s.o.b. something to think about when he wakes up," he said. "I'd love to hear what he'll yak about, and I'll bet anything it's stuff Borg wouldn't want anyone to hear."

I took Arley's pill bottle. I took out one pill. I showed it to him. "Are you going to swallow your medicine like a good little dog—or do we hold you down and force it down your throat?" Whittington, grinning, brought a tall glass of water from the kitchen. "Hold your head back!" I ordered.

Arley tried to wriggle, gave it up, obeyed.

"Way back!"

I dropped the pill all the way back, and Whittington followed it with half the water. Arley had to swallow.

"Now, let's take one more precaution," I said, and I fired a tranquilizer dart very deliberately into each of them. "They're very mild," I told Arley. "They'll just make sure your friends hibernate for a couple of hours after stun-gun time. As for you—" I pointed at Rhoda. "—you're going to be like that for quite a while. Dan, give him a light stun-gun shot just to make sure he doesn't do anything foolish like trying to chuck up that pill or phone people before the stuff takes hold."

And that was it. I went outside, and waited until Janet came in sight, driving slowly and casually. I signaled her. We brought Rhoda out. We locked up tidily behind us. "Dan," I said, "I think it'd be wise for you and Rhoda to do on *Owl* what Saul did aboard *Cupid's Arrow*—move in and set up housekeeping. And I mean tonight. Janet can drive there with you, and help Rhoda make it out of this. As I understand it, there's no instant antidote, but there are counteracting agents, and *Owl's* medicine chest is pretty much complete. I'll have Sousa guarding her apartment tonight, and tomorrow you can move more of your stuff over."

Janet and I took one car, with Dan and Rhoda in the back seat. Sousa and Whittington drove the other. We went by different routes, and arrived at the yard within minutes of each other, and no one bothered us.

I showed Dan what would be their cabin aboard *Owl*, then reported back to Laure, who was waiting, quite unruffled, in her office. I told her what had happened, in detail, and we played that cassette of Arley's. It was disgusting. We heard Arley pleading with Rhoda to help her little brother, just to give him a few useful bits of information, because he was scared, scared to death of what *they'd* do to him; and we heard Rhoda's anguished answers, crying, telling him she had a headache, and she couldn't see, and what was *wrong* with her? And when was the doctor getting there? And she couldn't tell him anything, how could she? Because everybody knew—here she laughed crazily—that submarines couldn't fly up to the stars. Then she was weeping once again. Then she became completely incoherent. That must've been when we came in, because there was no more.

"Now," I said, "I'd better tell you all about *Owl's* flight."

"Geoff—" Laure shook her head. "—you've had a long, hard day, and you don't need to tell me anything. Ever since you returned, I've been aboard the ship with Franz and Tammy. They've told me everything—what Gilpin's Space is like, and how wonderfully Saul's drive works, and what it feels like, with mankind still not quite out of the cave, to circle another star. Tomorrow, if you want, you can tell me more. It's been a tremendous day, a memorable day—and not the least of it is that we have Rhoda back safe and sound. Besides—"

I looked at her, and in her eyes I saw the ice and fire of her determination.

"—Besides, we've learned two things about Borg and his crew. First, they're *certain* that we have something that they want. Second, they feel more confident, more willing to take risks, but they still don't feel that they can go all out. We're going to have to speed things up, Geoff, even if it means fewer precautions. So far we've been lucky—it's not often a secret so many share stays secret. By this time, Macartney's already taken off for Ireland with his list—a long list—and at this end we're just going to have to go ahead and load everything we can think of aboard *Owl.*" She stood up. "Geoff, I can see that you need sleep, and need it badly. Is Janet still aboard *Owl,* taking care of Rhoda?"

I said she was.

"Then why don't you join her there? If Rhoda's going to be all right, she can drive you home, but if she thinks she's going to need more expert watching over, you can both use the captain's cabin." She smiled at me. "After all, the starship *Owl* is *your* command."

9

JANET AND I SPENT the night aboard *Owl.* She sent me to bed first, staying up until she was sure that Rhoda was coming out of it and could safely be sedated, then joining me—or so she told me next morning, for I was sound asleep the instant I hit the pillow. I slept—and dreamed of Gilpin's Space, that Universe of precise, faint, sharply delineated ghosts, and of the world which I knew some of us at least would soon be leaving, with its hordes of power-hungry ayatollahs, political and otherwise, its maniacs, its Whalen Borgs. Nevertheless, I awakened rested, grateful that I had Janet there with me.

The next day went well. We held two conferences, one in the morning, the other in the afternoon, both aboard *Owl,* which seemed appropriate. We decided, or perhaps I should say that Laure decided and we went along, that we had to firm up the roster of *Owl*'s crew. Was Tammy Uemura sure his wife would come with us and bring their kids? Was Franz sure his girl down at Stanford would want to give up her teaching assistantship in anthropology to visit stars instead of look at them? And what of Sousa? Dan hadn't briefed him fully, but Sousa had practically told him that he guessed the rest and would be eager to go along; for a few years, until something to do with depth perception had grounded him, he'd flown charter flights; he'd sailed single-handedly to Tahiti and down to Suva. He'd be a good man to have with us. Both Franz and Tammy assured us that their women wouldn't have to be asked twice. As for Sousa, we let the question rest, for there still would be the matter of choosing another crew for *Pussycat,* something that could not be deferred much longer, for the components of her Gilpin's drive already were arriving. I counted five couples so far for *Owl,* Janet and myself, Dan and Rhoda, the Uemuras, Franz and his lady, Macartney and his wife, plus five teenage and near-teenage kids, the Uemuras' boy and girl, and Jamie's boy and two girls. Fifteen, plus Laure, made sixteen, which was all right because *Owl* could sleep twenty or more comfortably. Strangely assorted? Perhaps, but no more so than the complement of *Mayflower*.

For the next three days, work went on, and between working sessions we conferred again and again. We spent Laure's money like water. We bought everything we thought the well-stocked spaceship might require, and loaded it aboard both vessels. Meanwhile, Dan kept a close watch on our warehousemen, and we transferred to other chores one or two who seemed to be too curious.

Nobody bothered us. Arley made no attempt to get in touch with Rhoda, and we simply rode our luck.

On the second day, the newspapers reported that a Dr. Harkis Vlachik had been found dead in a gutter in a ghetto area, beaten to death. The police blamed muggers, but a cold chill went down my spine when Dan showed me the item, and we began to wonder what might have become of Arley.

On the second day, too, Franz's girl, Bess Mayhew, showed up, tall and forthright and athletic, a girl to love and not to trifle with. She and Laure took to each other instantly, which told us more about her than Franz ever had.

On the third day, Laure and I had a long conference with Placek, who quite clearly was starting to understand that something out of the ordinary was going on. She told him exactly what we had and what we planned, and what we could expect when the IPP moved in against us—as they were absolutely sure to do. When she spoke of space, of actual traveling between star and star, I saw the flare of anticipation and excitement in his eyes.

"In a few days, *Captain* Placek," she told him, "your vessel will no longer be a simple submarine. She will be a spaceship, a starship—the third one of its kind in the history of our Earth. Her new drive's components have all arrived; the last of them, with their associated computers, will be aboard tomorrow, and you will have detailed instructions regarding them. Then, if events happen too suddenly, it will be up to you. Commander Cormac and I can help you choose your crew. I would suggest that you consider Sousa, but also what of the men who were with you on your trial run?"

Placek frowned. "Latourette and Singer, yes, definitely.

Maybe Alwyss. Then there would be my wife and boy. And my—my brother's wife, with her two kids. This isn't just for men?"

Laure assured him that it was not. "You and Latourette can do all the drive installation, or almost all of it, at sea if you have to. Then, if you do need a good, safe place to finish it, I'd suggest Taiwan. You'll have Swiss francs and bullion in the safe. As I've explained to you, Saul Gilpin arranged matters so that the whole world will have the information necessary to duplicate the drive. The IPP in our country and other totalitarian groups abroad will of course do their best to monopolize the knowledge. They will not be able to. Therefore it would be sensible of you to show your crew—whomever you decide to take—that they'll have far more to gain as pioneering astronauts than by betraying you. Captain, I am going to *give* you *Pussycat.* Will you accept her?"

"Good God, *yes!*" Placek cried, incredulous. "But—but there's no way I can pay you for her."

"You can," said Laure. "You can take her to the stars."

I was thoroughly surprised—and disturbed. "Placek's a good man, Laure, a very good man," I said after he had left, "but aren't you putting a hell of a lot of trust in him? Have you thought of what rewards the IPP is going to offer?"

"Geoff, of course I have," she answered. "But I guess you've forgotten, haven't you? Do you remember who his brother was?—the captain of that tanker rammed by a conglomerate vessel three or four years ago. They'd clearly violated the rules of the road at sea, and he tried to fight them in the courts. The IPP railroaded him on a perjury charge, and in prison two of their thugs killed him. The verdict said he was fomenting riot. If anyone can be trusted to work in silence and take *Pussycat* to the stars it's Placek."

I looked at her a little ruefully, thinking that after all the years I should have known better than to question the soundness of her judgment. I never dreamed that very, very soon I not only would question it again but would, against her will, take the decision into my own hands.

We worked hard, and I slept soundly—so soundly that, when the phone rang at almost 3:00 A.M. on the fourth night after *Owl*'s return, Janet actually had to shake me awake to answer it. It was Garvey at NavIntel, and sleepily I did what he told me to about the scrambler.

"What's up?" I asked.

"Geoff, for you it's red alert. We just got word here that "Ham" Smithfield's committed suicide. All very tidy and made to order, with a .44 magnum, and in his office, too, leaving a typed suicide note. His confession—how he ratted on Good Ol' Breck, and how he'd made scads of dinero selling out the IPP. Also, he implicated a few more of Marrone's enemies, the attorney general, for example. And Good Ol' Breck was all prepared. Two hours after they found the body, he'd appointed Marrone to Defense. And you know what that means."

"I can guess," I said.

"Exactly. After that ship of yours disappeared, or got stolen, or whatever, all of us here figured you had *something*, but because subs aren't worth a tinker's damn these days we didn't care. But that's not the way our friend Borg figures it. From now on, he'll be where he can bring the whole national security battering ram down on you—and there'll be damn well nothing I, or anyone else around these parts, can do to help. I'll be expecting my retirement orders anytime now—if I luck out, that is. Give Laure my love."

I thanked him—what else could I say?—and hung up.

"The fat's in the fire," I told Janet. "I've a feeling there'll be no use our trying to get back to sleep."

"They murdered Smithfield, didn't they?" she said. "And now?"

"And now we're going to have to move, and move very fast indeed. Do you want to get breakfast going while I call Laure?"

She slipped into a housecoat, and I woke Laure and told her what had happened. She answered me without a tremor. "I think you and Janet had better get all your things packed, hadn't you?"

"Right," I said, "packed and aboard *Owl* as soon as possible—and not just Janet and I, but all of us. I doubt somehow whether Borg will make his move immediately, but let's take no chances. Incidentally, we've got to get Placek off to sea. Probably we can't get him out of here before late tomorrow, but anyhow, let's try. He can tell Latourette anything he wants—after all, he'll be the engineer—but maybe he'd better cook up a cover story for the others, at least for now. We'll have to leave that up to him. How close is *Pussycat* to ready?"

"Geoff, she has everything *Owl* has except the drive and

some of the medical supplies Janet's been bringing in. Anyway, can't Placek rendezvous with Jamie Macartney when you do?"

"Not if they don't have her converted."

"Well, there's enough money aboard to buy them anything they need, either in Taiwan—I've told him to get in touch with Henry Kwei—or any other reasonably safe place. Are you going to call the Uemuras and Franz, or shall I do it?"

"Could you call Franz, Laure? Then get him to put through the call to Tammy. The fewer calls I make from here the better. I hate to wake Placek at this time of the morning, but I'm afraid I'd better, so he can pass the word along. But I'm going to tell him not to show up before regular opening hours."

"I think," said Laure, "that that applies to all of us. We can't remain completely inconspicuous, but at least we can make all our activity seem reasonably normal."

I phoned Placek, who understood immediately and said he'd get things rolling at his end. Then Janet and I dressed hastily and ate a hurried breakfast. After that, we spent a difficult three and a half hours selecting things we'd need and things we simply couldn't bear to leave behind: a fragile Sung dynasty bowl, pale celadon, a Royal Doulton kitten, books and diaries, small gifts of love from long ago, a kachina doll Saul Gilpin (of course) had once given us, all sorts of things that seemed utterly nonfunctional, yet essential to our humanity. I was astounded at how many of the really necessary, really useful things Janet had already transferred.

Finally, we felt that we had done our best. We took leave of treasures we couldn't abandon without a twinge, a tear. We drove down to the yard, and found that everyone else was just arriving. We need not have worried. The day passed, and nothing happened. The work went on. By three in the afternoon, Placek—very much to our relief—had put to sea. In addition to his family and his brother's, Sousa's wife and Latourette's girlfriend had been added to the complement. Placek, wisely, had hinted only that there was going to be a lawsuit, and that Mrs. Endicott wanted *Pussycat* well out of lawyers' reach, and that therefore they were going to get a long first-class cruise for free. They were delighted. They knew there'd be some work to do aboard, but they also knew that both *Owl* and *Pussycat* were about as automated as a ship can get, and that nobody was going to have to man the pumps or holystone the decks.

The day passed, and I found myself wishing that we, too, could leave, running on the surface with the tide, submerging far out at sea, then resurfacing at nightfall to enter Gilpin's Space. But Laure, I suppose wisely, would have none of it. She had not packed her things. She alone among us was not ready. In her office, Rhoda kept looking at her anxiously—Rhoda who for good reason was even more eager than the rest of us to get away.

"You're quite right," Laure said to us. "Speed is of the essence, and you should be ready to leave at a moment's notice. But I am determined to find out what Borg is going to do, for it is I who'll have to give the word to publish Gilpin's data, to send it out by satellite autofax and through all the other channels we've prepared. As you said when you called me, Geoff, Borg probably will not move immediately, and I will tell you why. Because his motive is revenge, against the admiral first, then you and me, it will taste especially sweet if he's back in naval uniform—as Garvey said he surely would be if that man Marrone got Defense. Well, Smithfield has just been done away with; other heads have rolled; Marrone's in. Just wait and see."

And she was right. The work went on. At five, we closed down as usual, but now we went to dinner in two shifts, with all gates closed and locked and Dan's men doubling up at every post. All that night and all the next day we waited. Laure went home as usual, but the rest of us slept aboard. Then, late that afternoon, when Janet had taken Rhoda and Tammy's wife into town for some last-minute shopping, the phone in *Owl*'s control area rang, and I answered it.

It was the nightspot-owning retired CPO, who had served the admiral and served him well. "Commander Cormac?" he growled.

"Yes," I said. "Pat Garrison?"

"Aye, sir. Commander, a friend of yours just called. He said to give you a message. I got it all wrote down. He said, 'Tell the commander the order just came through. The bastard's back in uniform, reinstated by executive order, all pay and allowanced since he got his board, and the members of the board all censured and dropped a few numbers on the promotion list.' And that ain't all, sir—" Garrison's voice was outraged. "He's—they've jumped him up to rear admiral!"

"My God!" I whispered.

"Me, too!" Garrison echoed me. "And there's just one thing more. Your pal said, 'Tell Commander Cormac he'd better start counting his minutes now. And I mean *now*,' he said."

I thanked him, and told him how grateful the admiral would have been, and how grateful Mrs. Endicott would be; and when I hung up he was almost weeping.

I went over to the office immediately and gave Laure the news.

She sighed. "Well," she said, "I suppose that means I'll have to get Mrs. Rasmussen to finish all my packing, doesn't it?" She stood up. "Geoff, I'll go home now and attend to it. I'll be back again tomorrow morning."

Both Rhoda and I tried to persuade her not to go, to let Mrs. Rasmussen do all the packing and bring her things down to *Owl* that night or the following morning. She would have none of it. "I'm sure that nothing will happen at least until tomorrow,' she declared. "He'll be too busy looking at himself in the mirror in his new uniform. Anyhow, what can he do that we can't counter legally, at least enough to slow him down a little? I'll be here right after breakfast, my luggage packed and ready to take off, so don't you worry, either of you."

She left the office, and presently, out the window we saw her car sweep through the gates and turn off toward the bridges.

"Rhoda," I said, "what the hell is she *thinking* of? She may understand Whalen Borg better than I do, but I still don't like it. With a guy like that, she's plain crazy to take any close chances. Could it be she has something entirely different up her sleeve?"

"Geoff," Rhoda replied unhappily, "I *feel* she has, but I simply can't imagine what, and I'm worried for her. I'm worried sick. She knows we've got to be ready to—to escape—just as—as Dan's explained to me. She told me so herself. *We* are all ready. We're all on edge. But look at *her.*"

All of us had dinner aboard *Owl* that night, and all of us slept aboard—all except Laure. We slept anxiously and lightly, armed, alert to every sound, to any hint that there might be trouble at the gates. I'd doze, and wake, worrying about what would have to happen if the morning came *without* Laure, what if she simply disappeared as Rhoda might very well have done if Dan and I had not taken such prompt action. Then what would we do? I would take command, certainly, but would I be justified in ordering the immediate publication of Saul Gilpin's stuff—and in ordering *Owl* and all her people into Gilpin's Space?

10

MORNING CAME—LIKE any other fog-free summer morning—
and after breakfast I stepped out onto the dock and looked at
Owl. She was certainly not beautiful, not as a clipper ship or
a sleek ocean liner could be beautiful. Her hull was bulbous,
with even that minimum of deck space considered *de rigueur*
for submarines broken by her massive control tower, with barely
a foot and a half of decking so that you could edge around it.
Her viewing ports were like the eyes of a gigantic insect, and
her starboard pair of twenty-foot articulated servos—those with
which Dan was so fascinated—were folded back into their
retaining slots. There was another pair to port and two more
forward and two aft; those amidships controlled directly from
the tower, those fore and aft from their stations. I knew that
when necessary they could accommodate and use all sorts of
special tools, but still their huge pincer ends, so terribly powerful, so precise, always made me think of hungry lobster
claws.

Owl showed no outward signs of either her capabilities or
her journeyings; it was more difficult than ever, not to believe,
but to *accept* what had occurred, where she had been, and the
whole situation in which we found ourselves. Janet came out
and stood there, on the ridiculous little two-foot gangplank,
thinking the same thoughts. Then we saw Whittington open
the gate for Laure's car and for another following it, and went
to join her at the office.

Rhoda was already there, of course; and Laure greeted the
three of us cheerfully as she came in. "You see," she said,
"nothing's happened yet. But you'll be pleased, I know, to hear
that I'm finally packed. All the luggage is in my car and in
Mrs. Rasmussen's. You see, she and her daughter and young
Keithy are coming with me."

I was surprised, but I couldn't see that any harm was done. *Owl* had enough room for all of them, and Mrs. Rasmussen would be especially useful. Besides, it *was* Laure's ship. "Shall I go tell them to drive down the dock and load the stuff aboard?" I asked. "The boys can lug it in for them and show them where to stow it."

Laure held up a hand. "Geoffrey," she said softly. "Geoff and Janet. And you, too, Rhoda. Please sit down. I have something to say to you."

We sat down apprehensively.

"I very much want you to understand what I have planned. The luggage is not going aboard *Owl*. In a few minutes I'm going to start the machinery of disclosure and publication going. Then I and Mrs. Rasmussen and her daughter and grandson will say good-bye to you. Oh, Geoff! I'm too *old* for space. Besides, this was my husband's fight, and now it's mine. I'm *not* giving up."

"God in Heaven, Laure! Have you any idea what you're saying? Have you any notion of who you're up against? You'll not have a chance. They'll butcher you."

Janet added her voice to mine. Rhoda stared silently, in shock.

I pleaded with Laure Endicott. We all did. We tried logic; we spoke of love and loyalty. She remained inflexible.

"I'm not going to try to fight them here, on their own ground," she declared. "In less than two hours, we'll catch a flight for Ireland. *That* is where we and our luggage are going to go. The IPP has made scarcely any headway there."

"And Adolf Hitler had made almost none in Denmark or in Holland when he invaded them, nor the Russians in Latvia or Lithuania or—"

"It is *still* my fight," she stated evenly.

"At least," I said, and I could hear the bitterness in my own voice, "at least you'll come down to *Owl* and say good-bye to all of us?"

"Geoff, dear, I may or I may not. Don't think that I'm not torn by this—I *am*. But now I have to pay my debt to Saul."

We left, Janet and I. Deeply troubled, we went on back to *Owl*. We told Franz and the rest about it, and they were as disturbed as we.

"She *knows* she's committing suicide," Franz whispered. "She *knows*."

We talked about it, back and forth, getting nowhere; and when the central control area phone rang, Franz answered it.

"For you," he said, handing me the phone. "A woman."

"Cormac here," I said.

"I have a message for you. Please do not ask me who I am or any other questions. It was considered wise to get in touch with you very indirectly."

It was a level, very professional voice, a high-level secretary's voice perhaps, or someone with even more responsibility.

"Commander Cormac, your time is almost up. A federal warrant has been issued for Mrs. Endicott's arrest and for your own. A seizure order has been issued against all her property. A Coast Guard vessel is moving to make sure nothing leaves your yard, and the party that intends to make the arrests is on its way. That party is not composed entirely of federal officers, and it is led by Rear Admiral Whalen Borg."

"How soon?" I asked.

There was no answer. She had hung up.

I turned around. I repeated the message just as she had given it. I stood up. "We're going to have one more stab at persuading Laure," I said to them. "We owe her that. Janet, get down to the parking lot. Mrs. Rasmussen will still be in her car. Tell her anything you like. Tell her that Laure's in danger, that she's been threatened, that the airline reservations have been canceled, that she's already decided against Ireland. Tell her anything, but get her and her daughter and Keithy and the luggage aboard *Owl*. Hell, kidnap them if you have to. No time to walk. Take the shop car."

"I'll go with you," said Franz. "They'll believe both of us easier than one."

Impatiently, I watched the old Datsun pickup scuttle off. It didn't take them long, and whatever Franz and Janet said was at least effective. In minutes, they were back, with Mrs. Rasmussen's sedan following close behind them. A moment or two more, and an excited Keithy was hauling the first suitcase in.

"We got 'em all! Grandma got Mrs. Endicott's out of her trunk, too. Gosh, I've never been aboard a submarine before!"

I watched until everything had been unloaded and brought aboard. Then I myself drove the sedan back to Laure's office. I went upstairs, and walked in unannounced.

She looked up. "Geoffrey," she declared, "everything's on

its way. All Saul's data is now going to every space organization in the world—not just to the professionals, but to the space-oriented groups—you know, younger scientists in other fields, science-fiction fans. And everything they need to know is going to all the mass media everywhere. Nothing can stop it now! Now I can leave for Ireland with a clear conscience. Now I can fight my battle!"

"Laure!" She was so absorbed that I almost had to shout it, to make sure I had all her attention. "Laure, you aren't going! Not to Ireland. Laure, you'd never leave the yard." I told her about the message I'd received. *"Please,* Laure, give it up. Borg will be here any minute now!"

She stood, facing me squarely. "In that case, Geoff, I shall fight them here. I shall fight them in the courts. Ne—" For the first time, just a touch of her native French came through."—nevaire shall I give up!"

"Laure, listen to reason! Look, we already have your luggage all aboard. Mrs. Rasmussen, too, and Keithy and his mother."

Suddenly, she was furious. "In that case, we will go to the ship together, Commander Cormac, and I shall order everything they brought unloaded and put back in the cars! Now!"

I saw that it was useless to argue with her, useless and time consuming. I bowed my head, and followed her down the stairs, and I could hear Rhoda coming after us.

She refused to ride. She walked. Perhaps it would be better to say she strolled, taking her time deliberately, defiantly.

She gestured peremptorily to Rhoda to precede us up the gangplank.

And that was when it happened.

Looking down the dock, past the offices, and at the gate, I saw the first of four huge cars turn in toward it. I saw Whittington try to do his job. He stepped out into the open gate, his hand held up.

And the driver of the first car gunned his engine and ran him down, leaving him motionless and broken in the road. And the following cars simply continued over him.

"Christ!" I exclaimed. I turned to Laure. *"Now* will you come with us?"

Her face was bloodless suddenly, but her jaw was set. *"No,"* she said coldly. *"Not even now."*

Then the first two cars were screaming to a stop twenty feet

from us. One of the cars following had dropped out to take
over the guardpost. Another halted at the offices.

The first car's doors opened and spewed out men. Whalen
Borg, in full summer uniform, was coming around the front,
an envelope in one hand, a laser pistol in the other. In his car
there had been three other men, in the next car, five. There
were no Navy types among them, and only one had the look
of being a federal man, a U.S. marshal, possibly. The rest were
members of Marrone's private army, all in their monkey suits.
All were armed.

It was Borg's big moment, the moment he had waited and
connived for ever since the admiral had, quite justly, ordered
him before his board. He came forward slowly, waving the
others back when they followed him too closely. I thought again
that he was a man who should never have worn a uniform—
any uniform, except perhaps an executioner's. No tailor ever
could have fitted him. The naked triumph on his massive face
was counterpointed by the dead coldness of his eyes.

Ponderously, he advanced toward us. "Mrs. Endicott," he
announced, in a strangely thin, high, raucous voice, "I have a
warrant here for your arrest. I have another for the arrest of
Mr. Cormac. If you make no resistance, no harm will come to
you, though we will for the time being—" He made a gesture
to the federal type, who hauled out handcuffs, "—restrain both
of you. Now—"

That was as far as he ever got. The upper starboard servo
moved. It moved up and out, and down again with the swiftness
of a striking snake. Its terrible lobster claw seized Whalen Borg
by *and through* his huge neck and chest. It lifted him, as he
grotesquely gurgling. It shook him as a terrier shakes a rat.
Then it flung him like a dead rag admiral doll against his
paralyzed retainers. I knew exactly what had happened. I realized that Dan had studied those fascinating servos well—and
suddenly I knew that there was only one thing I could do.

I slugged Laure Endicott. I slugged her as gently as I could.
I caught her as she fell. Then I pitched her bodily across that
two-foot gangplank and through the door and, with the sound
of weapons going off wildly behind me, threw myself after
her. I pushed the button that ordered the massive door to close.
I dogged it shut.

Moments later, we were in Gilpin's Space.

• • •

That was the only time in my life I ever slugged an elderly lady, or for that matter anyone of whom I was so deeply fond, and for a time afterward it was very hard for me to face her.

But weeks later, and two thousand light-years out, when we had found our first water-planet—all green and blue, and richly brown, and white with mountain snows and drifting clouds— she forgave me for it.

BOOK II

Laure's World

Janet Cormac

1

THAT WAS WHEN Laure *formally* forgave Geoff, though we all knew that, in her heart, she had forgiven him before we had been in Gilpin's Space a week. Her pride would not permit her to tell him so, even while we were finding out what that Space was like when we had penetrated far enough from Earth, not until she had achieved the triumph of her self-discovery and an understanding of her new role in life.

At first, of course, there had been the euphoria of undreamed-of adventure, very much as we had experienced it on *Owl*'s maiden flight, and our own natural preoccupation with all unexpected intimacies and revelations that surprise you when, for the first time at sea with a new crew on a small vessel, you realize that you are utterly alone with one another and with your ship—a realization psychologically compounded because we knew we were isolated, not on an ocean, but in the Universe. We reminded ourselves that our risks on alien worlds would, at least in certain ways, be minimal. We had sensors to tell us the composition of atmospheres and liquids; we had our diagnostic surrogates, those wonderful half-living gels, triumphs of genetic engineering and microelectronics, which made it possible to detect almost instantly the presence of anything organic or inorganic harmful to man. We also reminded ourselves that we could return to Earth at any time, but I'm not sure that any of us believed it—not after we had touched down on our first two alien planets, and especially after we had had our first taste of the agonies and terrors, the consuming hungers, the devouring loves that started to touch our minds out of the Far Reaches of Gilpin's Space.

We went nowhere near the Alpha Centauri system, knowing it would be the first target of the Earth invasions which, now, were sure to follow. Our first landing—after we had approached and retreated from more than a score of hostile worlds, barren as Mars, great and gaseous as Jupiter or Saturn, or cold as icy Pluto—was on a planet perhaps as large as Venus, the fifth in a crowded system circling a dull red star, and even from Gilpin's Space we could see that there were living creatures there in the vast strangely writhing growths which, like live precipices, assailed the marshy shores of its soup-thick seas. Geoff decided immediately that those seas were not for *Owl* in her submarine configuration, and then put her into as low a normal space orbit as he dared, letting her cameras and telephoto lenses record what they revealed of continents and oceans, dark-green, solidly overgrown mountain ranges, huge, sluggish serpent-rivers, and endless bogs which, over enormous areas, a perpetual rain was doing its best to drown. Finally, unable to resist the pull of the unknown, he shifted back to Gilpin's Space and came down on a narrow beach of uncontaminated sand. We did not realize how really alien an alien world could be.

The air tested out as much heavier than Earth's, unbreathable. Therefore, though we detected no microorganisms harmful to us, and though the temperature was not much more than tropical, he and Franz suited up to go exploring. Dan, as unofficial second-in-command, was not expendable. He ignored every plea to go along with them, especially Keithy's. They went out through the starboard lock—and even as they did, we saw that from the beachhead behind the ship mottled tendrils as thick as anacondas were groping out toward them. Geoff alerted Dan to make sure he was recording everything. Then I heard Franz's voice.

"Don't look now," he said, "but I think our hosts are here."

He was pointing beyond the slow, heavy rollers pressing from the sea. I looked, and saw two things rising ponderously— two heads, two necks. Each head had two separate mouths, articulated so that they could actually face each other, jaws sharply serrated. Each had one large eye amidships, two smaller ones to port and starboard, and several ragged orifices like open wounds expanding and contracting spasmodically. Their hides—if they were hides—were grayish pink, and crusted with, apparently, parasitic life forms. And each head was half the size of *Owl*.

Then their bodies, loosely limbed and powerfully fingered, began to rise behind them—and Geoff, thank God!—didn't wait for them to emerge fully. He and Franz hurried back through the lock, then let its pumps evacuate the alien atmosphere so they could unsuit. Dan, of course, had taken us into Gilpin's Space immediately, but not until we all had felt those unbelievable fingers touch *Owl*'s hull.

"Well, Stout Cortez," Jamie said to Franz, "you look awfully glad to be inside again. But weren't you rather impolite? Possibly they were intelligent. Shouldn't you have stayed just long enough to get acquainted?"

"Franz wasn't cut out to be a good ambassador," Geoff told him. "He's much too impulsive."

We laughed, but we were all shaken, everyone who had watched, everyone except the younger kids, who were complaining because we'd robbed them of a visit to the zoo. It was not simply the idea of monstrous critters cruelly fanged—after all, we were from a world which, in its time, had evolved *Tyrannosaurus rex* and all his kith and kin. It was simply that now we *knew* that there were alien life forms, that they came in shapes we couldn't even understand, and that they could be dangerous to us.

Geoff, or perhaps Laure, had already begun the practice of gathering all of us, except the two on watch, in the ship's wardroom twice a day—usually right after breakfast and either just before or after supper—to discuss how things were going and what we would do next, and to plan the routines and activities essential if life aboard ship was to proceed normally. Things were shaping up well. Mrs. Rasmussen, automatically, had taken over the running of the galley, with the help of her daughter Linda and assorted children. Franz's beautiful Bess Mayhew, announcing that she was the only qualified schoolmarm anywhere around, had started planning classes for the kids. Jamie and Tammy Uemura, with Dan and Tammy's tall Hawaiian wife, Malia, as disciples, had been busying themselves learning the intricacies of the computer and of astrogation. We all were just beginning to realize what a complex project we had undertaken when we fled Old Earth, how much work there'd be to do, and the range of challenges we'd be forced to meet.

The afternoon of that first touchdown, we got together at the cocktail hour. Dan, officiating at the wet bar, waited until everyone had a drink or tea or coffee. Then,

"Things have changed, haven't they?" he said.

"They have for me," I answered. "Maybe because every world we'd seen before was lifeless. I'd almost taken it for granted that when we did find life at least it'd be no thicker than on Earth. I never thought it could be such a—well, such an *infestation*."

"Nor so abominably ugly, Janet," Geoff added. "Let's have another look at it."

I brought the screen to life and played back the recording, but when it ended we understood the life we'd seen no better than before.

Franz shrugged. "We came, we saw, and we learned absolutely nothing. Great space explorers, we!"

Laure smiled at him. "No, Franz, you're wrong. We've learned—or will have when we come to realize that we're not explorers. We're refugees—settlers looking for a home." She pointed at the bulkhead behind the bar, where I had hung a framed photo of Saul Gilpin with Polly Esther and his Lillian, together with the kachina doll he'd given us. "Let's all pretend we're Hopi, and never try to play conquistador," she said.

From that time on we avoided any star not closely similar to our own sun, and even then we suffered one disappointment after another. Only once did we dare to land, on a strange planet whose sea-girt continents reminded us of Earth, but of an Earth virtually mountainless and seemingly without weather. We saw no frozen poles; pale cloud banks drifted lazily across its pallid surfaces; and all its colors, its greens and blues and browns, even its red ochres, appeared pale, as if the millennia had depleted them.

We landed in a valley where pale-gray grasses grew, and we saw slow, amorphous creatures moving, all colorless, only relatively alive. And instantly our sensors and our surrogates cried their shrill warning, telling us that the air, the soil, the growths all harbored death for us.

We stayed only long enough to record what we had seen. Then, disheartened, we took off again; and again, in the wardroom, we discussed our prospects. We knew now that most stars had their planets, and we knew that at least on some of them life had come into being. What we did not know was how many, or how few, had gravities we could tolerate, air we could breathe, life forms we could live among. And there was only one way we could find out—try, and try, and try again. Of us all, Rhoda was most discouraged; Dan told us she was getting homesick for Old Earth, with all its viciousness and all its perils, and it was worrying him. But, that evening, when we talked about our future, even she agreed we should go on.

We had not yet entered the Far Reaches of Gilpin's Space, that illimitable area which seems to start roughly fifty light years from our solar system, and which even today no one really understands. We hadn't even suspected its existence, and had no inkling of how strange it would turn out to be until three days later, when Saul's second message suddenly turned on to warn us of what he thought might happen there.

Tammy and his Malia were standing watch, and the rest of us were talking things over in the wardroom. Red-headed, happily untidy Anne Macartney had been worrying over her two daughters, VeeVee (or Valeria Vivian), and the Gnat (more properly known as Natalie). They were cute nine-year-olds, identical twins, as red-headed and ordinarily as carefree as their mother, but they'd been having nightmares.

"You know how these carbon-copy twins are," Anne told us. "Like two halves of the same being. Half the time, those kids don't have to say anything aloud; each knows what the other's thinking. Now, God help me, they're sharing nightmares! Last night, VeeVee woke up suddenly, scared half to death; she didn't know what about—just plain fear. And the Gnat woke up at the same time, having had just a taste of the same thing. Mavis and Mutton were sleeping on their bed, as they always do, and they must've taken off straight up—"

"Those fat cats still haven't gotten used to half a grav," put in Jamie. "When they're woken suddenly they can't believe that now they weigh less than any very thin cat does on Earth."

"Anyway," Anne went on, "I heard the commotion and ran into their cabin, and got everything quieted down. But it just wasn't like them, and it's the second time now something like that's happened. I don't like it."

"Don't let it worry you," Franz told her. "I used to have nightmares all the time. It's natural."

"Not for *my* kids, it's not," Anne retorted. "Oh, they have bad dreams once in a while, but those aren't nightmares, really. They disturb; they don't terrify."

"Franz just meant it was natural for *him* to have them." Bess Mayhew laughed. "It's his Magyar blood—probably dreaming he was a Transylvanian werewolf and somebody was giving him the stake treatment."

We all—even Anne—laughed with her.

And it was exactly then that the ship's computer network alerted us. It flashed every screen three times, and then brought us Saul's voice calling out, *"Oyez! Oyez!* This court is now in session." Then it showed us Saul himself, with Polly Esther, Lillian, a tall young man whom we took to be Polly Esther's boyfriend, and another couple we had never met, both dark and grave and obviously Amerind, all in the control tower of *Cupid's Arrow.*

"Attendez! Attendez!" cried Saul. "This recording would never have turned on unless you had come at least fifty light-years from Old Earth. Therefore you have done well, *mes enfants!* Be proud!" He pulled at that weird moustache, and it was as if it had been connected to an emotional valve. His whole manner changed. For the first time in our experience, he suddenly was completely serious. *"But—"* he said, "but it is my duty, because I am responsible for your being here, to utter a reluctant word of warning. I say 'reluctant' because the warning may not be necessary. But I have reason to believe it is, a reason I can not explain in detail."

He turned to the two Amerinds, put an arm around each of them. "These are my friends," he said, "Paul and Louisa. Of course, they also have Hopi names. Paul's grandparents helped to raise me, and then I helped to raise him, so we are very close."

They both smiled at him.

"Now listen carefully. Louisa is a sensitive—a psychic if you prefer that term. She tells me that the Universe is alive with beings whose minds can and do reach out through the space we are now in. She has been able to feel them, though very faintly, and she believes that once you have left Earth far enough behind they will become much more powerful. She doesn't know whether they will actually communicate—she does not think so—because it is not concepts they will project, but raw emotion."

He asked her a question, swiftly, in a language alien to us all, and she answered in the same tongue. Then, in unaccented English, she said, "Please. Please do not be afraid. I know it—I have been told—that if you are not afraid no harm can come to you. How can I say this? No matter what comes to touch your minds, you must not echo, you must *not* reverberate."

She spoke again to Saul. He nodded. "The best way to put it is to think of a crystal glass and how it can be shattered by certain high notes of a violin string—and then to remember that the glass is inanimate, without free will, and that you are free to choose and have the power to do so."

Louisa looked upon us once again, and her dark face was kindly and concerned. She spoke again in her native tongue.

"She has blessed you," Saul said. "She has blessed you one and all. She has met you through me, and she says you are her white brothers and sisters, and someday, somewhere, we all shall meet again. Because Laure's such a special person, I'll blow her a kiss, which she can share among you." He did, and smiled at us, and said, *"Au revoir!"*

And the screens went dead.

We sat there in silence, staring at each other, while slowly the warmth of Saul's personality dissolved, leaving a sudden chill where there had been none before. Until then, I had felt safely insulated from the Universe's apparent infinity of strange living things by the enormous distances of Gilpin's Space; now I was unprotected, vulnerable—to what I did not know. I thought of subtle mind-tendrils reaching out to me, out from the burning suns, the icy darknesses.

Anne was the first to speak. "So *that's* what's behind those nightmares!" she said, an abrupt little quaver in her voice.

Her husband laughed. "Oh, come on, love. Don't jump to catch conclusions by the tail. The man didn't say it was a *fact*. Neither did that little Hopi friend of his. The whole thing may turn out to be a tempest in a teapot."

"Jamie, it's *not*. I feel it in my bones. Identical twins are telepathic—you know that. They'd be the first ones to feel anything like this. And don't think I'm getting the wind up about it. We've got to be prepared to cope, that's all."

"Anne's right," Laure said quietly. "If it turns out to be a false alarm, we've lost nothing by trying to prepare."

"Besides," Geoff added, "Louisa did say that we *could* cope. If what she said about alien minds touching ours is true, chances are she's right about that also."

Dan's arm had gone around his Rhoda protectively, and Geoff and I and Anne exchanged glances, all wondering whether she, too, had been troubled while she slept.

Then Tammy's voice reached us over the intercom. "Hey, just what was that all about?"

"Tammy, you know as much as we do," Geoff said, and I thought of VeeVee and the Gnat. "Well, almost as much. You and Malia hustle down here—the ship'll do all right without you for five minutes—and we'll fill you in."

They came, and we talked about it for a while, all of us pretending to take it lightly, knowing that we were really deadly serious. What else can you be about the threatening, the almost incomprehensible, even if it is just a shadow in the background?

The pattern didn't become clear all at once. It took form sporadically. For the first few days, it was simply a matter of more children having nightmares, most of them quick assaults of terror, of panic, followed by awakenings, tears, parental soothings. After that, for nearly a week, there was almost nothing, and we began to think what they had experienced was nothing more than out-of-the-ordinary coincidence. We tried to argue the improbability of human minds being invaded by the emotions of utterly alien beings God only knew how far off in space. We were, of course, whistling in the dark. Only Geoff and Laure and Tammy's big Malia refused absolutely to let down their guard—and Dan and Rhoda only looked at each other and said nothing.

Then, abruptly, it began again—and now it was affecting, not just the children, but some of the rest of us.

We argued. Franz, obviously disturbed, insisted that such things were psychologically infectious, and he repeated what he had said before—that nightmares were natural and nothing to get upset about; and Dan came to tell me that Rhoda had started having terrible dreams at the same time as VeeVee and the Gnat. She must've heard the kids telling each other, he insisted. It wasn't like her, it wasn't like her at all, and he wished Saul Gilpin had never left us that damn message.

I questioned him as gently as I could, but he couldn't give me any details. Rhoda had awakened in the night, and for a moment he'd wondered whether she'd somehow caught malaria or something—she was shivering so hard the whole bed was shaking. She was pale; her pupils were terribly dilated; her fists were clenched so tightly that later, after she had relaxed a little and become aware of where she was, he found tiny drops of blood in the palms of her hands. When he tried to find out just what had done it to her, she had simply come apart. Finally, clinging to him, she had sobbed out something about *abandoned, abandoned, l-left all alone,* and he, knowing what had happened to her in her life, hadn't pressed her. Instead, he'd soothed her as patiently and gently as he could, and she had made him promise to tell no one, even after Saul's appearance and his speech. Now, however, he felt he had to tell me—after all, wasn't I a doctor? He felt he owed it to her because maybe I could help.

It was my turn to soothe him, and I did my best to do it honestly, with a minimum of pseudo-psychiatric gobbledygook. I told him that even if he was right about the psychological infectiousness of this nightmare syndrome, still we weren't sure, and therefore I hesitated to suggest tranquilizers or sleeping pills. I asked him to be sure to keep in touch with me, and I suggested that, if possible, he should wake Rhoda at the very first sign of a nightmare. Knowing him and how he felt about her, I was sure he'd be a very light sleeper from then on.

He left me shaken, convinced despite myself that what Saul had warned us of was true; and later in the day I talked to Laure and to Geoff. Neither was surprised, and both were glad that at last I was taking the problem seriously. Malia and Jamie had both felt intrusions in their sleep, but had managed to awaken before the nightmare took hold. They had not told Dan, but they had told Laure, and they had not told me because they thought that I was firmly committed against the notion.

"See what comes of having too good a bedside manner?" Geoff smiled wryly. "You talk them out of catching cold, and when they catch one anyhow they go to a doctor who believes in colds."

"No doctor," I told him, "wants to believe there's going to be an epidemic. I'm taking this seriously, yes, but I'm still not convinced."

I may not have been convinced then, but two nights later I was, completely.

I woke. I did not know who I was. I did not even know *what* I was. All I knew was that I *was,* that I existed, that my existence was endless, stretched unendurably through frozen infinities of space-time, and that I was utterly inert, utterly helpless. Somehow, in my sleep, I must have managed to cry out, because the next thing I knew was Geoff shaking me, and that my own identity—at first only a faint pinpoint at the end of an endless dark tunnel—was coming back to me, slowly and very painfully; and as I woke, I wept with joy at the pain of it, and at the fact that I could *feel,* and know myself, and where I was, and Geoff.

I slept no more that night, and Geoff, too, stayed awake. After a while, after I was calm again, we talked about it, and I described the experience as fully as I could, realizing that what I myself had felt had been only an approximation, only an analogue, of feelings my soul and mind and body were not built to feel—and that, too, was something to be thankful for. We knew then what I suppose we should have realized long before: that all men are innately telepathic, but that our cultures and our associations with others—parents, other relatives, even casual passersby—force us, in varying degrees, to suppress this faculty.

We decided then that in the morning we would discuss it all again, first with Laure alone, then with the rest. We held each other very closely while we talked about it, and finally, as an affirmation, we made love.

We waited until after breakfast to get Laure aside. She was not surprised, and she agreed with the tentative conclusions we had come to.

"I'm certain," she said, "that there are ways for us to cope with these intrusions. Why is the telepathic faculty suppressed on Earth? I think it's because none of us is prepared to cope with it when it is experienced—as I'm sure it must be—let's suppose, at first, quite suddenly in childhood. A child is walking in the street. Abruptly, a hideous thought enters his mind. As we all now, there are innumerable people—cruel, sick, horrible people—whose minds we'd never want to know. Knowing only his own thoughts, a child *must* assume that any thought is his, a part of him, something for which *he* is responsible. Do you wonder we turn it off, or do our best to?"

"It makes sense," Geoff said. "But there must be ways to protect ourselves."

"That's why we'll have to talk it over with the whole ship's company," Laure told him. "Tammy and Malia come from different cultural backgrounds. So does Franz. Bess Mayhew is an anthropologist. I know techniques have been developed

for dealing with nightmares, with what are called delusions
and hallucinations. Let's get everyone together—all except the
kids—and see what we come up with."

We did, and after I had told them of my own experience,
after we had, much against their will, persuaded Franz and
Dan and Rhoda of our total seriousness and of the reality of
what was threatening us, then Laure outlined her theory of
what was happening and why.

And they accepted it almost immediately. Instead of questioning it, they started telling of their own experiences: the
usual ones, how people really close to one another could anticipate what each would say or want, how over great distances
triumph and tragedy would announce themselves, how comings
and goings, unexpected and unsignaled, would be foreseen.

Franz, after grudgingly surrendering his insistence that it
was all superstition, told us of his great-aunt in Hungary, who
never needed to be told of important family events, no matter
how far away they occurred.

Malia related a long and complicated story of a *kahuna* who
had been her father's friend, and of his telepathic talents.

Tammy, smiling a deliberately superior smile, declared that
his Uncle Hiroshi, the Buddhist priest, had taught him how to
liberate himself from his own thoughts when meditating. "It
works, too," he said. "All you need is to be Japanese like me.
Then, if you can learn not to pay any attention to your *own*
thoughts, think how easy it'll be to ignore other people's!"

Malia slapped him on the rump, said something to him in
Hawaiian that made him snort, and then, thank God, we all
laughed. We needed it.

Bess Mayhew, black hair flowing spectacularly, brought us
back to seriousness. "Have you ever heard of the Senoi?" she
asked. "They're a Malaysian people, known especially for the
lack of violence and the high degree of cooperation in their
lives. They've evolved a way of handling dreams, especially
nightmares. They teach their children to *confront* whatever's
most frightening in a dream—to confront it and conquer it;
and every day they get together and discuss their dreams of
the night before. Their idea seems to be that the content of the
nightmare stands for something in your own personality, and
that you can't dispel it as long as you let it frighten you and
flee from it. Maybe *we* can learn something from them."

"That may be all very well for nightmares that start within

us," I objected, "but we're dealing with something entirely different—nightmares from *outside*."

"That's true, Janet. But we don't *know* that all Senoi nightmares are born in their subconscious minds—that's simply what they think. Isn't it possible that some of them, at least, are telepathically inflicted, perhaps not even by their fellow Senoi? After all, the world is full of people thinking nasty thoughts. And maybe the same principle would apply, that business of confronting the content of the nightmare. Why not?"

"It makes good sense," said Laure slowly. "From what we know so far, part of the problem is absolute identification. Janet didn't tell us of her experience as if she'd been getting someone else's message. It was *she* who didn't know who or what she was, *she* who was stretched unendurably through space-time. If these Senoi actually have a technique that trains kids to recognize that they and their nightmares are *separate*, that the content of each nightmare *is* something they can face and fight, surely we can put it to good use."

"It'd at least be worth a try," put in Jamie; and Dan echoed him a little dubiously.

"We can get together every morning," said Geoff, "probably with separate sessions for the kids. I know that people can be trained to remember dreams, and this implies that no matter how deeply we may sleep, there must be a residual consciousness no dream can quite submerge—we hope."

"And maybe we can teach that consciousness to remain alert against intrusions," Bess added, "to wake us at the first hint of anything. I'll dig into my references and see what more I can find on the Senoi, and also other ways of handling dreams. There's no point in messing about with conventional psychotherapy. No predictability, and about a zero batting average."

Franz laughed. "And that's God's truth. But you talked about absolute identification, so how about Korzybski?"

Bess feigned astonishment. "Imagine this ski-bum/physicist knowing about Korzybski! Next he'll be telling us he's read *Science and Sanity*—I mean, really—and that he knows all about the Structural Differential."

"That is correct." He looked at her condescendingly. "I, unlike you, my love, haven't just acquired a superficial knowledge of General Semantics from Hayakawa's greatly simplified primer. I have read the good Count's *magnum opus* twice, as he recommended, and the Structural Differential is just what we need. It looks like several pieces of pegboard hung together with strings, and with other strings dangling from it; and it teaches Korzybski's three basics: consciousness of abstracting; awareness of structure and process on all levels; and the tremendous influence of such compulsive concepts as *allness* and *identification,* which our languages force on us. It teaches us that A is *not* B, that A_1 is *not* A_2, that A-now is *not* A-then."

"I haven't gone beyond Hayakawa either," said Laure. "But give him credit—he does mention the gadget. And I can see that it may be of help to us—depending, of course, on how much time we can devote to it, and how we react to it as individuals."

"Mightn't it be especially useful with the kids?" Geoff suggested. "They've not had time to get as language-conditioned as the rest of us. Laure, why don't we ask Franz to go ahead and make up a few of the things. You could, couldn't you, Franz?"

"Sure, especially if Jamie and Tammy and a couple of the boys help me in the shop."

"Fine," Laure said. "Then we can start sessions almost right away."

Jamie shrugged. "I'll be glad to help, but do we really have to go to all that trouble? After all, all we have to worry about are some scary dreams. They're no fun, but they aren't really dangerous."

That, of course, was what I had been telling myself and Geoff before I myself was hit.

Less than two weeks later, we found out otherwise.

We started holding morning sessions immediately, and Franz had his gadgets ready in time to get the kids started with them next day. On Bess' advice, we began by coaching everybody in how to remember dreams, how to go to sleep aware that we would dream, and—or so we hoped—how to remain aware while we were dreaming, aware that we *were* dreaming.

It seemed to work, especially with VeeVee and the Gnat. They reported waking up just as nightmares started, half-scared but not overwhelmed. But it didn't seem to work as well with adults and some of the older children, especially as the days passed and the intrusions intensified, coming with greater frequency. Franz and Bess Mayhew both had a taste of it; they reported that they never before had known the meaning of pure terror. Geoff, too, of all people, woke up in the small hours, utterly desolate, weeping; he told me he had found himself a thousand fathoms deep in a despair so absolute that at first he *knew* there could be no escape from it. Then Rhoda experienced two more attacks, each just as traumatic as the first.

"I think," Laure told Bess, "that how we respond to your Senoi therapy and Franz's Korzybskian approach—and also how we react to these invasions—is a function partly of our cultures and partly of what has happened to us as individuals. Tammy and Malia and, for that matter, Anne and Jamie, come from cultures not really hostile to the extrasensory; so does Franz. Besides, they all had family backgrounds in which a child would have run no real risk by suddenly becoming telepathic and letting his folks know about it. Rhoda's parents, on the other hand, lived lives of suspicion, jealousy, and downright hatred. From everything she's told me, I'd not have wanted to peep into either of their minds. That's the sort of thing that could reinforce the resonance Saul's little Indian friend warned us against—a resonance that may make the sense of identity almost unbreakable."

In our sessions, we listened to how one or another had been wakened by—by what? In many cases, the emotions reaching us were too alien to be directly understandable; our assailed minds could only struggle to translate them into our own idioms. Most of them involved suffering—sometimes with vague implications of physical agonies, sometimes as a direct message of terror of the unknown, the unknowable, sometimes screaming the fear of death, sometimes the fear of *never* dying. Then there were others which we translated into bleak bereavements, into the cruel destruction of high hopes and cherished loves, into yearnings so acute and deep and completely hopeless that only the emptiness of nonexistence could put an end to them.

And, worst of all, this was *all* there was. No data came, nothing to tell us the nature of those suffering beings, or their environments, or what it was that hated them, or had abandoned them, or thrown them into the terrors they screamed at us. Yes, we would awaken cold as ice—but did we really know that it was *cold* we were responding to?

Our reactions differed widely. After that first nightmare hit me, I usually managed to wake instantly—or almost instantly—at the first painful touch; so did Geoff and Anne and Jamie; so did Bess. Mrs. Rasmussen and Linda each told us that they really had to struggle to awaken. Franz had a terrible time for days; then suddenly, somehow, managed to turn it off—he credited the Structural Differential. Tammy and Malia and their boy and girl pretty much took it in their stride— perhaps with the help of that uncle priest of his—but they didn't claim to be unaffected. Keithy and VeeVee and the Gnat still were wakened by nightmares, but they declared they weren't scared of them anymore.

Strangely, it was very seldom that, except for the twins, more than one of us had the same nightmare or even simultaneous ones that were in any way similar; and all of us seemed to be affected differently. All of us except Tammy put it down to differences in personality structure and background. He attributed it smilingly to karma.

Another odd thing was the behavior of the two cats, Mavis and Mutton. Both Anne and Jamie told me that they'd seen them, just before the kids had a nightmare, crouching with all their hackles up, growling deep in their throats, protective but not at all afraid. Malia explained it by saying that everybody knew cats were telepathic; they had to be in order to find scared mice; they understood that the thoughts that came to them in the night were neither cat nor mouse thoughts. Then, as she often did when she wanted to emphasize a point, she dropped her habitually meticulous English for Hawaiian pidgin. "Hey," she said, "you listen. Those *popoki* got sense. They say, 'Those no my thoughts, no *popoki* thoughts. Maybe they been reading this guy Korzybski. Anyhow, all of us get same kind sense, no more *pilikia*, no more trouble.'"

But strangest of all was the fact that, from the beginning, Laure was immune—completely so. Her sleep was never troubled. Her dreams, she told me, were now either of her life when the Admiral was alive or of a planet she had never seen, an Earth-like planet, but one—here she groped for words— very *different* somehow, as though a different spirit hovered over it. She told us all, and I think that, because all of us were doing our best to fend off our nighttime assailants, we hated her a little for it. Aloud, we wondered whether we ever would find such a planet, and how long the attacks would persist, and whether they depended on the fabric of Gilpin's Space; and then, invariably, Franz would demand to know how we knew Gilpin's Space *had* a fabric? And, in relief, we'd start arguing about that.

But at least those morning sessions kept us pretty much on an even keel, those sessions, and Laure, and Geoff, who held us to our routine of searching, making near approaches when a system seemed likely, and once—only once in sixteen days—almost landing on a planet which did not show us its true, unfriendly face until practically the last minute. He also made sure that the ship's log didn't miss a change of course, or how long each passage took, or any of the other data we might need just in case something diddled the computers.

And then things got worse, much worse.

2

DURING THOSE SIXTEEN days, we began to think we had the situation more or less in hand. Then, at the breakfast table, Keithy's mother dropped a bombshell. Clearly distressed, she had kept him with us when Bess Mayhew, as usual, herded the kids out to their morning class, and now she told us that he had had a very different sort of bad, bad dream. "Tell them about it, Keithy," she said.

"Do I got to?" He was terribly embarrassed.

Mrs. Rasmussen patted his knee. "Now, it's not like it was any fault of yours," she told him. "You heard about what Mr. Gilpin and his nice Indian friends said, and you know what we've all been going through, so your dream's real important to everybody here, like Mrs. Endicott and the Commander and all our friends."

"Well—" He hesitated, shuffling his fork around on his empty plate. He flushed and dropped his eyes. Then it all came out. "Well—it—it was like I suddenly woke up—*and everybody hated me,* and everybody was—was just out, I guess, to *kill* me—and I—I was plain scared to death, and *awful* cold, and I—I couldn't run—*and all of a sudden I just knew I wanted to kill everybody too.*"

"Who was everybody?" Laure asked gently.

"Gee, Mrs. Endicott, just *everybody.*" Keithy squirmed, choking a little, and I could see tears forming at the corners of his eyes. "It—it was only for a—a second. Then somehow I woke up, sort of half way. And I pinched myself as hard as I could to get away from it, because I didn't want to believe it was *me* thinking like that—and Gosh! I lay there and thought about it for a while, and I—all of a sudden I was real scared of *me*—and I—I didn't *want* to be!"

He was crying openly, and for a few seconds there was

97

absolute silence at the table. My own mind was throwing me a terrible, troubling question; and I learned later that everybody there had reacted similarly, at least with variations on the theme: what might have happened if such a telepathic compulsion, instead of striking happy, well-balanced Keithy, had hit Whalen Borg, or Rhoda's brother, or any of the IPP's twisted hit men? Or—or *whom?*

Mrs. Rasmussen gathered Keithy to her, and comforted him, stroking his hair and telling him, in English and in Danish, that he'd been very brave, and there was nothing now for him to worry about; and Laure said we were all very proud of him because what he'd done had been exactly right. Then she asked him not to tell the other kids about it, not for a little while.

Still sniffling, he wiped his eyes, and apologized because he hadn't meant to cry, and Geoff—God bless him!—told him how a few nights before he'd had a dream that set him crying a lot harder than Keithy had. Finally, he went off with his mother and grandmother; and for a few moments we all simply sat there staring at each other. It was the first time we had ever looked at husbands, wives, friends in just that way—the first time that doubt—yes, and fear—had ever entered into our relationships. But it was there. Laure sensed it instantly.

"All of our nightmares so far, she said, "have been negative, but because of what's just happened we now know that there are far more vicious ones. Still, to my mind, the situation hasn't changed—except that now the most important, the most urgent thing is to avoid the trap we're all looking at—"

"And that is?" Franz asked.

"Paranoia."

We exchanged glances, shamefacedly. Nobody answered her.

"Paranoia," she repeated. "An unreasoning fear of each other and of ourselves. Let us remember that all of us are friends, close friends, that we're alone in a vast and possibly hostile Universe where uncounted unknown beings dwell. Let's remember, too, that not one of us is hostile, not the way Whalen Borg was hostile, that we're all stable individuals . . ."

I thought of Rhoda.

". . . individuals who can, and *must* rely on one another."

She stood. She smiled regally at all of us. "Let's go about our business," she said. "We've a ship to run, and a world to find."

As we left the table, I looked at Geoff, and saw his own conflict expressed on his face. All men and women have the germ of violence in them, and men in the profession of arms are more aware of it than most men are. In Geoff, it had been disciplined as perfectly as Wolfe and Montcalm had disciplined it, but still he knew that it was there.

"I'd hate to have to go to bed wearing a straitjacket," he said, half to himself and half to me; and when I told him I didn't think I had to worry, he gave me a wry smile and kissed me very softly on the cheek.

We held our usual discussion session later in the morning, but its entire atmosphere had changed. All of us were on edge. We were guarded with each other, even though we tried hard not to be. I could feel Laure watching us, weighing us, and, behind the curtain of her half-closed, almost translucent eyelids, letting her mind plan a course of action.

We all, I think, would have been happy to shelve the problem of Keithy's dream, hoping there'd be no recurrence, but she would not allow us to. After we had talked over our own, now seemingly inconsequential dreams, she brought us back to it. "As I said at breakfast," she declared, "we're threatened with a new and greater danger. But let's consider what we have going for us. First, not one of us is even potentially a sociopath, and we are extremely compatible; I've never encountered any group where—even among the children—there's so little envy and jealousy and spite and unhealthy rivalry. But there's one thing more—"

She stood. "As you know, I have not been touched by these emotions that have troubled you. I seem to be impervious to them—why, I do not know. But this doesn't mean that I have not been dreaming. I have. Here in Gilpin's Space, where its Far Reaches start, I've dreamed more clearly than I ever have before. In my dreams, we find a planet—a planet very like Old Earth, but unharmed, uncrowded, unpolluted. I have seen it, and in my dreams I've walked its surface, on the sands of its blue seas, and I have seen its cloud-piercing mountains— a lovely, lovely world. No—" She smiled. "—I won't tell you that a voice spoke to me out of a burning bush. But I do *know* it's there—there for us to find. This Universe we live in is no dead machine. It lives, and everything that lives is part of it. Not everything that lives is harmless. Not everything that lives is friendly. That we cannot expect. But as for those invasions of your minds, I am certain—*absolutely certain*—that, as one great man said long ago, we have nothing to fear but fear itself."

She stood there. Her aura, her personality, overshadowed all of us. None of us said a word. Of course, all of us did doubt her, to some degree. But how, after what we ourselves knew of Gilpin's Space, could we dispute what she had dreamed?

Silently, we looked at her, and then we looked at one another. In our hearts, we were still afraid.

She left the wardroom, and two or three at a time, all of us went about our business expect Geoff and me and Franz and Bess. For a few moments, nothing was said. Then Bess spoke, her voice vibrant with excitement. "Laure has changed," she said. "She *is* changing. Gilpin's Space is changing her. It's changing all of us, but Laure especially, perhaps because she's ready for it and we are not. And it's good—it's a *good* thing."

"What do you mean, Bess?" Geoff was puzzled.

"Geoff, I'm an anthropologist, as you know. On our Old Earth, where for millennia man has been wallowing deeper and deeper in his own artificialities, it was my job to try and understand what our less involved ancestors felt and knew of the world and its forces, of the Universe in which they found themselves—our ancestors and some of those whom we call savages, our less involved contemporaries. Because they lacked the scientific method, they had to use direct perception—and all of them interpreted what they encountered, not the same way exactly, but similarly. They evolved animistic religions; they found and followed those among them whose perception appeared to be more complete and clearer—shamans, witch doctors, all sorts of oracles and clairvoyants, call them what you will. Here in Gilpin's Space, in its Far Reaches, we've burst the man-made cocoon we were brought up in, and we're being forced into a new direct perception, perhaps one no man or woman back on Earth ever could have known. On Earth almost all of us had shut off that telepathic ability we now know we possess. Gilpin's Space has opened it again, probably more for Laure than for the rest of us. Somehow, she's armored against the Universe's agonies and sorrows, while we aren't, and somehow she can see and hear and feel those other messages to which we're deaf and blind." She paused, tossed her head to send her hair flying. "Let's listen to Laure. Whatever she suggests, let's do it!"

"You're *serious!*" Franz reached out a hand to touch her. "Do you really mean that our Laure, our Admiral's widow, has become some sort of witch-wife?"

She took his hand in both of hers. "No, not a witch-wife. Nothing so crude. Nothing so vulgar. And may I never sleep with you again if I'm wrong! She is becoming what perhaps she might have been two thousand years ago, what perhaps in a less artificial world she might have been all along—"

"And that is—?"

"A priestess."

Images flooded through my mind—silly ones, I suppose, a mélange of Fraser's *Golden Bough* interpreted by Arthur Rackham, by Burne-Jones, with just a touch of Delphos thrown in.

"A priestess," she repeated, "a woman born to mediate between the Universe and man. A woman like Saul Gilpin's young Indian friend." Then suddenly, "Don't laugh at me," she pleaded. "I *know* I'm right."

"I'm sure you are," Franz told her. "Considering the alternative you gave me, I have to be."

"We aren't laughing, Bess," Geoff assured her, and I echoed him.

She thanked us, and she and Franz left together.

Geoff, his gray eyes somber, turned to me. "Doctor Cormac," he said, "I hope you won't think I'm nuts. But it makes sense to me. With all the due caution of a ship's c.o., I say let's follow where Laure leads. Priestess or no, she has something the rest of us don't have."

Onward and outward, *Owl* flew through Gilpin's Space, and those raw emotions continued to assail us. Mostly, the invasions were still as negative as they had been before Keithy's dream. But now there were enough nightmares of writhing anger, and despairs and vengeances, of imperatives abrupt and terrible, so that no matter how we tried we could not shake off our awareness of their existence and our fears. The first after Keithy's happened to Anne two or three days later. She woke sometime in the early hours—woke to Jamie's harsh breathing and the pressure of his hands around her throat.

"I really thought he was going to do me in," she told us, still pale and drawn and shocked. "But he'd barely started squeezing, so I screamed—not a real scream, but some thing like *'Jamie, you dirty bastard!'* Then there was a long, awful moment while his hands stayed where they were, while in the glow of the nightlight I saw his eyes slowly opening. Then his hands dropped, and he said *'Jesus Christ!'* in an absolutely tortured voice. After a bit, we talked about it, and he made me feel a little better by assuring me that he'd already started to wake up and fight against it." She shuddered. "I hope it doesn't do it anymore, either to him or me."

"The most important thing," Laure said, "is that he did wake up, and that he'd already started to. Even asleep, he knew the impulse simply wasn't his. I think our Senoi sessions and the exercises with the Structural Differential really are helping. I'm glad we started them before this sort of thing began."

So she encouraged us. When Tammy woke to find Malia wandering round their cabin, growling like a wild animal in her sleep, and shook her awake only to have her collapse, weeping uncontrollably, so that he had to carry her back to bed to weep out her horror at a hunger so ferocious that it could be appeased only by some warm, living thing, Laure patiently pointed out that she was wandering, not actively seeking, and that plainly she, like Jamie, was already fighting against whatever clutched her mind.

We all suffered, in one degree or another, and though for a wonder there were no tragedies, our fear of each other grew with each reported nightmare. And with that fear, the tension mounted. We feared to sleep. Sleeping, we feared that we might never wake. Even though Laure kept pointing out that we were responding much more quickly to alien entries, even though she insisted—and actually, I suppose, we knew—that we were ourselves becoming, if not immune, at least impervious to domination, our fears still heightened. They became almost unbearable.

Partly this was due to Rhoda, for of us all she was the hardest and most often hit. Once Dan had a nightmare, a vicious, violent thing. She had awakened in the midst of it, sure that he was going to tear her to pieces. Her screams had wakened him and the whole ship. Three or four times, he came to me, asking me if I couldn't let her have some sleeping pills.

"Christ, Dr. Cormac," he told me, "the poor kid's not getting any sleep. She's scared of me. She's scared to death of what sort of dream she's going to have. This Senoi stuff and the rest is helping everyone, but it just isn't getting through to her. Can't you give her *something?*"

I explained why I hesitated to use any opiates. "We don't yet know at what level we're most vulnerable, Dan. It may be that we'd be worse off under sleeping pills. I hate to take the chance."

Finally I did give in. I shouldn't have. She took the pill, Dan watching until he was sure she was sound asleep, even though he himself was tired out. Two hours later, Franz found her, absolutely unaware of what she was doing, clawing at the starboard lock, trying to throw herself out into Gilpin's Space. He had wrestled her back into her cabin, while she struggled against waking; then he and Dan had listened to her raving incoherently, her nightmare compounded of terror and horror and despair, commanding suicide.

Next day, we talked to Laure about it, Geoff and I and Dan; and Dan was beside himself. "What the hell are we going to do, Mrs. Endicott?" he pleaded. "I know we can't abort the whole thing just to get her back to Earth. All we'd be doing is sticking our own heads between Brother Breck's jaws and hers with 'em. But we can't just keep on the way we've been and watch her fly apart."

"I was hoping, Dan, that she'd start improving like the rest of you—" She raised a hand at a hint of protest. "No, don't say you aren't. You've been adjusting, not all in exactly the same way or to the same degree, but adequately. You've been too close to it to notice. You really have things pretty well defused, not to the point where you can take them lightly, true, but at least so they aren't dangerous. Rhoda's another matter." She paused for a moment, thinking. "Geoffrey," she finally said, "is there any reason why we can't set down on the next suitably safe planet or a moon big enough to have adequate gravity, revert to normal space, and stay there a few days to give her a chance to catch up on her sleep and get leveled out a little?"

"No, of course not," Geoff answered. "But after that—?"

"We'll all get rested, and Rhoda will have had a lot of TLC, but mostly we'll have had a chance to think the whole thing out, carefully and not under pressure. I'm certain it'll not be too long before we find our own new world—a week, or two, or three—but we'd still be wise to take time out. A few days out of Gilpin's Space will give us all a respite."

It took us two days only to find a suitable planet. All through the period following Keithy's dream, we had reconnoitered one system after another, finding nothing interesting or noteworthy, and always circling onward in the general direction of a glowing cloud behind which a clutch of stars shone, and to which Laure was drawn. The stars themselves were too faint to see from Gilpin's Space; and we were able to see the cloud only when, in normal space, we turned the ship's eyes in its direction. The planet we found to rest on was not quite as large as Mars, and from space, once we had gone into orbit, it looked worn and bleak and desolate. We could see nothing growing there, though there were vast, murky, shallow seas; but once we were down, on the rounded ridge of an eroded mountain chain in the middle of one of its innumerable mini-continents, we could see vegetable life forms, rather like Earth's lichens, clinging precariously to every inch of soil. Our surrogates and sensors told us there was nothing there to endanger us, chemically or bacteriologically. Its sun was a dull, ill-tempered red, and the temperature of the atmosphere around us was like that of a Scandinavian winter. Geoff had deliberately chosen our landing place so that we came down into twilight—to keep us from getting curious and trying to go exploring, he told us. But he need not have worried, not then. The time coincided nicely with ship's time, which meant that after supper and perhaps some conversation, we'd go to bed; and I was surprised at how terribly eager I was, suddenly, to get there—to go to sleep, to dream no dreams other than my own.

We stayed there for five days—our days, doing our best to ignore the planet's, which were about nineteen hours long—and we slept beautifully, even Rhoda, especially Rhoda; Dan told us that she was asleep as soon as her head hit the pillow, and she slept more than half the clock around, sixteen hours or so at least. When we wakened, the sun was up, and we looked out upon our refuge. There was no color in that world, or almost none. It was all dull gray, dull brown, streaked with spines of black basaltic stone, mottled with muddy yellowish, greenish lichens—if that's what they were. Nothing moved. No whisper of a breeze. No creature flew or crawled. And down in the low valley far below we could see, quite clearly, indisputably, a ruined city, a city so destroyed by time that only its massive walls, black and rounded and rectangular, showed that it had been purposely constructed, and by a race who, in their day, had had the power to cut and move enormous stones and to arrange them by some strange geometry.

We knew that it was dead. We knew that possibly it held the secrets of its long-past life and death within it, but we felt no urge to go investigating.

"Let it rest in peace," Laure said. And Franz echoed her with a profound "Amen!"

We were content to rest, knowing that here we were safe from all intrusion, but we did not forget our problem or our purpose. No longer under stress, each of us gained a new perspective on our nightmares and ourselves—all of us but Rhoda. She brightened. Her eyes almost lost their haggard circles. But we could tell that, when it came to confronting Gilpin's Space again, she had made no progress whatsoever. She turned pale, trembling even at the thought of our reentering it.

All of us came to realize that we had indeed built up effective defense mechanisms, that now we could, even in our sleep, distinguish between alien emotions and our own. We knew that we would not sleep as comfortably in the Far Reaches as we were sleeping here, but we also knew that nothing there—at least nothing we already had encountered—could injure us.

All of us except Rhoda.

As those days passed, we became more and more concerned. Dan, of course, was almost frantic. He kept appealing to Laure, to Geoff, to me. And we could offer him neither comfort nor encouragement. Rhoda's life and background, everything that had happened to her as a child and as an adult, seemed to have doomed her to resonate emotionally. She could no more help herself than a glass, vibrating under the assault of high-pitched sound waves, can prevent its own destruction. We could see that Laure was as concerned as we ourselves, and as much at a loss for a solution.

Yet the solution, when it came, was beautifully simple. From the beginning, we had agreed to let the older kids, Keithy and the Macartneys' Jamie, Jr., and Tammy and Malia's, stand watch with us, knowing that they'd find it interesting and exciting, and also learn from it. Keithy especially always begged to stand watch with Laure, to whom he was devoted; and it was he who, on the fourth day of our stay and right out of the blue, showed us the answer.

He had been on duty with Franz and Bess, on one of the night watches, and he had simply blurted it out without guessing its importance. Bess, astounded and excited, had asked him to repeat it, and had questioned him in detail. Was he sure? Was he absolutely sure?

"Gee, Miss Mayhew," he'd replied, "sure I am. I been with Mrs. Endicott a lot of times when almost everybody else has gone to sleep, and while *she's* awake Miss Rhoda *never* had bad dreams. You know how usually when she'd dreamed something real scary, whoever's on duty hears about it right away. It's *never* happened with Mrs. Endicott."

Keithy's awareness of Rhoda's problem didn't surprise Bess; he was an observant kid. She hurried down to find me, leaving Franz on duty.

"Janet," she asked, after she'd told me, "is there any way we can check up on this? Has anyone entered Rhoda's nightmares in the log?"

"I have," I said. "Geoff asked me to when it began to look as if they were going to be a serious threat to her."

"And of course there's a record of when Laure had the duty?"

"Of course."

"Well, for God's sake, let's go check it! Janet, it makes *sense*. Remember what I told you about Laure? What's been happening to her? What she's become? She can protect us if anybody can—even if she herself doesn't know she's doing it."

I didn't buy it, not immediately, but I called Geoff, and we got the records, the written ones and those in the computer's memory—and it checked out. Rhoda had never had a nightmare when Laure was awake.

Bess was triumphant. "I knew it!" she exulted, her Gypsy eyes flashing. "I knew it as soon as Keithy told me. While Laure's awake, she's been protecting her. It fits. It's *right*."

I still couldn't accept it quite so readily. Maybe it's just coincidence. She's certainly not been protecting any of the rest of us."

"Why should she? Probably she knows what we're all starting to understand—that we don't *need* protection, that we're building up our own, and that we *should* simply because we *can*. But *Rhoda* can't. Gilpin's Space has changed us, but it's not been able to change her—life's rendered her too vulnerable, too fragile. Maybe someday she can grow to meet the challenge if she has to, but not now."

I said nothing, recognizing the truth of what she'd said, and suddenly my mind was flooded with compassion, with pity for poor Rhoda. I thought—and so did all the rest of us except perhaps Laure—that we were the human norm and she the exception to it. We did not discover until much, much later that the reverse was true, and that humanity would find crews like ours so difficult to put together that the Far Reaches would be declared taboo, not to be entered by any official or governmentally licensed expeditions into space, and that those adventurers who, unsponsored, dared to enter and survive them would be regarded with suspicion and with actual fear.

"Well?" Bess said. "Janet, what are we going to do about it?"

"Let's talk to Laure first. Maybe she'll want us to keep it to ourselves and not let anyone know except, of course, Dan, and Franz—because by now he's surely guessed where you ran off to, and probably Geoff because he's the skipper."

We found Laure in her cabin, and showed her all the evidence, and though she seemed as surprised as we had been, she accepted it with equanimity. "I hope it's true," she said. "I hope so from the bottom of my heart, and I feel it is. How I protect her, if I do, I do not know. Nor, at the moment, do I care. It's not important. Let's get Geoff in, and reschedule the duty so that I'll be awake at least eight hours every night. I don't think it'd be wise to bring the subject up when we're all together, but we should let the word get around individually. It'll be good for everyone's morale. Both Dan and I will need a little time to prepare her, to assure her that when we're back in Gilpin's Space she'll not need to fear."

We brought Geoff in, and Franz and Dan, and briefed them. Then Laure had Keithy paged, and praised him for his astuteness, telling him that no one else had noticed it. "And now, Keith," she said, "I want you to wait until tomorrow before you begin telling the other kids about it, but you can tell your mother and grandmother right away. And tell them I said I wish I had another merit badge to give you, a very special one."

He left, and she turned back to us. "Geoffrey," she said, "when we leave this planet would you mind very much if we headed directly for the Cloud, not bothering to hunt up any systems on the way? You'll know the first night out whether Rhoda's going to be all right, and if she isn't we can always find another place of refuge for whatever time she needs to level off again. It'll be a longer run than most of ours, but we have all the speed we need."

"There's no reason why we can't," Geoff told her. "And I hope we find your planet first crack out of the box. I for one won't be sorry we're leaving this one. Every time I look out of the port and see those ruins, I can't help wondering what sort of agonies poured through Gilpin's Space when their builders perished." He looked at Laure. "No wonder that even on Old Earth men have always felt the need for special people to intercede for them with whatever gods govern the depths between the stars."

3

WE SET OUR course for that far, far distant cloud, and from it
we did not deviate. At velocities greater than any we had ever
reached, we shot through those Far Reaches, and for the first
three or four days it was as it had been before. Our sleep was
again being violated; the only difference was that now, with
Laure standing her long night watches, Rhoda, with Dan beside
her, slept peacefully. No one, not even Dan, minded that she
kept their cabin door locked. We all were simply grateful that,
each morning when she joined the rest of us, she was more
rested, more relaxed. We still were not.

The change, when it came, was so sudden that it was unbelievable. We slept that night, all of us except Laure and Dan
and Franz, and some of us remembered that we dreamed—I
and Malia, and Malia's daughter Julie, a twelve-year-old, and
Bess Mayhew, and Keithy and the twins. The dreams came to
us as all those others had, out of the immensities of Gilpin's
Space, but they did not rend us, did not send us crying out or
weeping from our beds. My dream was a dream of joy, not
my own but that of some supernal entity capable of a triumphant, embracing, all-encompassing joy and love that seized
me, swept me up within itself, soothed all the fears I had been
carrying with me, then gently laid me down again. I did not
know whether it knew that I existed, nor did I care. For moments I was wide awake, but for moments only. I went back
to sleep immediately, because I knew it was the thing to do,
and slept beautifully almost till breakfast time, when Geoff
roused me.

I told him, poured it out to him, my excitement growing;
and it was he who told me about Bess and Julie and Malia and
the kids. I joined them in my bathrobe. We compared our
experiences, our accounts cast in the individual terms of our

ages and our backgrounds, but essentially the same. Strangely, the others, those who had not dreamed—or who couldn't remember that they had—showed no disbelief, no envy. They also had been visited in sleep, and were aware of it.

"I don't *think* I dreamed," Geoff told me. "But somehow everything seems changed. When I woke up, it was like a six-year-old waking into a beautiful spring morning."

That was pretty much the way they all described it, all those who could recall no dreams. Mrs. Rasmussen told us that, during the night, both she and Linda had felt the old, horrible dreams nudging at them, but as though from behind an impervious wall, powerlessly. Anne and Jamie's story was the same. Even Rhoda, emerging from her cabin with tears in her eyes, had awakened with a memory—one long buried, of her father and mother before they had changed so cruelly, loving her, cherishing her.

VeeVee and the Gnat poured out their dream to Laure and to their parents, and then just stood there, faces glowing. I could see that they were simply bursting to tell something more. Tall Malia stood between Tammy and their golden-skinned, handsome children. "Listen!" she said, her mock pidgin cast aside. "Everything *has* changed. Though some of us may not know it yet, *we've* changed. As for me—" Her voice was at once humble and triumphant. "—I shall never fear anything again!"

Julie nodded her agreement, and Tammy looked at them with a look almost of reverence in his eyes.

Then VeeVee piped up again. "I—I can close my eyes," she told us, "and I can see everything just the way Mutton does. I can see just what *he* sees."

"And Mavis, too," put in the Gnat. "They don't see colors the way we do, and the way they see is different—they're always watching for things that *move*. We didn't use to be able to do that."

"My God!" Jamie said, under his breath. "This is a new kind of second sight. What *has* happened?"

"I think we've all passed a boundary," Franz answered. "But it's more than that. We've been touched by—how can I say it? A mind, a tutelary spirit?"

"Yes," Bess answered, speaking very softly. "And it has seen into us, and through us, and—and—" Her voice almost broke. "And we have received communion."

Then she went up to Laure, and kissed her on the cheek. "Thank you, Laure," she said.

She spoke for all of us.

For the next hour, during breakfast and afterward, we scarcely said a word. We, the adults, were overwhelmed by the sudden realization that, no matter how long we had been friends, how long we had been married, or whatever, we had never before really *seen* each other, known each other. Between us, even between me and Geoff, there had always been a subtle screen, a veil, composed of all those little fears, those small reservations and deceptions, which our individually isolated lives on Earth had made an absolute condition for getting along together. Now these were gone, dissolved, and we were bemused by the openness and beauty of their absence—all of us except the youngest children, who had not yet learned not to see too clearly. For my part, it was as though the Far Reaches had opened each of us up telepathically, not to the point where we could penetrate the privacy of each others' minds—though we were to find that even this, as time went on, happened more and more frequently, as if by agreement—but on a very deep subconscious level where we could meet one another, as I said, needing no defenses. It manifested itself in varying degrees, for we were, after all, very different individuals, but its essence was the same.

During the course of that first day, we thought only of our new selves and our new knowledge of each other—that, and our new understanding of those Far Reaches, for we no longer felt that Gilpin's Space was an endless emptiness stabbed through haphazardly by tormenting thoughts. Now we recognized that it was here that the infinitely complex strands of the web of life met and interlaced—the living nervous system of a living Universe, an infinity of minds with gradations of awareness, gradations of volition, and ultimately, ultimately and above all, conquering and triumphant, the power to rejoice and love. We had felt love utterly without fear, and the terrible, solemn beauty of existence had been opened to us in a song of love and joy.

That night, when Geoff and I made love, it was as if we never had before, not so totally, so wholly *for* each other.

•   •   •

Laure had listened very calmly to our excitement—for a time, it must have seemed to her as though we were all chattering at once—but never, not for a moment, were we unaware of her presence. Finally, though, she told us that she was going to get some sleep.

As she arose, Bess asked her the question which must have been in the minds of most of us. "Laure," she said, "tell me— what we felt last night, it has something to do with that planet we're heading for, doesn't it?"

"I *think* it does," Laure answered. "Remember, I don't *know* any more than you. I can tell you only what I've felt and what I feel. Remember the null zone we went through extending those first fifty or so light-years from Earth? I think we've entered something of the sort."

"How can that *be?*" Bess protested. "How can anyone compare what we've experienced with—with how things are back on Earth? Laure, we were greeted, welcomed. Nothing like that kissed us good-bye when we left Earth's null zone. What is the difference? *Why* is it?"

Laure smiled. Very quietly, she said, "Perhaps it's a matter of fallen angels, Bess." And with that she blew us all a kiss and went off to bed.

We spent the day doing the ship's work, somnambulistically, taking time off whenever possible to exchange impressions and speculations. We knew, of course, that we were close to the vast cloud that veiled the star cluster we were heading for, and during the afternoon Geoff announced that we had entered it. Later, Laure joined us again, and before supper she gathered us all together, kids and all.

"Please don't take what I'm going to say to you as gospel," she began. "That's the last thing I want. I simply want you to know what I feel, and what I believe has been communicated to me, perhaps not even deliberately. We are very near our planet now—near in terms of Gilpin's Space. But in spite of what we felt last night, in spite of what I myself have felt and dreamed, we mustn't expect to find Eden ready-made. We won't have to face the hazards of Old Earth and what our fellow men have done to it and to each other, but we'll still be on our own, free to make all the mistakes men can make; and our new world will have its hazards, its storms and waves, harsh winters and broiling summers, and very probably its earthquakes and tornadoes. It will offer us, not a haven only, but also its perils and its predators, and we'll be free to meet them and to solve the problems offered us." She laughed. "What would life be like without that challenge? Would it be any fun at all?"

"In other words," Geoff said, "we'd better figure out our SOPs before we try to settle down—watch out for serpents, don't eat any strange apples, that sort of thing."

"Exactly. We know how strangely life can develop on worlds other than our Earth, and no matter how friendly our planet may appear, we can be sure that it'll have innumerable life forms, hundreds and hundreds of thousands of species ranging from the microscopic up to, conceivably, the absolutely gigantic. We'll be moving into an ecology with its own survival rules, its own evolutionary patterns. So no matter how lovely it may be, even if everything we encounter closely parallels what we've left behind, let's not forget that it is we who are the strangers and who must walk carefully."

We did not feel deflated by her warning. On the contrary, our enthusiasm was fired by it: first there had been the blessing, the benison; now would come the adventure. For the rest of that day and half the next, we slowed the ship deliberately, and spent our time discussing possibilities and procedures, bearing in mind that we had nothing to go on but Earth's experience and our own brief encounters on the few worlds we had landed on.

Our route through Gilpin's Space had been wandering, circuitous. We had looped back and forth from one likely looking star to the next, sometimes far, far from Earth, sometimes nearing it again. Now, as we emerged from the tenuous cloud of stardust that had veiled our destination, we were moving like the penpoint on a pair of draftsman's compasses, and *Owl's* computer told us that in actuality the stars we were aiming at were scarcely two hundred light years from Earth's null zone.

Then, during that second afternoon, Geoff called us all to the control room. He and Laure were there, awaiting us. The computer displays told us that now *Owl* was almost motionless. Without a word, he threw the ship back into normal space. He turned out all the lights.

There was our cluster. The heavens were alive with stars, and we could see that here they dwelt much closer to each other than in our own segment of the sky.

"Look!" Laure cried.

There, dead center, brighter than the others, burned a single golden sun, very like Sol but of a purer gold.

"That is *ours*," she said. "That is where we shall find our world."

The lights went on again. Geoff shifted us back into Gilpin's Space. The displays told us that we were again accelerating.

It took us only hours to reach that new sun and its family of planets, and even from Gilpin's Space we could tell that it burned with a steadier fire than Sol's, that no enormous spots marred its surface, that its corona was infinitely more placid.

Around it, fourteen planets wheeled in their orbits, huge gas giants with their attendant moons, others like frozen Pluto but far larger; then, as we came in closer, a congeries of smaller ones, glowing red and white and an actinic green, two of them retrograde, and most of them with a moon or two.

We surveyed them cursorily. They were not what we were looking for.

"It will be the fifth one out," Laure said, and she said it with absolute certainty.

We had to scribe a circle round the sun to find it, a bright pale-blue disk which, as we came up behind it, broadened, first to reveal its brilliant polar caps, then to begin the differentiation of its continents and seas, plains and mountains green and granite-gray and brown, broad forests and widely rivered jungles, and the shifting line of day and night. We could not see the colors from Gilpin's Space, but the evolving patterns told us what they'd be. It was so much like Earth—but still different, totally different.

We decelerated until its Gilpin-ghost filled half the sky; then, at a velocity which would put us comfortably into orbit, Geoff shifted *Owl* back into normal space.

There our new world loomed, like a vast jewel, its seas glowing with deep greens and blues, its golden sands, its cloud-crowned, snow-topped peaks. We saw now that it had two moons, one lemon-yellow, the other twice as large and rusty red. They looked as though they were chasing each other in the same orbit, and we didn't find out until later that, while they moved in the same plane, their paths were far apart.

Back we went into Gilpin's Space, shifting to a lower orbit still, where our new world *was* the sky. Its array of continents and islands bore no resemblance to Old Earth's. The continents were smaller and more numerous. If Europe and Asia and the

Indian subcontinent had been split up and set apart, they would have conveyed some idea of its northern hemisphere. Two narrow continents, heavily mountained, stretched down toward the south, and we discovered eventually that there were eleven continents all told, almost all of them with outpost islands, some as large as Britain or Japan, others forming endless sea-girt archipelagoes.

"It—it's *lovely!*" Bess whispered.

No one else made a sound.

It was Keithy who finally broke the silence. "Gee! What are we gonna name it?" he asked.

Geoff turned around. For a moment, he simply looked at him. "Keith," he said, "there is only one name we possibly *can* give it. We'll call it *Laure's World.*"

Laure started to protest, but our voices immediately outvoted her.

"Laure's World it is!" Geoff announced.

It was the first time I had ever seen Laure Endicott so deeply touched. She seemed about to speak, hesitated, dabbed at her eyes.

"You—you're being awfully nice," she told us, and her sudden smile warmed us all. "And you, Geoff—" She walked over to him, took his face between her hands, and kissed him. "—I want to thank you. I want to thank you for—for everything."

She knew how to forgive very graciously.

We spent three days in orbit, recording everything, monitoring the electromagnetic spectrum to make absolutely sure that no advanced autochthons were beaming anything at all in our direction or at each other, monitoring for those fires and smokes which are the first signs of a polluting culture, watching for indications of lights at night and movement in the daytime. We saw four or five widely separated active volcanoes and a few scattered forest and prairie fires. And we made measurements.

Laure's World was a little larger than Old Earth, with a diameter about three percent greater, but its gravity was just below Earth-normal. It had much less axial tilt, and a daily period of 25.6 Earth hours. The proportion of land to ocean area was roughly the same as Earth's.

At Geoff's insistence, we were being very cautious, not that he did not believe Laure's assurances—he did—but on general principles, which she herself agreed was wise.

We could see that it was summer in the northern hemisphere, winter in the southern. We could see storms stirring in the equatorial tropics, dark, angry clouds massing to sweep down on rain forests; and we discussed the question of where we were to make our first landing.

The general consensus was that we'd do best trying an island for a permanent base. "One like Great Britain, or perhaps Ireland," suggested Jamie. "Chances are the fauna will be limited—I'm sure there will be beasties—and in a temperate climate, if it's anything like Earth, the other biologicals won't be as rambunctious as they might be in some continental jungle."

"How about a really nice island like Honshu?" put in Tammy.

"With earthquakes and tsunamis?" Jamie retorted.

Bess pointed out that neither Ireland nor Hawaii had any snakes. "We certainly don't want any serpents in our Eden," she said. "Just Franz is bad enough."

"I will ignore that," Franz told her loftily. "This is a time for our best sober judgment. In principle, I agree about the island, especially if it's a nice little one. However, may I point out that we started to talk, not about our eventual base but about a spot for our first landing? We really ought to get around to that. But while we're on the island subject, have you noticed how a few of them, and not just in the tropics, have weird reefs—sometimes only one, then again an entire reef complex, like north of Australia? Quite a lot of them aren't at all like reefs on Earth. They look geometrical—angles, and long straight stretches. Who ever heard of tetrahedral lagoons before?"

"You mean Laure's world got coral?" Malia laughed. "Hey, that's good! Means maybe we got fish, all kinds. Maybe porpoises."

"Maybe big sharks?" piped up VeeVee or the Gnat or both of them; and Anne quelled them with a glance.

"An island would be the best location for our base," Geoff said, "especially if it's relatively isolated. It'd limit our problems with assorted life forms, and we wouldn't feel we were trying to swallow a whole world at a gulp." He grinned. "I'm sure you've all noticed how vast a sun—scarcely a speck in the Universe just days before—becomes when one comes close to it, and how much larger a planet that wasn't even a speck is when one lands on it. On the other worlds we've touched,

I've been able to avoid feeling overpowered by the realization, probably because we had no intention of staying on them. But here I can't. Now we are facing a vastness like that the first Phoenician navigators faced. Though we have the advantage of being able to chart our world ahead of time and hop around through Gilpin's Space, they always knew they had a home base to return to—and we are going to have to *be* our home base. So, before we settle on our island, let's spot-check the continents, and get as good a general picture of Laure's World as possible."

My own concern, of course, was less with the larger creatures we might encounter than with the microscopic ones. We were well protected: immunized against just about everything the human race had encountered, and with our computer-linked diagnostic surrogates which would not only tell us almost instantly whether anything menacing was present, but also provide the means for dealing with it. Theoretically, that was fine—but what of the unknown, the unguessed-at? Then there was always the question of bites and stings, and swiftly acting systemic poisons. I told myself that catching insects—any, at least, who looked as though they had offensive or defensive weaponry—was going to be high on our agenda.

"Where do you think we ought to start touching down?" Franz asked.

Geoff looked at Laure. "I'd say definitely in the temperate zones. Laure, what do you think?"

"Definitely," she answered. "If the rules here are anything like Earth's, temperate zone ecologies will be much simpler than tropic ones, but in the arctic and subarctic regions they'd be a bit too simple to give us much of a perspective."

"And how do you *feel* about it?"

She laughed. "I gave you good logical reasons, but that was just to justify how I do feel."

There was a little more talk about where and when, and it was agreed that, until we'd found our base, we'd stay with ship's time instead of trying to accommodate ourselves to the planet's. As Geoff pointed out, with instant access to Gilpin's Space, we didn't need to worry about when we'd arrive at a destination—we'd simply wait until local planetary time was approximately the same as ours, then hop. We'd eliminate what back on Earth we'd called "jet lag."

For two days, we remained in orbit, shifting our orbital plane occasionally for maximum coverage of the surface under us. There still were no signs of any advanced culture; indeed there were no signs of any sort of any reasoned activity, not at least within our frames of reference—no canals, no constructions, no roads, no agricultural geometries. As far as we could judge, too, the temperature extremes between the zones and between the seasons were not quite as pronounced as they had been on Earth. Except on the highest mountains, snow and ice did not extend as far into the temperate zones. Neither did the equatorial jungles. From orbit, we could detect no signs of residual glaciation.

Clearly, there was some sort of continental mass at either pole, more or less coinciding with the frozen areas. Besides these two, there were four continents wholly or almost wholly in the northern hemisphere, two straddling the equator, and three in the southern hemisphere. Straight-line oceanic distances out of sight of land were not as great as Earth's simply because the land area was more broken up. Besides, at least half the continents had attendant archipelagoes as thickly islanded as East Asia's.

We chose the largest of the continents for our first landing, a great rugged land mass ribbed with mountain chains, extending from the icy north down through the temperate zone and several hundred miles south of the equator. Topographically, it was as varied as North America: enormous plains all green and golden, cut by at least a dozen major rivers, vast areas of low, rolling, thickly forested hills—thickly forested or at least covered with what on Earth would have been forests—and one enormous, jagged desert cutting halfway across the lower temperate area, below which, suddenly, more mountains rose, then llanos, then rain forest, and finally a dry, reddish continental tip broken into rough islands.

Looking at it with our own eyes and the ship's, we took a long time to arrive at a decision.

Jamie laughed. "It's worse than trying to decide where to holiday in Europe when you have free tickets and just one week. Here we have all the time in Laure's World, but without a guidebook."

Franz spoke up. "Why not just pick a place that looks like somewhere down on Earth—somewhere nice, like Colorado."

"My God!" Bess exclaimed. "Here we've just arrived and already the bum wants to go skiing!"

"Well, it'll be a while before he can do that." Geoff chuckled. "There'll be a lot of things to get checked out before anybody can go ashore without a suit—"

Franz groaned.

"—but still, mountain country's not a bad idea. It ought to be ecologically cleaner than any bottom lands, except, perhaps, a desert. Laure?"

"How easy it was to pick a landing site on those other worlds we've visited, and how hard it seems to be now we're here." She was amused. "And that's natural. We know this one's important. But let's go back over those close-up views. There's that range Franz kept referring to as 'the Rockies' yesterday. Malia, will you show it on the screen?"

I looked out of the viewport at the immensity that filled our sky, and I thought, *How can we ever, in our short lives, hope to know even a little bit of it. We'll have our maps and we'll have named the continents, but what of the myriad living things this globe must hold, its mountains and its caverns and its canyons? How many of them can we ever see or name, the few of us who are here?*

And it was then I realized something I should have understood long before: that we could not hope to sever all our ties with Earth, that if we were to survive—and not just survive, but survive as civilized beings—we would have to find and bring others like ourselves. Some of us at least—and I understood it with a pang—would again have to brave the passage through Gilpin's Space and return to Earth.

The screen glowed with the image of Franz's mountains, and they were truly reminiscent of Colorado.

"Okay," Geoff said, "what is your pleasure?"

"You are too kind," Franz answered. "I could not be so presumptuous." He bowed to Laure. "Madame shall choose."

She did not hesitate. She stepped up to the screen. She pointed at a tiny spot of green. "There," she said; and Malia recorded the coordinates. "How does local time there gibe with ship's time now?"

"Within a couple of hours, I'd say."

"Then we could put down there tomorrow morning, couldn't we? Without breaking our sleep schedule?"

"Right."

Bess was standing there with her eyes closed, her lips moving silently.

"What *are* you doing?" Franz asked her.

"I'm praying," she replied, "to the spirit of this planet, or whoever it was that we communed with. I hope it hears."

4

THAT NIGHT IT was hard for us to sleep. We spent the evening speculating. What would we find once we had landed—a world where we could live, or utter disappointment? At dinner, Anne had pointed out that the ship's supplies wouldn't last forever, and that eventually we would have to determine whether any members of the local vegetable and animal kingdoms were edible. "We do have seeds, I know," she said, "but it'll be a long time after we get them started before we find out if they'll produce crops at all, and we didn't bring along any livestock—unless we count Mavis and Mutton."

"Mummy!" screamed VeeVee and the Gnat, outraged; and Jamie had to assure them that nothing serious was intended.

But the subject did reinforce my own awareness of the absolute necessity of a return to Earth and some sort of continuing ties, however tenuous, with our mother planet. I mentioned it to no one except Geoff, just when we were getting ready to go to bed, and he just shrugged it off. "We'll cross that bridge when we have to come to it," he said, and I could see that his whole mind was preoccupied with Laure's World and what we would so soon encounter, so I didn't mention it again, not then.

We breakfasted, and immediately afterward Geoff set us down, all of us in the control tower, all of us with our noses glued to the viewports. As we touched, we could see the planet's brilliant Gilpin-ghost around us, the mountains rising up at every side, a rushing river a hundred yards away, and an encircling forest of tinsel trees.

Then, abruptly, it was real, alive with color: the blueness of its clear sky adorned with a few streamers of white cloud and with a pale-yellow quarter-moon half the size of ours hanging overhead, the green carpet on which *Owl* was sitting, the vivid greens and pale greens and painted reds and golden splashes of the trees towering over us—if they were trees, and the dark granitic crags above them streaked dramatically with startling quartz outcroppings and veins of what looked like porphyry.

I stared—all of us stared—at those trees. Those that were dominant resembled giant conifers, tall and straight, their glowing ochre trunks and major branches bearing a profusion of, not leaves, not needles, but what seemed to be very thin pendant tubes, some a foot or more in length, others rather smaller; and these were green and red and golden, but very delicately so, hanging straight down like icicles on a well-ordered Christmas tree, almost translucent in the sunlight as they moved gently in a little breeze.

In their shade, we saw broad-leaved bushes—bushes?—each crowned with red and ivory, with long-stemmed ivory mushrooms set brilliantly with rubies.

We stared. I doubt if any of us even noticed that, as we reverted to normal space, the planet's gravity—about ninety-five percent Earth-normal—took instant hold of us.

"What a beautiful, *beautiful* world!" Anne said, her voice very small.

Then, as we stood there watching, out of the greenery a tall creature came, tall as a small horse but far more finely fashioned, with very long fetlocks, as though designed for some special purpose, and delicate small feet. It was completely alien, but still it was, in some strange way, familiar. It had two enormous eyes, gleaming amethysts, two ears like tufted narrow spikes, a stiff silver mane starting as a crest and continuing halfway down its back, a fantastically deep chest, and very powerful haunches. Its coat was buff and silver, its tail a tuft. Its broad forehead melded into a long, sharply narrowed face, with flaring nostrils a third of the way back from its small mouth, and fantastically long whiskers.

It tiptoed out toward us. Stood still. Sat back for a moment on its hind legs, but without taking its front feet off the ground, looked us over carefully—then, suddenly alerted, with one prodigious leap back it sped into the cover it had come from.

"I think what we're seeing," said Laure, "is a demonstration of parallel evolution. This world is Earthlike, and so its living things are also. Completely different from our own, yes—much more so than the animals of Australia were from those of Europe or Africa or America—but still infinitely closer to us than the creatures we've seen on really alien planets. We'll find enormous differences, but most of them will probably be unexplainable—at least without a paleontological record, which we won't be in any real hurry to go after, I'm sure."

"*I'm* sure," breathed Anne, "that I'd like to go out right now and run over to that river with a fly rod."

"Not till the sensors and the surrogates give us their reports," her husband told her. "An hour or two, love. So just be patient."

"He's right, Anne." Geoff turned away from the view reluctantly. "We can afford to take no chances—especially now. So first we're going to have to find things out. After that, a couple of us can suit up and go out for a follow-up."

"But Mutton's meowing to go out right now," protested VeeVee. "He knows there's nice clean sand down by the riverbank."

"Nonsense!" Anne told her. "He'll have to use his cat-box. Anyhow, how would he know about the sand? He can't see out."

"I held him up to the window to look out," the Gnat retorted.

Anne herded them, giggling, out of the control area, and the rest of us went about our chores, recording, adjusting the ship's sensors, making sure that the surrogates were all in place and functioning. The sensors were extended on their stalks; the surrogates were extended into the atmosphere, into the soil, and among the green "grasses" where *Owl* rested.

We waited, and the sensors began to give us their reports. The air was almost identical to Earth's, but with a rather higher oxygen and CO_2 content, a slightly different balance of inert gases, and a very much lower incidence of dust and other foreign matter.

We waited, impatiently. Only Laure was totally serene, as though willingly serving the interests of good sense. Had she been alone, she probably would simply have opened the lock and walked outside. Had she done so, she would certainly have been followed, first by Bess, then by at least half the ship's company, and she knew it.

Then the surrogate reports started to appear on the screen. One by one they came, and each seemed to take longer than its predecessor. And all were negative—even more so than they would have been on any Colorado or Wyoming mountain meadow, or even higher still, in the Andes or Himalayas.

As they came in, telling us that that immediate area of the

planet at least was safe, our impatience grew—especially after Anne spotted a swift flash of blue and silver-gilt as a swimming something broke water a hundred yards away. "Look!" she cried out. "Oh, Jamie, *look!* It—it was some kind of trout. I *know* it was!"

"Let us be accurate, Anne," Jamie answered. "All we can say that probably it was, if not a fish, something very much like a fish. Perhaps I should enunciate Macartney's Law: When both life and water exist on a planet, fish will come into being. If I were on Earth, I'd write a paper on 'The Universality of Fish,' and make my undying scholarly reputation."

"Oh, shut up!" his wife told him. "How can you chatter on like that when we've just found a whole planetful of unfished streams?"

Geoff chuckled. "Any ex-Marines here who'll volunteer to suit up and do a close reconnaissance?"

"Sounds like somebody means me," Dan answered with a grin. "Only, Commander, there's no such thing as an *ex*-Marine."

"Sorry, Dan. These strange planets make us forget important things. All right, who else?"

"Me," said Tammy. "Only why do we have to suit up? I feel like I could go out there in my bare feet."

"Like the *haole* say before he find out about scorpions." Malia snorted. "You no want suit up? Okay, *I* go."

"How about me?" offered Victor eagerly.

"And *me?*" cried Keithy.

"Hold it, hold it! Victor, we're going to have a rule until we're sure it's absolutely safe that only one per family can go. And I'm sorry, Keithy, but we just don't have any suits your size. Anyhow, I think two's enough for this first patrol. All they'll need to do is watch out for each other while they scout around the riverbank and those great trees over there, putting out more sensors and surrogates and testing things like that mushroom bush. We'll be recording all their findings here. Oh, yes, if they can catch any insects it'll be a help."

"How about putting out a few small snares?" Dan said. "Don't we have some with beepers that'll holler if anything gets caught?"

Geoff told them to take half a dozen. "Sooner or later we'll have to find out what the critters here are made of. The insects won't tell us whether we're likely to find compatible proteins, but anything bigger will at least give us some idea."

The question was not a pressing one, not while we had supplies aboard for months, but still it was important, one to which we needed a reasonably early answer.

We got that answer much sooner than any of us expected, and from a completely unexpected source.

Dan and Tammy went off to suit up, while VeeVee and the Gnat, now back in the control tower, made pests of themselves by demanding to be taken along, and were shushed with no notable success by Anne. Geoff checked out the equipment, and—at his insistence—sidearms. Finally they were ready. The lock admitted them, and closed, and its red light went on to show that it had opened to the air of our new world. We watched the two of them step down. We saw their feet sink into the verdure that carpeted the ground. They surveyed the clearing, the river, and the trees. They turned and waved at us. Dan's voice announced *All clear!* Then they went off about the business of that first exploration, placing the snares and the sensors and the surrogates, making sure that they were linked to the computer system.

Then suddenly, when each was about thirty or forty feet away, "Hey!" Malia exclaimed. "What's *that?*"

"What's what?" I said.

"I saw something move! It was running after them!"

"Me too! I saw it!" Victor put in excitedly. "Looked like it had a tail."

"It *has.*" VeeVee giggled.

"You saw it?" Geoff demanded.

"Uh-huh. It was just Mavis."

"You mean that cat got out?"

"She wanted to," said VeeVee.

"She meowed," contributed the Gnat. "When she saw them go inside the lock she meowed because she wanted to go with them."

"Good God!" bellowed Jamie. "So because she meowed, you brats let her slip in without a word?" He looked at Geoff. "I *am* sorry, Geoff. I suppose that's shot just about all our precautions?"

"Not all." Geoff frowned. "But we're really going to have

to go over her when we get her back in here. I'll alert Dan and Tammy and tell 'em to grab her as soon as she shows up, and pop her back into the lock."

VeeVee was standing there with her eyes squinted almost closed, concentrating. "They won't catch her right away," she announced. "She's too smart, and she's having a fine time."

"Uh-huh" said the Gnat, squinting hard and snickering. They nudged each other and their freckles danced. "Don't worry, Mr. Geoff and everybody. She's going to be all right. Cats *always* know when they're going to be all right."

Anne glared at them disgustedly. "That King Lear business about *how sharper than a serpent's tooth* must've really referred not just to thankless kids but to little vermin who pretend they can read cats' minds. Just wait till I get you in your cabin, you two."

Geoff gave Dan and Tammy their instructions, and they reported that Mavis was nowhere in sight. Then, for perhaps a half-hour, they went on scouting the immediate area. Twice, tail high, she dashed out of cover and ran around them, daring them to catch her, knowing that suited as they were they didn't have a chance. Finally every device had been planted, and Geoff summoned them back. They came, pausing every few feet to look back for Mavis—and, of course, at the very last instant there she was, running as fast as a fat cat can run, eluding their grasping hands to precede them up the boarding gangplank, and squeezing through ahead of them when the lock's outer port opened to admit them.

"When you get unsuited," Geoff told them, "see if you can grab her in the lock before she can get back inside. Then our good doctor here can put her through a battery of unpleasant tests to find out if she's brought in anything pernicious. I guess we'll just have to take a chance on some outside air getting in. We can't exhaust the lock completely with that fool cat in it."

"We're all going to have to start breathing it eventually," said Laure with a smile. "Somehow I doubt that we'll want to start looking for another, safer planet."

We waited until Dan and Tammy had shucked their suits, and Dan's voice had reported, "Okay, cat secured."

The lock door opened, and he stepped out, carrying Mavis by the scruff of the neck and her rump. "Would you believe it?" he said. "She's purring. She must've had herself a real nice run."

VeeVee and the Gnat were squinting hard and giggling. "That's not why she's purring," one of them said. "She caught a mouse."

"She ate it, too," declared the other. "It wasn't a real Earth mouse, just sort of." She shut her eyes even more tightly. "But it was *good.*"

"Not people good," explained her sister, "only cat good."

They both opened their eyes. "Can we take her now? Please? So she can tell us about it?"

"That," declared Anne, "is just about enough of *that*. Mavis is going to have to go with Dr. Cormac to make sure she didn't bring in anything that'd hurt us. Maybe you can have her back when she's been vetted—if you're good and quiet, that is."

"She didn't bring in anything that's bad," said the Gnat positively. "It was a nice, clean mouse."

"And *please* don't do anything to hurt her," begged VeeVee. "She—she's going to have kittens."

"Into your cabin, both of you!" snapped Anne. *"Right now!"*

She took each by an arm, marched them off, and came back just as Dan was turning Mavis over to me. "Those little demons!" she declared. "Identical twins are pretty telepathic, but that was just too much. Mavis and her mouse indeed! And having kittens! Jamie, if they keep on faking this sort of thing— I suppose to get attention—we're going to have to do some bottom-thumping."

She came with me when I carried Mavis into what she and her husband called my surgery, and held her while I applied assorted surrogates to what I thought might be critical points of her anatomy and inflicted one or two other indignities of the sort doctors and veterinarians habitually perpetrate upon their patients.

Happily, everything was negative—everything except the X-ray. It revealed, indisputably, the remains of some small creature in her stomach.

"Good Lord!" Anne whispered. "She *did* eat a mouse."

"Or *something,*" I said.

"Janet, hadn't we better make her upchuck it?"

"I don't think so," I replied. "Really, she's performing a very useful experiment for us, and everything seems to be going well so far. Remember, VeeVee and the Gnat said it was a good, *clean* mouse, and they've called the shots pretty well so far."

"But—but— Do you mean those kids really can do the telepathy bit with Mavis? Janet, they're *my* kids, and—Oh, *dear—*"

"Anne, relax," I told her. "After Gilpin's Space, which those two survived very nicely, their development of such a talent should neither worry nor surprise you. Just think how useful it may turn out to be." I rolled Mavis over and scratched her tawny tummy, and she bit me playfully. "Look at her nipples."

"They—they're *pink!*"

"That's right," I said. "She's going to have kittens. Your kids were right on both counts."

After an hour, Dan and Tammy suited up again, and went out to retrieve the gadgets they had planted—this time making absolutely certain that neither child nor cat sneaked past them. Two or three of the snares contained small many-legged creepy-crawlies and one a delicately winged insectoid with triple antennae fore and what looked like a small sting aft. Handling them with forceps, I killed them chemically, then gave them surrogate tests. The stinger turned out to be exactly that, but whatever venom it was equipped with would, judging by the readout, have been no more than an itchy nuisance, and everything else was as negative as the air and vegetation and Mavis herself had been.

"Well," I asked, when the reporters were in, "what do we do now?"

"That, I think, is obvious." Laure stood, stately and serene, smiling at us all. "We must celebrate our new world. We must embrace it, and allow it to embrace us. We have white linen tablecloths, big ones. Let's spread them on the grass outside and have a picnic lunch."

"Swell!" shouted Malia. *"Le déjeuner sur l'herbe*. Me, I'll take off all my clothes and be the model."

"She's always finding an excuse to take them off," her husband said. "Though, considering what a handsome, intelligent man she's married to, who can blame her?"

"You *pupuli*, Tammy Uemura—you *pupuli nui*. It's only that I admire beauty, even when it's me. Okay, just for that I won't take 'em off."

Geoff was hesitant. "Laure, do you think we should forget all precautions and—well, just go out there?"

"Yes, I do, Geoff—at least all those extraordinary ones we

have been taking. Sooner or later we're going to have to, and everything's tested safe so far. I'm sure the Navy and Marine Corps can protect us against any hostile critters."

Geoff was still reluctant, but he did give in; and I could tell that actually he was as eager to get out there as the rest of us. The hustle and bustle started automatically. Mrs. Rasmussen suddenly appeared with three enormous tablecloths and, of all things, a wicker picnic basket big enough to hold a dozen bottles and a whole suckling pig. Cups and plates and knives and forks and spoons made their appearance. A ham showed up and a cold smoked turkey. From the galley came laughter and salad-making noises; and I could hear VeeVee and the Gnat nagging at their mother. "But why *can't* Mavis come? She's been outside already." And, "Please, Mummy, please let Mutton come along. He's not been out *at all.*"

"Absolutely *not,*" said Anne very firmly; then she repeated it not quite as firmly as before. Finally she told them that they could take the cats, "But only if you put their harnesses on and hang onto the leashes every minute. You hear?"

Laure gestured to us, to Geoff and me, and we accompanied her to the lock's inner door. He threw it open for her. Then he stepped through and opened the outer port also.

There was a gentle breeze outside, and the air of our new world started to drift in, bearing its total freshness and its subtle scents, scents disturbingly reminiscent of Earth's forests and yet, quite literally, with a world of difference.

Laure stepped out and stood at the gangplank's head, breathing deeply, feeling the warming rays of our new sun through the cool, moving air. She walked down the gangplank, and we followed her, Geoff and I. Then the parade started, Keithy with the basket, his mother with the tablecloths, others with the provender and plates, cats and children and huge salad bowls. Dan came out, to stand guard like a good Marine. Franz came, decked out in a tall chef's cap and starched white apron, and Bess followed him bearing a lute which I knew she had aboard, but which I'd never heard her play. Her eyes were wild with pure joy, and I saw her nostrils delicately testing the wind's subtle messages.

And there were sounds. We could hear the river, like all mountain rivers anywhere, and the almost crystalline rustle of the trees, and all those not-yet-familiar background sounds that are the voice of every living world.

The tablecloths were laid out on the golden-green verdure which, for lack of any native name, we were to call grass from the beginning. The food was piled high—more, I thought, than we could ever eat until I remembered the many young appetites among us. Glasses were passed from hand to hand, even VeeVee and the Gnat each getting one. Then, wonder of wonders, out of the basket Mrs. Rasmussen began taking magnums of champagne, and passing them to Victor and Malia, who promptly popped their corks and started pouring.

When they had made the rounds, Geoff lifted a hand for silence. "Let me propose a toast!" he said, raising his glass. "To Laure! To Laure Endicott!"

"Thank you, Geoff. Thank you very much indeed. But first—" She looked all around her, at the mountains towering over us, the ardent, playful river, the growing things among which we were seated. "—first let us drink to our new world!"

Geoff bowed. "Very well, then—to Laure's World!"

He drained his glass. We all drank. But Bess barely sipped hers, then very carefully, murmuring something we could not hear, she poured the rest gently on the ground.

"What *are* you doing?" Franz asked.

Laure answered him. "Franz, that was a libation. It was to acknowledge and to honor the being, the spirit, who brought us here—Bess, wasn't it?"

Bess nodded very seriously, holding her glass out to be refilled. Then we drank toast after toast, to Laure first and foremost, then to our gallant captain, to one another, to Mutton and to Mavis and her mouse. We ate and drank and laughed, and Bess began very softly to strum her lute, softly, softly, an air of Thomas Campion's. Then presently she sang, her voice very low and sweet, the love song's words. Then Laure joined with her, and Jamie Macartney in a well-controlled baritone.

When she had finished, she made the lute speak again, William Byrd's "Wolsey's Wilde," originally composed for a keyboard instrument but losing nothing in her rearrangement. It spoke to us of springtime and garden shadows and songbirds and Old Earth's blossoms. The songs that followed were, most of them, the songs of England when the first Elizabeth sat upon the throne, and all the glories of the Renaissance, fresh from Italy, were taking root in that rich soil. She sang the songs of Shakespeare, and pastorals by poets I did not know, and country airs about the rites of spring, vibrant with the joy of being alive, tremulous with the sudden hungers of young love.

We ate and sang and talked, and Malia danced an impetuous hula for us while Tammy and Victor accompanied her on drums they'd made by turning buckets upside down. We were completely happy, and the Earth-nostalgia awakened by our songs only accentuated our happiness. Only Mutton and Mavis were disgruntled—no proper cat likes being restrained by a leash—but once they'd been well stuffed with turkey and cold salmon and other not-good-for-cats delicacies, even they decided to enjoy themselves.

We felt, all of us, that we were home.

Then, around mid-afternoon, I happened to look up at a bare jutting quartz crag forty feet above the river. On that crag, forefeet relaxed in front of it, its long, strange head cocked slightly to one side, a huge creature lay. Its pale eyes glowed like opals under the cavernous arches of its broad forehead; its reddish pelt gleamed in the sunlight; large nostrils on either side of a wide, curved muzzle dilated and contracted as it breathed; deeply cupped ears were adorned with pairs of what could only have been feelers.

Geoff saw me staring. His eyes followed mine. "Good Lord!" he whispered. "That thing is bigger than a tiger—it's like a tiger and a half!"

By now, everyone was staring at it, and it, impassively, was staring back at us. Then, very slowly and luxuriously, it rose and stretched. It opened its great mouth, and we could see that each jaw was doubly fanged. There was no doubt about its being a carnivore, swift and lithe and magnificently muscled, a predator as perfect as any on Old Earth.

Logically, we knew we did not need to fear it, that Geoff or Dan could, with a laser pistol, destroy it in an instant. But still I myself did feel a twinge of fear, just for a moment when it looked at me, fear and wonder and, yes, respect. Just so, I thought, must the Masai have respected the lions they slew, the Amerinds the grizzly bears they encountered.

For another half-minute it posed there for us, then uttered a curious, undulating, whickering cry, and turned its back on us and slowly walked away.

I looked around. Laure was watching it with open admiration. Dan and Geoff, hands hovering near their sidearms, were—I think—trying to do their best not to look like a couple of trophy hunters. Rhoda had taken instant refuge behind Dan's back. And now all the rest were chattering at once—how glad they were it had decided not to join us for lunch, and how they'd hate to run into it on a dark night, that sort of thing. Mutton and Mavis who, busily digesting, had slept through the whole business, now were testing the air, looking puzzled, and growling softly to themselves.

For the moment, VeeVee and the Gnat were saying nothing. They had their eyes squinched shut, facing the crag where the creature had appeared.

"He's gone, kids," said Anne soothingly. "You can open your eyes now."

VeeVee opened hers first. "Why is everybody *scared?*" she asked. "*He* wasn't trying to scare anybody."

"Uh-*uh,*" her sister echoed. "He was *nice*. He was just sort of listening to us. He knew we aren't good to eat."

"He's going home now," VeeVee added. "Maybe he wants to tell his wife about us—his wife or somebody."

"That is a *great* comfort," Franz declared. "He'll tell her not to put us on the menu. As for me—" He reached for the champagne. "—I need a little morale stiffener. Anyone else?"

The champagne went round again, and once more Bess poured a little on the ground; and we went on singing for another hour or so, songs from Spain and Scotland, from France and Wales, songs mostly of revelry and pleasure. Franz, not very melodiously, favored us with a tragic Magyar ballad about a goose girl whose lover had the misfortune to be thrown by his horse into the middle of her flock of geese, where he was pecked to death. "My mother taught it to me," he explained as he translated each verse for our benefit. "She used to get annoyed because I always asked whether, back in Hungary, people were often goosed to death."

At that point, out of the sky dropped five great birds. They came down smoothly, their wide wings swept back like a swallow's, their silver silken plumage contrasting vividly with their veridian stilt-like legs, yellow sabre-beaks, and red-rimmed golden eyes in round pumpkin heads. They landed in a line at the meadow's edge, eyeing us, opening and closing their savage beaks as if in a supersonic conversation. Finally, each raised a ruff of feathers up around its head, and all took off simultaneously.

Somehow we all knew that the show was over, and, laughing, we set about our packing up, none of us too eager to get back into the ship, but knowing that there was much, much more to do, what with other continents to check, and—ultimately—our island base to find.

"I suppose we ought to name this continent before we leave it, hadn't we?" said Jamie. "Laure, what do you want to call it?"

"Why don't we call it *Mavis?*" piped up the Gnat.

"You can't name a continent after a cat," her father told her.

"I don't see why not. It was *Mavis* caught the mouse."

Laure patted her on the head. "Be patient, dear," she said. "We won't forget Mavis and Mutton. They're going to have whole islands named after them."

5

WE SPENT THE next two weeks methodically checking out the other continents, getting a general idea of climates, terrain features that appeared particularly interesting, fauna and flora. Those areas which, from our knowledge of similar areas on Old Earth, promised to be either dangerous or decidedly unpleasant—vast swamps, too-thick jungles, harsh deserts, and polar ice-caps—we mapped from low orbit, but otherwise left alone. But we could not resist forested mountains, well-watered plains wide as half a continent, rolling meadowlands. We made our landings short, allowing none of the lighthearted carelessness which had made our first arrival such a joy, staying just long enough to see what our sensors and surrogates would tell us about the air and soil, the water and the living things. And all we saw contributed to a single message: parallel conditions contribute to parallel evolutions. We found enormous herds of grazing herbivores, some cloven-hoofed, some not, all as curiously specialized as their analogues on Earth. (After all, who would expect the same veldt to produce creatures as dissimilar as the giraffe, the wildebeest, the zebra, and the tiny dik-dik?) This was true also of the predators who killed and ate them. No, they were not great cats, nor were they wolves or bears, but in a hundred different ways they filled similar ecological niches. We recorded everything, putting off all attempts at classification until later—much later.

Naturally, there were some creatures that were far out, just as the duck-billed platypus is far out. For instance, we saw a group of flying things that looked half-bird, half-mammal, with rubbery beaks hooked almost like a macaw's, huge dull-orange wings covered with what looked like inexpensive carpeting, and teats like harpy's breasts. They must have had hollow bird-bones, for despite their size—they were as big as condors—

they were able to take off almost vertically. We saw flocks of birds such as Earth had not seen since the last of the passenger pigeons were exterminated, flocks half-darkening the sky, and flying, not in Vs, but in ordered helixes.

Then there were reptiles: lizards and snakes and others who seemingly had not been able to make up their minds what to be, snakelike creatures who looked as though they had been derived from frogs, and weird amphibians whose flying surfaces were controlled by their front legs and folded back along their wet, scaly bodies when not in use.

Oddly enough, while there were arboreal animals aplenty, we saw nothing even resembling a simian, let alone the more anthropoid of the apes—and somehow I found this rather comforting.

The evolution of the flora had followed the same course as that of the fauna. The trees were trees; they simply were not Earth trees. Similarly, we could look at a shrub, a fern, a succulent, but we could never give it an Earth name, not accurately. We found entire forests of giant tree-grasses like bamboos, but they were not bamboos. There were trees and vines bearing fruit, but it resembled no fruit with which we were familiar—or rather, sometimes it resembled Earth fruit just enough to emphasize its strangeness. Only the insects, at first glance, seemed almost eerily like those of Earth, but that was simply because most of us pay very little heed to bugs unless they bite or get into the cooking or spatter on our windshields. We were to find out eventually that even the insects, though they had developed along parallel lines, were analogues, never duplicates.

Wherever we touched down, too, our instruments reported favorably. Nothing more dangerous was encountered than we might reasonably have expected back on Earth; the small life forms we snared and examined harbored nothing really deadly either within their own chemistries or as parasites. For the time being, we had decided not to seek out things like poisonous snakes or the equivalents of crocodiles. By the time our primary reconnaissance was finished, when we were ready to begin searching for our island base, we had pretty much decided that many of the native species of flesh and fowl, fruit and vegetables would ultimately turn out to be edible. Mavis had suffered no ill effects from the ingestion of her "mouse," and Anne and Jamie had demonstrated, with rod and line, that the

fish were indeed fish and that they would strike a lure like their
distant cousins back on Earth. So far, we knew that to be true
only of freshwater fish in the streams of a mightily fjorded
continent—icy streams that proved too enticing even for Geoff,
who really isn't that much of a fisherman. We did not yet know
what we would encounter in the oceans, though we were sure
that, as on Earth, the sea life would be wilder and weirder than
anything on land.

Finally we started searching for our island. We had noted
some in passing as worthy of investigation, and now returned
to them. We landed on ten, a dozen, all in the more temperate
zones; none struck us as quite right until, off the northeastern
shore of a long arrowhead-shaped continent extending from
south of the equator more than two thousand miles, we found
what we were looking for. Far from the mainland, at least five
hundred miles away, they formed a tiny archipelago: two large
main islands, one forty miles long, the other slightly smaller,
the two shaped curiously like the Chinese symbol for yin and
yang, a pair of mighty tadpoles trying to embrace each other.
They were mountainous, but not too ruggedly so, and showed
no signs of vulcanism, and they were attended, to the south,
by a host of very much smaller islands and tiny atolls. The
broad channel between the two major islands formed a lagoon
varying from one to about twelve miles in width, and its two
entrances were battlemented by multiple reef complexes, all
beautifully geometrical and each geometrically broken by the
channels that gave admittance to the tides and currents of those
seas and whatever lived in them. And every visible lagoon,
every atoll, however small, shared this geometricity. We speculated on it, naturally, on the enormous coral populations which
must have been responsible, and whether instinct drove them,
like honeycombing bees, to build their lives in such well-ordered
shapes and then, dying, leave their skeletons for their descendants to keep building on.

We chose a sheltered cove on the lagoon side of the bigger
island, an inlet rimmed by white beaches a hundred yards and
more in width with a gentle curl of surf sweeping their rims.
Those beaches rose gradually, to end, not in dunes, but in
rolling hills, small at first, then getting larger and more impressive. The trees were very different here, very tall, their
trunks as white as birches, but with spreading palmate leaves

and splashes of varicolored blossoms; and down between them a river ran, broad and clear and even where it joined the sea, edged with unbelievably neat rows of glass-green, grain-bearing grasses, for all the world like carefully cultivated giant rice. We brought *Owl* out of Gilpin's Space on an open hillock from which we could see up and down the river, from where it emerged out of the trees to where it surrendered to the sea; and impatiently we started the routine of our tests. To make waiting easier, we breakfasted while awaiting the reports.

"Let's name our islands," Laure suggested suddenly, joyously. "I feel they *are* our islands. Let's name this big one Mutton, and the other Mavis."

"After the *cats?*" said Jamie.

"Of course, you idiot," laughed his wife. "Don't you remember? Laure promised the kids we'd name islands after them."

VeeVee and the Gnat crowed with delight; Keithy rubbed Mutton's jowls until he purred; Victor and Julie clapped their hands in glee.

"Mutton Island it is, then," declared Geoff. "With Mavis Island next. They'll be the first names on our charts."

"*Mavis* should be first," the Gnat protested. "It was she caught the mouse."

After breakfast, the results started to come in, and they were uniformly negative. We adults waited more or less patiently because we had to; and, waiting, I think we all began to get a better idea of just how great a task we'd set ourselves. The exploration of Mutton Island, which previously—against the gigantic and infinitely complicated backdrop of our new world— had seemed a petty thing, now assumed formidable proportions. Forty miles of strange terrain is nothing to sneeze at, not when you have to get to know it intimately.

During our journeying, we had, of course, gone over *Owl*'s inventory many times, wondering whether we had brought enough of this or too much of that, and whether in the forced haste of our departure we had completely forgotten absolute necessities. We knew that, sooner or later, we would have to start building, for all of us had read enough science fiction in which a spaceship, used as habitation and refuge by generation after generation of its crew's descendants, remains a ship no longer; and we were determined to avoid this at all costs. Now that we had our site, we agreed to go over everything again and reevaluate in terms of Mutton Island and our exact spot on it.

Everything about our location suggested a climate something like New Zealand's, neither too tropical nor too cold. We had seen no signs of heavy storm damage; the tall trees were untorn; the beaches showed little or no driftwood; where beaches ended and, for instance, low cliffs began, the waves seemed to have done little damage over the centuries. We familiarized ourselves with the immediate area for a day or two, then set to work listing everything we knew would have to be put ashore more or less permanently—everything redundant to *Owl*'s safe operation as a spaceship and as a submarine—and we were astounded not only at the variety and quantity of necessities we'd brought aboard, but at the ship's cargo capacity.

First, on the leeward slope to the hillock, we set up two geodesic domes roughly thirty-five feet in diameter, driving their anchor pins into hard rock and giving their assembled skeletons impermeable, translucent double skins. Into them, we put the two extra nukepaks, knowing now that *Owl* wouldn't need them. We stored kitchen gear, power tools, pieces of furniture for future housing, two inflatable boats with their motors, the small copter, the cross-country vehicle, and the duplicate computers. We also brought out several smaller packaged domes. Deliberately, we set out to make *Owl* seem less like home. That, we knew, was essential.

Actually, our main difficulty in the beginning was in persuading the kids, especially the twins, that Laure's World and Mutton Island were not yet home for us, that we were strangers still and would have to behave as though we were on sufferance. Usually with Dan leading, and with transport now available, we adults and the older kids took turns exploring, always expanding our perimeters a bit beyond where we had gone before, setting up electronic systems to notify us of any critters larger than a mole and to have the computer record what they looked like. We couldn't cover every square inch, of course, but we did cover those places that seemed most likely: springs where animals came to drink, anything that looked like a worn trail or showed hoof or paw prints. Also, we dropped sonar receptors in an area perhaps half a mile in radius from the river's mouth, to tell us what swam in those waters and whether it might plausibly be considered dangerous. Geoff had been eager to do a little submarine exploring, and now, with *Owl*'s cargo unloaded, there was no technical reason not to. However, he put it off until we could make a sonar chart of our little inland sea. "I very much doubt," he said, "that we'll find any major reefs like those weird ones at either channel, but coral's odd stuff—if it is coral—and you never can tell. We've gotten a pretty good picture of the sea life here, at least in the lagoon, and judging by what the screen's shown us there's nothing to compare to Earth's sharks. The big fish are nowhere near as primitive, and the aquatic mammals seem as tame as porpoises. When Dan and Victor took their boat ride yesterday, the critters tagged right along, splashing each other and the boat and doing no one any harm."

Those first water creatures eventually turned out to resemble king-sized otters almost as much as they did porpoises, having retained some use of their front paws, but with a porpoise's ability to stay submerged. At first, Dan had been reluctant to try fishing, worried that one of the mammals might strike his bait, but at Victor's suggestion he cut the hooks off two trolling lures, a Japanese bone jig and a more recent wiggly minnow. Several of the mammals zeroed in on them, looked them over, then swept off with disgusted swishes off their tails. We learned later that they much preferred shellfish.

At any rate, Dan and Victor caught two splendid fish, one weighing twenty or more pounds and shaped like a green-and-orange pompano, the other glossy black and red and swift as any skipjack. Both turned out to be biologically no more dangerous than any ordinary fish on Earth, and that night Mrs. Rasmussen served them both at dinner. Mutton and Mavis thought them simply wonderful.

The days passed swiftly, and they were working days for everyone, so much so that even Geoff's subsurface exploration kept getting deferred. As our picture of Mutton Island's life filled in, we began to feel more and more secure, more at home. We became acquainted with birds of sea and shore, small and large strangely convoluted shellfish, some of them astonishingly mobile; little mammals who seemed to come to life only after sunset, and small birds of prey, night-fliers, who lived on them and on even smaller birds, calling eerily to each other after one or both moons had risen to cast their oddly tinted shadows. There were long, yellow singing lizards like miniature dragons, and funny little froggy creatures with ears like bats and voices like bull-roarers. We saw no snakes at all, a circumstance which led Anne to speculate that Mutton Island must have been on St. Patrick's itinerary. Nothing appeared that offered any serious danger to any of us. Some distance from the sea, where the grazing was especially lush, we encountered herds of ungulates similar to those we had seen on one or two of the main continents, but smaller, no larger than fat sheep, and they, too, had their attendant predators, lone hunters with huge night eyes and long hind legs with which to spring, but so timid, so terrified of the unfamiliar, that one of them, happening to encounter Mavis, fled panic-stricken as soon as she hissed and growled and raised her hackles.

"Too bad no *pua*," Malia said, after she had seen the almost ovine herds. "No pig for good *luau*."

"Couldn't one be a pretend pig?" suggested Tammy.

"They just look too much like sheep," Jamie said. "You know, everybody's going to think they're why we named the place Mutton Island. All I can say is we'd better not let the word go out on Earth. This place would be overrun with Aussies in no time."

Rhoda laughed. "Well, at least there's no way the word *can* get out on Earth," she said. "Who'd ever want to go back there?"

There was a silence. Then Laure spoke, very quietly. "I'm afraid, Rhoda, that some of us are going to have to, and probably before too long."

So there it was at last, out in the open. The certainty I had foreseen. The certainty none of us had wanted to confront in the excitement of finding our new world. But I could see it on their faces, Geoff and Franz, Malia and Anne and Bess, Tammy and Jamie, all of them. Only Rhoda and the smaller kids seemed genuinely surprised.

"Isn't it obvious?" Laure went on. "We could probably survive here well enough, if that's all we wanted, just those of us who're already here—but what of our children and our children's children? Of course we have computer access to a vast store of mankind's knowledge, but is that enough? No, unless we are content to backslide, we must have more people, and they can only come from Earth. Our gene pool is too small for us to be able to avoid the dangers of inbreeding, and there are not enough of us to ensure that we'll even be able to use the knowledge we have access to—not effectively. Consider how fearfully complex our technological civilization has become—and consider, too, whether we really want to take a chance of losing any more of that inheritance than we absolutely have to. No, that journey back to Earth must be made. Only a few of us will have to make it, for *Owl* needs only a small crew. So let's all think about it and discuss it. Let's consider who, on Earth, we would like to bring back here, and let's list, very carefully, all the things we know we'll need and either do not have or may run out of."

"But—but that—means going through Gilpin's Space again, doesn't it?" Rhoda was almost whimpering.

"Not you, Rhoda dear. You and Dan will be needed here. But I'll have to go, and there'll be others who have reason to."

All the while, Bess had been looking at her strangely. Now she said, "Laure, why would *you* have to go? This is *your* world. It needs you, and—and so do we."

"I—well, I feel I have unfinished business, Bess. Let's just say I hear kachinas calling me. Besides, I'm vain enough to think I'm a fair judge of men and women, and we're going to have to choose those we bring with great care."

Bess didn't like it. Nor did I. But Laure's final argument was one we could not very well dispute, not after what we had all gone through in the Far Reaches.

So we talked it over. Geoff said at once that first off he'd do his best to find Placek and *Pussycat*. "If they're still on Earth, or back on Earth after having a look around, by now he'll have put a really solid crew together. Anyhow, we can try to raise *Pussycat* by radio as soon as we get into normal space, and if we can't, well, we can always put a tracer on her through your people in Taiwan or Brazil."

Laure nodded. "Let's hope we do find him. It'd save us a lot of time and trouble. But we'll have to plan on doing our own recruiting, too. First let's go over the people we'd really like to have, friends and relatives and, of course, specialists in areas where we feel we're short of competence."

Jamie and Anne, almost with one voice, spoke up for his brother Alec and his family. "He's a hell of a good all-around engineer," Jamie declared, "and there's hardly anything Maeve can't do, from fixing electronic gadgetry to teaching math. Besides, their four kids are bright as buttons, and they aren't afraid of a spot of work." He grinned. "Also, he's got that lovely ketch of his. We could really use her here, and she'd give us a lot of extra cargo space."

"You're joking!" Geoff told him. "We never could install a Gilpin drive in her, even if we had one to spare."

"Ah, the naval mind, the naval mind!" Jamie shook his head. "The man thinks I'd actually try to fly her! What I had in mind, sir, was carrying her as deckload. Couldn't we get below her, pick her up, blow our tanks, and then lash her down? We've had other stuff on deck, and the drive's field seems to have taken care of it well enough."

"By God, it might be worth a try," Geoff admitted. "As I understand it, the field extends wherever there's metal, and we can take care of that without too much trouble. How long is she, about forty feet?"

"Forty-five. She'd just about fit on *Owl*'s afterdeck."

"And would he and his family like to come?"

"Would they?" replied Jamie. "Would Mavis eat a mouse?"

We thought of friends whom we were sure were stable. We thought of acquaintances who had the skills we knew we'd need. Tammy and Malia suggested people from their own academic and professional backgrounds. So did Franz and Bess. Dan remembered close friends in the Corps. Mrs. Rasmussen, urging her blushing Linda forward, asked if we'd mind trying to pick up her young man in Minnesota. They'd been talking about getting married, and even though he wasn't a scientist, he wasn't scared of anything and he could top trees with any lumberjack anywhere.

Rhoda, at Laure's suggestion, listed them as individuals and by their specialties. "What we'll end up with," Laure said, "is sort of an optimum list. We don't know what's been happening back on Earth, but we can be absolutely sure that there's been a great rush by all sorts of groups and enterprising individuals to build Saul's drives and put them in anything that even looks like a submarine—and also that every major government, and probably a lot of petty ones, will have instituted repressive measures to keep them from doing it and to make star travel an official monopoly."

"Of that we can be sure," Geoff put in. "They'd do it partly to keep an authority they feel threatened, but even more because they'll see a Gilpin ship as the most perfect weapon of surprise ever invented—a vessel which can appear anywhere, instantly and without warning, do all the damage in its power, and instantly be gone, perhaps to reappear thousands of miles away in minutes. Probably scientists from Moscow to Monrovia are sweating away at a Gilpin's drive detector, and if there were such a thing as a paranoia gauge, I'll bet the needle would be bending itself around the post. The chances of somebody starting a major war will be higher than ever—unless they've already started one."

"It's sure not going to be a healthy situation to walk into," Tammy said. "They'll have a price on all our heads—Laure, on yours especially. So we'd best be sure, not just of our candidates' qualifications, but of their reliability. One bad guess, and—" Graphically, he illustrated the cutting of a throat.

"I'm not so worried about that—about our being betrayed by people whom we know. Remember, we learned a great deal about ourselves and about people generally in the Far Reaches. We've all noticed that, while we have all our old emotions, while we can still get irritated or annoyed or anxious, we no longer let these things build up through feedback, through resonance. To that extent, we've become telepathically conscious, and this is going to serve us well on Earth."

"Especially if we keep our fingers crossed," laughed Franz.

After that first conversation, our work pace changed. One by one, we erected the smaller geodesic domes we were going to live and labor in, putting off further exploration indefinitely; and in a week, surrounding the two main domes, we had a settlement. Geoff and I had a dome to ourselves, but it had to double as a clinic, lab, and (though we hoped not) small hospital. Franz and Bess, Dan and Rhoda shared another which they'd divided into two apartments. One of the larger domes became our shoreside wardroom, with adjoining galley and quarters for Mrs. Rasmussen, Linda, and young Keithy. The other housed our computers, machine shop, and the two nukepaks. The Uemuras had a dome to themselves; so did the Macartneys. We jury-rigged a shed to act as a hangar for the copter and garage for our FWD, making it as wind- and weatherproof as native bamboo analogues and modern plioplastics permitted, and finally we installed a water system with an upstream intake.

By the time we were through, *Owl* was gutted of everything not absolutely essential to her safety and the safety of her so-soon-to-be-much-smaller crew. On Earth—if all went well—

she would be reequipped and reprovisioned, and her complement brought back to more than full strength.

We knew—all of us—that time was short, that every wasted minute would make the task on Earth that much harder. Regretfully, those of us who were staying, Bess especially, had resigned ourselves to Laure's going. With infinite regret, I had forced myself to accept Geoff's, simply because he was *Owl*'s captain and, in every way, best fitted to command. Actually, while we had talked over who would go and who would stay many times, expressing our anxieties and concerns, it was Laure's choice that prevailed.

Dan would stay, of course, because of Rhoda and because he was at least informally second-in-command. Jamie and Anne and the twins would also stay, but Jamie Junior would go along because his parents felt he would be helpful with his uncle Alec, and besides, he was familiar with the ship, had stood his watches. Linda had pointed out that her young man would never leave unless she was there herself. The last was Franz. Laure chose him—partly, she said, for his temperament and partly for his languages—and, to his disgust, Bess backed her up.

"I'll be casting spells," she said, "for your safe return—for *both* of you." Then she burst into tears.

No one made any further objection to Laure's leaving, for we all knew that, after all, it was she who had the connections in Taiwan and Brazil, she who had access to Swiss accounts conspiring governments might not have confiscated, she who—even more than Geoff—might still have friends in high places.

Finally, all the work that we could do was done. It was mid-afternoon and, though that would have made no difference to *Owl* in Gilpin's Space, we decided to put off departure until next morning.

"I know that time's wasting, Laure," Geoff said, "but there's one more thing I'd like to do before we leave your world. After all—"

He broke off. After all, there was no point in saying that nothing was certain about *Owl*'s return, or his.

"And that is?" Laure asked.

He grinned. "Laure, I'd like to take *Owl* out just once as what she was and is—a submarine. I'd like to have one close look at those reef complexes of ours. Maybe we can find out why they're geometrical, and I won't have to wonder about it all the way to Earth and back."

"I don't see why not," Laure answered. "The computer's got a detailed chart of every inch of our lagoon now, hasn't it?"

"Just about. There are no true reefs except at the two channels. Inside the harbor, there are what seem to be eroded reefs, far below the surface, and even they look geometrical. What I'd like to do is slip into Gilpin's Space, come out again just inside the western channel, then dip down and have a look around."

"Couldn't we all go?" Anne asked. "Then, if we find anything interesting it'll give the rest of us something else to think about while you're away."

"Why not?" Geoff said. "Who's for it?"

Laure said she was, and Franz and Bess. Mrs. Rasmussen said she and Linda would be too busy fixing a going-away dinner, and Rhoda and Dan said they'd help them. So did Malia. Jamie said, regretfully, that he still had to write important Earthside letters, but Anne and Tammy and, naturally, all the kids were enthusiastic.

Geoff was first aboard, and I followed him; and now *Owl* seemed strange to me, as though stripped for action, every nonessential gone, everything that had made the ship our home, absolutely everything except the kachina doll and the picture of Saul and his family, which still looked down at us from the wardroom bulkhead.

All of us crowded into the control tower, the kids all pushing their noses up against the observation ports expectantly. Geoff, telling them to be sure and stay right there, brought the ship to life, her control panels reporting their readiness, her computer readouts glowing. We slipped into Gilpin's Space just as we had so many times before, but this time it took us minutes only to reach our destination. We emerged on the smooth surface of the lagoon, and for a little while just floated there, looking at the long white breakers beating against the outer ramparts of the reefs, breaking far more gently against the inner ones, and finally dwindling against the shore itself.

Then Geoff took *Owl* down. Some of us, the kids especially, had never experienced her doing her diving bit before, and we heard a chorus of *oohs!* and *ahs!* and twitterings.

The water was crystal clear, and every detail of everything for many yards around was completely visible. Geoff had brought us down in what, according to the screen and what we saw outside the ports, was a narrow channel—probably not wider than fifty meters—between two reefs, if you can call walls of vari-colored coral extending twenty or thirty meters above the lagoon's floor reefs, walls not roughly armed as coral usually is, but shaped and smoothed and pruned as though by some gigantic undersea gardener or pyramid builder. Attending us were myriads of suddenly frightened fish, some no stranger than the fish of the South Seas or Caribbean, some just as strange but in stranger ways. And romping all around us was a school of—well, I suppose I may just as well call them porpoises, despite their fingered flippers and slightly more mammalian faces. Where we came down, each reef wall had angled suddenly, almost as though to form a street, and down this street *Owl* made her way—and we could see that each wall, rectangular, was broken at regular intervals by ogival openings, by curiously vaulted, almost ecclesiastical passageways, not just on one level, but on two and three and four.

Very, very slowly, *Owl* moved between those walls, so slowly that the fish, no longer frightened, started to swim by, one or two at a time or in schools, and to halt, trying to peer in, only to be scattered by the playful porpoises. This went on for a quarter of a mile; then, suddenly and simultaneously, the walls each turned outward at an acute angle, and we found ourselves in what I can describe only as a courtyard. It had a floor of fine white sand, without a stone, without a seashell, without a sprig of seaweed. Now the reef walls enclosed us, straight again left and right, then once more abruptly angling inward to meet another, higher reef across our path. Geoff brought *Owl* to a stop, and let her settle gently to the bottom; and we saw what, I learned later, had made him do it. Deep in the reef ahead of us, deep down within those recesses and passages, lights were glowing, lights cold and phosphorescent like the distilled light of a pale-green moon, but not spread out as phosphorescence usually is at sea. I knew immediately that those lights were deliberate, contrived, used to illuminate the inner structure of the reef.

It was then that we saw the beings who lived there, a group of them, gathered together on the sand just outside a particularly large, arched passage entrance. Each individual was from six to nine feet high, and at first glance they looked like glorified terrestrial octopuses. Their heads were domed and ovoid, crested with what I first took to be helmets of some sort and then, as they came nearer, recognized as nacreous, apparently vestiges of what, much earlier in their evolution, must have been their shells. Their great eyes were astonishingly human, lidded like our own, flecked like fire-opals, and with descernible whites. Their mouths were ivory-beaked, and their bodies descended like mantles from necks garlanded with brilliant sea-stones, terminating in half a dozen tentacles equipped with sucking discs and, in the case of the foremost pair, with three finger-like appendages each. Their body colors varied, and it would have taken a great watercolorist indeed to have done them justice, for every part of the visible spectrum was represented, but always subdued, muted.

Erect in the water, they swam toward us, using no visible means of propulsion. They came, and the innumerable fish danced all around them, and the porpoises dashed gaily round them, quite unafraid.

For an interminable moment, no one said anything. Then, *"Look* at them!" Franz exclaimed. "Look at their necklaces— fabricated, carved! These—these—whatever they are, they're *intelligent."*

"And they're beautiful!" said Laure, awe in her voice.

The tallest of the creatures—the beings—moved out ahead of the rest. Twenty feet from *Owl,* it stopped. Using four of its tentacles, it made a curious bobbing gesture, almost like a curtsy. With one of its fingered forelimbs, it reached into some sort of underpouch, extracted a thin, pointed instrument, and sat down on the sand. In front of it, it scribed a circle a meter in diameter, with another, very light circle round it. Much further out, it drew a little circle emitting rays. It looked up at us. Finally, it drew quite recognizably the form of *Owl,* and a long curved arrow indicating a trajectory.

"They know we're from out of town," Franz said. "They must know there's nothing really intelligent living on the surface of their world, so where else could we have come from?"

The being straightened. Followed by four others, it floated to the level of our control tower ports. They glided forward. We looked directly into their enormous eyes, and they looked directly into ours—which must have seemed absurdly small to them. They moved from port to port, hesitating for a moment at each one. In front of the viewport through which VeeVee and the Gnat were peering, they stopped dead still. The foremost came forward until he almost touched the glass. VeeVee and the Gnat stared back, entranced.

An endless minute passed before Anne, now clearly nervous, snapped, "What the devil do you two think you're doing?"

"Sh-h-h! *Mummy,* can't you see he's *thinking* at us?"

Laure touched her on the shoulder. "Anne, Anne! Don't forget Mavis and the mouse." To the twins, she said, "Can you tell me what he's thinking?"

"Uh-huh. He thinks nice—I mean nicely. He thinks like Mutton does when he's purring, only it's more like people-think. Lots of it's pictures."

I never was quite sure who did the talking for the two. Sometimes, I suppose, it was Vee, sometimes the Gnat. "He— well, sometimes he sees like us, but sometimes he sees like we can't see, with noises."

Well, I thought, *that makes sense. If whales and dolphins back on Earth can "see" with sonar, why should this being be less gifted?*

The twins were getting excited now. "And he can see real *small*—like we can when we look through the mi—the microscope, only he doesn't need one. He—they all can see that way, with sort of noises, ones we can't hear. They can *feel* things real small too. They can make things grow the way they want them to. That's how they made these houses where they live, and how they make the lights and everything. That's how they scare off the big things out there in the sea." They broke off. "Now he's asking us to think at him—anyhow that's how it feels."

"Shouldn't we make suggestions?" Anne asked.

"Somehow I don't think so," Laure answered. She looked at Geoff, who nodded.

"Let the kids think their own thoughts at him—that way they'll ring true—a good way to get to know your neighbors."

I could see the two of them squinching their eyelids shut, concentrating. I could see the great eyes of that water-being watching them intently. And suddenly I realized that the alien countenance was not expressionless, and that even though the expression was one I could not read, there was no menace, no hostility in it. Then, for an instant only, I saw the world through *his* eyes, a very different world from mine—different, yet again analogous, and I remembered something that had happened to me when I was very small, something long forgotten. We had had an old cat whom I loved, a big silver tabby, and one day while I was watching him, abruptly I saw things through his eyes—a cat-world, where people towered over me, a world almost without color, but one in which the slightest movement was significant. I had run in to tell my dad about it, and had been good-naturedly but firmly told I'd been imagining things. But now I knew that I had not, that for one telepathic moment my mind's eye had been wide open.

We adults waited, listening to the fragmentary reports VeeVee and the Gnat tossed back to us. They were telling him how we had come through Gilpin's Space, and how scary it had been, and how people like us lived, in what sort of houses, and that we wore clothes, and how Mavis was going to have kittens, and that we liked to eat fish but not all the time—all sorts of very important things. How much of it he understood, we did not then know, but I was sure of one thing—that he knew there was no guile in them.

Minutes passed, and I could see that the kids were tiring, and apparently the water-being realized it, too.

All of a sudden, their eyes opened. "He likes us!" they cried out. "He wants us to come and visit him again."

"Try to tell him it'll have to be a good bit later," Laure said. "Tell him we're going to have to go back through space to pick up more people and get supplies. And promise him that, when we return, we definitely will visit him again."

There was a minute more of eye-squinching, and it seemed that at least the gist of the message had gotten over to our host. He backed away from the viewport. Then he and all his fellows repeated the curtsy gesture he had executed when first approaching us. Then, very slowly and gracefully, they withdrew, the many-shaped and many-colored fish swirling around them.

Nobody said a word while Geoff brought the ship back slowly to the surface. The impact of encountering an intelligent race, and one so vastly different from our own, was too great to absorb all at once. Only VeeVee and her sister were unimpressed, and they chattered to Keithy and anyone else who'd listen all the way back to base.

We came out of Gilpin's Space, and once again we knew our whole new world had changed. While the kids ran off to spread the news, Geoff looked at all of us. "What do we do now?" he asked. "Do we call off the trip till we know more about these—all right, I'll say it—these *people?*"

"No, No," Laure replied. "That we mustn't do. Don't you see that now it's ever so much more important to get whatever we can from Earth, more people, more equipment, more everything?"

Of course, we talked it over, the pros and cons, the endless possibilities ahead of us. We were not worried about the water-beings: they had their world, and we had ours, and the two were separated by eons of evolution. The great question was what we could learn from each other, teach each other. Finally, we voted, and everyone except Rhoda, who wept and begged Laure not to go, and only reluctantly let Dan persuade her that no sea monsters were going to eat her—everyone except Rhoda voted to carry on as planned, some of us—like I, myself—despite our fears for those we loved.

We knew that we might never have another chance. We knew the journey had to be made.

Next morning, after breakfast, we stood and watched as *Owl* dissolved and disappeared.

BOOK III

. . . And Back Again
Geoffrey Cormac

1

I HADN'T WANTED to return to Earth. I hadn't wanted to leave Laure's World. Above all, I had not wanted to leave Janet, even temporarily. All of us aboard *Owl* felt pretty much the same way. We left only because we had deemed it absolutely necessary.

Franz was the first really to talk about it. After we were well on our way, he confessed that he had even tried to argue Bess into persuading him to stay. "I told her I was only leaving because Laure asked me to," he said, "because she was a priestess and was never wrong. But was I man or was I mouse? I told her I felt like that old Hungarian song my grandmother used to sing. It was called 'Gloomy Sunday,' and it is dated back to around the Second War. It had sent the suicide rate in Budapest sky-high. I even offered to sing it to her. Well, we happened to be in bed, so she just called me a nitwit and started to nibble here and there. 'You're wrong about Laure being a priestess,' she said, 'She isn't. She's a sibyl. *I'm* the priestess. Who do you think invokes the deities of hearth and home? Who pours the libations? Who, with her sharp little teeth, can make you forget all about 'Gloomy Sunday'? Me, Bess Mayhew, that's who!"

"And then?" put in Laure slyly.

"Then? Well, I said *ouch!* but it was a pretty nice ouch, and somehow 'Gloomy Sunday' got pushed aside, and when I woke up come morning I was much too busy to let dark thoughts interfere, even when I was kissing her good-bye."

He laughed a little ruefully, and we laughed with him. Then suddenly he was completely serious. "You know," he told us, "Bess said something just before we left which I paid almost no attention to. I thought she was just trying to make me feel good. 'Franz,' she said, 'don't worry about our being out of

153

touch. We won't be, you and I—no, never again! You can take my word for it.' And the damn odd thing is that we *aren't*. I can feel her with me, almost as if she was *here*."

He looked at each of us as though he expected us to doubt him, but no one did, for all of us were having very much the same experience, though perhaps not yet quite so definitely.

I myself realized abruptly that the thread between Janet and myself had never broken, that no matter how tenuous it might be it was unbreakable; and later, when we compared notes, I learned that Linda was having the same experience with her mother and with Keithy; so was Jamie, especially with the twins; and so was Laure, with everyone.

Our course was not roundabout, as it had been. Now it was laid straight for Earth, but at Laure's suggestion we did not go all out. "Let's take our time," she said. "I don't mean forever, but enough to go over all our plans. Remember, it's been three and a half months since we left, and a great deal must've happened. Let's plan our approach. Let's go over our lists of people we'd like to recruit, and of supplies we know we ought to have. I know, and you know, that everything will have to be revised once we're there. But the more we can anticipate, the fewer adjustments we'll have to make."

"We're going to need information," I said. "When we get within radio and video range—when we're close enough so that all the news won't be months out of date—we can start popping into normal space and listening to Earth's voices. They should be interesting. We can record news and commentary in those languages we—that means mostly Franz—speak or understand. The information will be complete and distorted, certainly, but if we use our heads we can probably arrive at a picture of the actuality."

"Well," Franz remarked, "We aren't going to do much listening till we're almost in the solar system. What do we do in the meantime besides ship's chores?"

"You heard Laure. We try to foresee contingencies, and list as many alternative courses as we can ahead of time. That goes for people and supplies. It won't be time wasted, Franz. Not if we remember that everything's going to be subject to change at a moment's notice. Right, Laure?"

"Absolutely, Commodore."

I laughed. "You've been talking to Saul again. I wish the pay came with the promotion."

Young Jamie spoke up diffidently. "Mrs. Endicott—well, maybe I shouldn't say anything, but—" He hesitated, a stout, square, redheaded boy very proud of the first sprouting signs of a new moustache.

"Go ahead, Jamie."

"Well, mightn't it be sort of a good idea to hurry as fast as we can through the Far Reaches, then take our time *after* we're in the null zone. We—we'd sleep better there. Anyhow, I would."

The idea did make sense. Even if those screaming alien voices now had little power over us, there was no point in having our sleep broken by them.

"You're going to be as sharp as your father, Jamie." I slapped him on the back. "It may not work—remember how really high speeds multiply the number of intrusions and their intensity?—but I'm all for trying it."

"I'll stand the night watches," said Laure.

We spent scarcely a week of days and nights in the Far Reaches, and even with Laure watching over us, our nights were hellish. The assault was virtually continuous, and sleep, even for us, frequently impossible. But we sweated through, comforting ourselves with the knowledge that our attackers would probably turn out to be our best defense against those of our fellow men who were sure to sally out with dreams of loot and conquest.

We filled our days with work. We went over our equipment lists, trying to think in terms of years, of the long haul into a far future. We gave first preference to tools that would enable us to repair and, if necessary, replace electrical and mechanical gadgets that might go kaput, allowing redundance only where highly sophisticated things like computer elements were concerned—things we didn't think we could produce in any foreseeable future. It was Laure's opinion that, sooner or later, mankind would evolve a tribe of traders to the stars, composed of adventurers of many races, well balanced and unhostile enough—and strong enough—to travel the Far Reaches, but this was something we couldn't afford to count on.

We listed extra nukepaks, small solar power plants, advanced computer hardware, and books on primitive technologies. We assigned priorities and estimated costs; and we followed the same procedures with our lists of possible new people, only here it was Franz who led. I myself was swamped by the number of scientific and technical specialties he dreamed up.

"How in God's name," I exclaimed as we started, "can we ever hope to fill every slot?"

He was undismayed. "We can't—but we can compile three primary lists: one of what seem to be essential skills; another of specialists whom we know and may be able to recruit; and the third—well, that may turn out to be most important, even though we'll have to wait till we're back on Earth to compile it."

"And it will be?"

"A list of generalists, men and women who have specialties but who can cross over into other disciplines, other skills. You know, physical chemists who know how to weave Oriental rugs, or build brick outhouses, or make the bricks to build them with."

"Or whatever?"

"Or what*ever*. Any talent that might conceivably be useful, especially those that have been useful in Earth's past." And that brings up what we'll have to do when—and if—we locate *Pussycat*. We'll have to start all over, listing her whole crew and finding out what everybody's good at."

"Franz, you don't know Placek. By this time, he'll know everything about every man and woman aboard ship. All we'll have to do is combine lists. Let's just hope our luck holds and we're able to locate him. We're going to have to start trying as soon as we get within practical radio range. Without him, our job will be a hundred times harder. He'll know more about the situation down on Earth than we could gather from a month of listening."

"Will he be listening for us?" Jamie asked.

"*He* won't—but *Pussycat* will, twenty-four hours a day. It was built into her, and into *Owl*, too, before we even knew about Saul's drive. So we'd never be out of touch. And we won't have to worry about anybody intercepting; everything'll be too well scrambled. Anyhow, it won't be long now before we find out what kind of little trap we're rushing into. If we can't locate Placek, we'll just have to take our chances in Taiwan or Brazil, and I'll make a bet we find the craziest tangle of Earth and space surveillance in all history. Let's just hope the big guys haven't been able to coordinate too closely, and that lots of smaller nations are pushing their right to exploit Gilpin's Space—both openly, by screaming in the UN, and covertly, by building drives and sticking them in subs."

"You know," Laure commented, "after what we've experienced, after how each of us has changed, it's getting harder and harder for me to believe how Earth people behave."

"I know," I answered, "or to understand why."

We flew across the light-years, and buxom, cheerful Linda, singing Danish ditties, fed us well with food from Earth and fish from Laure's World. She, at least, wasn't concerned about the future. Her only worry, she told us, was for her Minnesota boyfriend, whose name appropriately enough was Lars, and who just possibly might've gone off to get a job in the Canadian North Woods or some place where we couldn't find him.

At mealtimes, partly because of her, we deliberately never mentioned the problems ahead of us. Instead, we usually talked of Laure's World, and of the people we had left there. We spoke of the beings of the reef, speculating on the sort of culture they had developed—a people who, in their entire evolutionary history, could never have known fire or its uses, unless perhaps they had encountered undersea volcanos. We tried to imagine what the possession of microsenses had meant to them. Could they, for instance, see genes and chromosomes directly? Could they manipulate them? Was that how they and their ancestors had been able to grow cities and walls of coral underneath the sea? And what of their mathematics, their beliefs regarding themselves and the Universe, their teleologies, their arts and crafts and music, their history and their literature? And, discussing them, we all agreed that, while it was important to protect ourselves and Laure's World, it was equally as important to protect these beings against men and weapons against which any sea-dwelling people would be powerless.

We knew almost immediately when we had entered Earth's null zone, not just by the vanishing of the night-voices, but by a subtle change in everything, a new tension, at first very slight. Laure put it neatly. "Things just aren't as *clean* as they were yesterday, are they?" she said.

As we came closer and closer to our mother planet, its mantle of tension, the result of millennia of hatreds and fears and suspicions, of plots and counterplots, of private murders and the slaughters and agonies of endless wars—that mantle descended on us all, trying to make us part of it again. And we fought against it, using the same techniques we had em-

ployed to free ourselves from the threat of alien agonies and
angers.

As soon as we felt ourselves within practical radio range of
the solar system, we began to listen, shifting into normal space
to do so, and recording news programs, political rantings, com-
mentaries on a variety of visual and audio channels, in all the
languages we understood: English and French and German,
Danish and Norwegian, Magyar and Spanish and Italian. Then
we'd slip back to Gilpin's Space and play them back, and
whoever happened to be best at it would translate.

We were careful. We spent four days at this, trying for a
coherent picture—and there wasn't any. Everything added up
to craziness and chaos. The major powers were doing all they
could to whip up public paranoia against anybody, nation or
individual, who might want to enter Gilpin's Space. Oddly
enough, it was not Saul but Laure who was their prime evil
genius. Their official and semi-official spokesmen not only laid
the blame first on her, but kept hinting darkly of alien plottings,
of Grade B movie Monsters from Outer Space out to enslave
Earth. Boob-tube evangelists shrieked of divine punishment
due to descend on a science-deluded planet. Tinpot dictators
brandished the modern arms given them by vying superpowers
and threatened their allegedly conspiring neighbors. Everybody
seemed to be blaming everybody else for anything and everything from plagues to hurricanes. There was, we heard, definite
evidence of atomic weapons detonating in the United States,
in Russia, in China, and in two or three nations which weren't
supposed to have any.

And, yes indeed, there was a price on Laure's head—and
on Franz's head and mine, and of course on Saul and his
family's. There was much less emphasis on the Macartneys
and the Uemuras. Bess was barely mentioned, and there was
not a word about Mrs. Rasmussen and Linda and young Keithy.
The head money offered was enormous, with the implication
that if we were brought in dead, so much the better.

I let it all slide off my back until I heard a Navy department
spokesman, a captain who didn't look as if he'd ever been to
sea, in an interview with an especially slimy Dugan Administration commentator. Commander Cormac, declared the captain, would face a naval court as soon as he was caught, as he
most certainly would be if he ever dared return to Earth. The
charges? Everything from desertion to using dirty words to

high treason. Commander Cormac, he explained, had been heavily involved with the late Admiral Endicott, whose own deep involvement with unnamed foreign powers had been proven; and he went on with nasty sexual innuendos involving Laure and the Admiral's career and advancement in the Navy.

The captain was soft and pudgy, with a small, nervous mouth and an unpleasant, wheedling voice which tried unsuccessfully to sound bluff and hearty. I could have strangled him easily with one hand, holding my offended nose with the other.

And at that point, Laure came up to me. *"Geoff,"* she said. "Pay no attention to him, Geoff. Think what would become of *him* in the Far Reaches."

Looking down, I saw that my fists were clenched, my knuckles white. I made myself run a hand through my hair as if I was combing the captain out of it. I said nothing, just touched her hand, but later I told Franz, "She's right. God knows we can't afford to blow up over anything like that, not back on Earth—and risk everything we have going for us."

I must still have seemed a little shaken, for he reassured me. "You won't, Geoff. You won't become impervious to that sort of garbage. Of course you'll feel it, and deeply. But you won't resonate uncontrollably, not now."

"That," I told him with a grin, "is precisely what Janet would have said."

"Janet or Bess or Saul or his two Indian friends, Geoff. And it goes for all of us."

"God be thanked!" I said.

We decided not to try to contact *Pussycat* until we were within Sol's planetary system. Then we planned to shuttle back and forth into normal space, sending out a scrambled message on each occasion, and waiting just the length of time it would take for a reply. We knew that *Pussycat*'s acknowledgment would be automatic, and each of our messages, unscrambled, would tell how much time would pass before we'd transmit again.

Then, before we could even start, and much to our surprise, *Pussycat* called *us*, first with Saul's built-in *"Meow!* This is *Pussycat,"* followed by Placek's deep voice. "Welcome home!" he said. "Anyhow, welcome back to the looney bin. Where can I meet you?"

"Where are you?" I asked

"Taipei Harbor, Commander—hey, it is you, isn't it?"

"It is indeed. Is everything secure?"

"In *this* world? Well, I guess we're as secure as we can be. Let me fill you in. Henry Kwei's built himself two brand-new covered docks, and we're in the south one. They're big buggers, big enough for a battleship. All you have to do is come in through Gilpin's Space and plop down once you're inside."

"Where are they in the harbor?"

"Right next to his old yards, which he's got going just about round the clock. Believe me, the sub business is roaring ahead right now, in spite of everything. You'll have no trouble finding us."

I've compressed all this. We had broken off immediately after our first contact, and had hurried through Gilpin's Space until we were close enough to Earth to make conversation practical. Then the only real delay came when we unscrambled each message spurt and listened to what it had to say.

"You'll have no trouble," Placek repeated. "Only you won't recognize old *Pussycat*. We've Q-shipped her—a false addition to her control tower, a false prow to change her profile, to say nothing of a different paint job, some Chinese characters, and a Republic of China registration number. Far as we know, nobody's been hunting us, but I decided we'd best take no chances. So the second you're down, get *Owl*'s name covered up or painted out—she's had too much publicity."

"We won't have to. She was due to get fancy bronze nameplates, but we took off before they reached us."

I looked at Laure enquiringly, and she nodded.

"Coming in," I said.

"Good deal," said Placek. "Henry Kwei will be happy as a clam." And he signed off.

"I've heard you talk of Kwei a hundred times," Franz remarked, "but I never thought to ask you what he's all about. He sounds like a real friend."

"He is," Laure told him. "He's an old, old friend—a naval architect and a superb engineer—Harvard and M.I.T. Years ago, the Admiral saved his fortune and possibly his life, and I'd trust him with mine any day."

"That makes me feel a little better," Franz said. "At least we'll have a hidey-hole."

Only minutes later, in broad daylight, I set *Owl* down inside Kwei's enormous shed-like dock, next to the now strangely disguised *Pussycat*, and shifted into normal space. Immediately, the vast dock doors closed, faster than I would have thought they could. I edged up carefully to close the gap between the ships, and even before they touched, a couple of Placek's crewmen were passing lines aboard. Placek didn't wait till we had tied fast. He leaped aboard, grinning, and knocked on the lock door.

When I opened it, he barreled in, a huge blond bear of a man, every inch a seaman, and obviously delighted to see us back alive. He grabbed me by the shoulders, hugging me. He embraced Laure, then apologized for it. He shook all our hands. "My God!" he shouted. "I thought the space dragon'd got you! Come on, tell me where you've been. I'll buy the drinks!"

"Hold it, hold it! Let's go sit down in the wardroom, then we can swap what's happened."

"My wife'll want to hear. So will Kwei. I sent him a message the minute I heard from you, and he ought to be here about now."

Seconds later, Sally Placek came aboard, tall and cheerful as her husband; then Henry Chao-Lin Kwei was ushered in, and there were welcomes all around. He was a really big man, and elderly. At first glance he seemed placid, almost sleepy, but once he spoke the illusion was dispelled. He was as keen as any bowie knife, and as practical. Clearly, he was very fond of Laure; tears came to his eyes when she kissed him.

We talked, Placek so eager to hear about our travels that he could scarcely tell us about his own. No one was making any sense until Laure took control.

"Listen, Captain Placek," she said, "and you, too, Henry. We have found a planet. We have found a *world*. Very much like this one before they spoiled it. It's a world we'd like you to share with us, and presently we'll tell you all we can about it. But now it's urgent that we learn what's been going on here, on *this* planet, so we can decide what we'll have to do and how to go about it. We listened to the media on the way in, but they've been putting out almost nothing but hysteria and rank propaganda. What *has* happened?"

Kwei smiled wryly. "Perhaps, Laure, it'd be better to say, 'What's *not* been happening?' Steve here and I have been puzzling over it almost from the start. Tell her about it, Steve."

"What's not been happening," Placek said, "is what we all expected *would* break out—war. A big war. Right away, the major powers started screaming at each other, accusing each other of everything from aggression to collaborations with alien invaders to plotting to destroy the Third World—and right from the beginning it's been obvious that they've been in cahoots, and their real push has been to make damn sure that no smaller nations make it into Gilpin's Space. They've rammed a treaty through the General Assembly giving the permanent members of the Security Council the exclusive right to build the Gilpin drive. They've forced resolutions through amending the Law of the Sea to permit UN licensing and inspection of all submarines."

"At first," Kwei put in, "the major powers went crazy trying to find ways to use Gilpin ships as weapons. They began by converting their mothballed naval subs as rapidly as possible, and that was followed by a regular little epidemic of atomic 'accidents'—in seaports belonging to the major powers, mostly, and with rather terrific losses of life. Finally everybody deduced that the Gilpin drive and atomic weapons simply aren't compatible. In the meantime, a lot of smaller powers flatly refused to obey the UN's licensing and inspection—small powers like the Republic of China, for example—because they were fully aware that Saul Gilpin had opened the way for them to escape Big Power domination and very possibly their own economic and demographic problems. And so far the UN hasn't been able to do anything much about it, even with the Security Council acting in concert for a change."

"It was real crazy," Placek said. "They threatened us with spysats—and suddenly there just weren't any. Whether they did it to each other, or whether other folks did it to them, we don't know, but it's awful easy to knock out *any* satellite if you have a faster ship that can duck in and out of normal space—all you have to do is drop a few bucketfuls of nuts and bolts where you know it's going to be."

"I suppose they threatened to use sub-killers?" I asked.

"They threatened, but that was all. Too much of the world's commerce is carried underseas, and sub-killers are just too indiscriminate. I guess none of them wanted to take a chance of really touching off the big one. The word now is they're all concentrating on finding a Gilpin ship detector—something that'll tell them instantly if anyone unauthorized turns on a Gilpin drive or slips back into normal space."

"And meanwhile," Kwei added, "Anyone who can beg or

borrow or buy or highjack anything that even looks like a submarine is getting into the act. A lot of them are going out as pilgrim ships, filled with the devout, some crazy and some not, some wonderfully well equipped, some with almost nothing but their faith. I hate to think what'll become of most of them, but, still it's a fine thing that nobody can yet stop them doing it. Then there are a lot of others whose only aim is to find an asteroid of pure gold, or a planet inhabited by ardent nubile maidens, or rich and appropriately decadent worlds ready for a conqueror. From what we've heard—indeed from what Steve here has himself experienced—after you get so many light-years out, the Universe will do its best to drive you mad. The Big Powers have been hammering on that in their propaganda, together with the peril of purple plagues from space, alien invasions, and the wrath of the KGB or the God of your choice. They're all starting Space Academies, to produce their various brands of supermen to overcome the dangers of Deep Space and stay sane while doing it."

"Like the Hobbit—" I grinned. "—we've been 'there and back again'—and their way isn't the way to go about it."

"You mean you've got a better one?" Placek said. "Boy, I had one taste of nightmare alley, and after I had to wrestle two of my crew into straitjackets, I turned *Pussycat* around and streaked for home and mother, or at least for nice safe places like the weird planets they've been finding around almost all the nearest stars."

"We have found ways," Laure told him, "very practical ways, to protect ourselves and to survive. But we'll tell you all about that later. When we found our world, we realized there simply weren't enough of us to settle it and stay civilized—*comfortably* civilized. We knew we'd have to return to Earth, regardless of the risks, and get more people, more skills, more supplies. From what you've told me, I'd guess the major powers will keep on trying, and sooner or later they'll be able to place an effective Berlin Wall around the Earth, if only temporarily. They'll probably not be able to stop those who are determined to emigrate, but they'll make life awfully difficult for anyone who plans to come and go. At any rate, I'd like to accomplish all we can on this one voyage."

"You spoke of risks, Mrs. Endicott." Sally Placek's voice was worried. "That's been on our minds ever since—ever since you went away. That's why we disguised *Pussycat,* and why we've all been so awfully careful. And they don't want us the way they want you."

Placek frowned. "It'd be bad enough if it was just Brother Breck, but it's a lot worse than that—Mrs. Endicott, Whalen Borg's still alive."

"He's *what?*" I almost yelled it—and I saw Laure turn pale.

"That servo didn't kill him. Damn near, but not quite. It tore him up pretty terribly, and he spent a long time in intensive care, but he's tough and they pulled him through. They've not announced it, but the gossip is they're giving him a boost again—to vice-admiral—and turning NavIntel over to him. That's probably why they've been making so much noise about you, and it means that anyone who'll find you for him—you and the Commander—can have just about any damn thing they ask for."

I sat there listening to him, and suddenly it was almost as though I was outside myself. There was no escaping the mental and spiritual miasma of Old Earth, that Earth on which I, Geoffrey Cormac, had been born and raised, where I had studied and made love and sailed the seas and built ships. I could feel it, and I could feel how it possessed even men as sane as Kwei and Placek, how it possessed me before I passed through the Far Reaches and then experienced the cleanliness of Laure's World. I knew that, before our mission was accomplished, we would have to contend with men whom it possessed totally, men like Whalen Borg, whom we had thought safely dead.

"Well," I said finally, "that seems to be the kernel of our problem—how to do what we have to do and still stay free. Steve, you and Henry know a lot more about the world as it's become than we do. What steps do you think we ought to take?"

Placek scratched his head. "You tell 'em, Mr. Kwei. You're the man who's really kept my head out of the noose."

"Not entirely," Kwei answered, smiling, "but I trust I helped. It seems to me, Commander Cormac, that the first thing we must be is thorough, no matter how impatient delays may make us. We must avoid false steps. That's critical. For the time being, you're safe here, especially on the ships. We on Taiwan feel very strongly about our right to sail the seas of space. No word of your arrival will be permitted to leak out. Even though they spout the same line as the Security Council, our mainland commies are too frightened of Breck and his cozying up to the Kremlin to want to help him in any way, and they'd be most likely to hear about you first—and we have moles over there who'd let us know. Your main problems will come when you start going about your business."

Laure nodded.

"Therefore," he went on, "I'd suggest that neither you, Commander, nor Laure undertake any missions personally, and plans must be made to give those of you who'll have to travel puncture-proof new identifies. I can arrange all that. Disguise in really a rather simple art, and the passports and other documents I can obtain are as authentic as the originals would be. Of course, nothing is ever completely foolproof, so even the contingency of being identified must be provided against. However, there'll be a lot of people helping out—people who won't even need to know it's you they're helping. When the powers started trying to suppress any space travel but their own, underground Free Space organizations started springing up everywhere, and some genius began coordinating them. Now in a lot of smaller countries they operate openly; in some others, almost openly. They have cells everywhere, even behind the Iron Curtain. They know that if they help us, we'll help them. They'll save you from having to take a lot of chances. Oddly enough, too, the fact that Borg's alive may be insurance for you."

"Come again?" I said.

"It almost certainly guarantees that assassination, so hard to guard against, will not be used in your case. Because of what he is, Borg will not want you dead. Nor will he, as long as you and Mrs. Endicott elude him, want to have any of the rest of you killed without questioning you. Not a pleasant subject, I know, but anything that limits his methods works to your advantage."

"You've summarized the situation beautifully," Laure said. "Can we discuss it in detail later on?"

He smiled. "I'd be hurt and offended if you didn't."

"Thank you, Henry. Now would you like to hear about *Owl*'s flight, and our new world?"

"Can I bring Sousa and a couple of the others aboard, Mrs. Endicott?" Placek asked. "Sousa especially'll want to know you're safe and hear where you've been."

"Of course," Laure told him; and in less than a minute he

was back with Sousa and with Latourette, who had also worked for Underseas, Ltd.

Laure and I shook hands with them, and I could see their eagerness to hear her on their faces.

"We've named our planet *Laure's World*," I told them. I motioned them to chairs, and sat down with them.

And Laure began.

2

LAURE TOLD THEM the whole story of *Owl's* flight, of the inhospitable worlds we'd visited and the creatures they had spawned, of our journey through the Far Reaches and the demonic emotions which had done their best against us while we slept. She described the methods we had used so successfully—even though most of us hadn't realized how successfully—to combat them. She told them about Rhonda, and that there were bound to be many other people who just couldn't cope. Finally, vividly and poetically, she painted a word-picture of Laure's World, of its beauty, its freshness, and of a new ambience holding neither living hatreds nor the not-yet dead residue of all our ancient cruelties. And the ship's screens accompanied her with their recorded realities: seas and continents, our picnic on the meadow, the beings of the reef. When her relations ended, even I, thoroughly familiar with it all, was surprised to find that she had been talking for two and a half hours, during which no one had interrupted her, not even with a question.

For moments, there was total silence. Then Placek, his deep voice breaking, said, "Mrs. Endicott, I—I think you're going to find a lot of people, people like me and Sousa here, trying to join you."

"And their wives," whispered Sally Placek.

"And their Chinese friends," said Henry Kwei.

"Would you come, Henry? Would you really come?" exclaimed Laure.

"I'm too old, Laure," he answered sadly, "too involved with this world. I was thinking of my second son, Chris—you remember him, don't you? He's married now, with a couple of teenagers. He's a marine biologist, with a vessel of his own, designed for his profession. She's only a few feet shorter than your *Owl*. We haven't installed a Gilpin drive in her—not yet—but we can in days. He's a space freak, too, and if you

won't let him join you, he'll probably stow away. Besides—
well, I'd like to see Chris and his family at least away from
Earth during the next few years."

"They'll be very welcome, Henry," Laure said. "All of you
will."

"But what of those of us who can't cope?" Sousa asked.

"Please believe me, all of you. Something happened to me
in those Far Reaches of Gilpin's Space. I am confident that I
can tell those who can't from those who can—I and Geoff and
Franz and probably all of us who, as Geoff put it, have been
there and back again."

When she included me, I was surprised; then I examined
the new self I had brought back from her new world and realized
that very probably I could.

"As for those who can't, well, the kindest thing would be
never to let them try. Captain Placek, what happened to those
men of yours who had to be restrained to get them home?"

"They leveled off okay, but you'd never get them out there
again. They were good men, and they signed aboard one of
Mr. Kwei's fleet after he promised they'd never have to go
that far again. Talk with them though, and you'd start believing
all that garbage Breck and his boys are putting out, and naturally
their wives and kids—both of them are married—feel the same
way."

"At this stage," I said, "it's probably just as well. We're
going to have to vet everybody very carefully before we even
extend an invitation, except for those whom we already know
well enough to judge instinctively. And that also goes for anyone aboard *Pussycat* who got into the Far Reaches and didn't
get too shaken up. Right, Placek?"

"Right, Commander. It wasn't any fun, but Sally and I and
the kids felt maybe we could've handled it, though we'd sure
like to have had a few pointers. There are more horror stories
going round than there are cockroaches in New York. The talk
is all of vessels vanishing, highjacking by their crews, diving
slam-bang into planets or even suns, and of whole shiploads
of brand-new lunatics hurrying back to Earth to assassinate our
heroic leaders."

"Speaking of that," Kwei interjected, "one of the first things
the powers thought of, naturally, was that a Gilpin ship was
the perfect terrorist weapon, not just for them, but for all their
enemies, home-grown and foreign. And of course that helped

to touch off the paranoia. But the odd thing is that there've been very few such terrorist attacks, and none have been too successful. Perhaps it's because once you have your own Gilpin ship you begin to see its true potential, and start wondering whether it might not be more fun and more profitable to fish for strategic minerals among the asteroids or dig for diamonds on planets no one ever visited before. We know that a great number of official ships have simply disappeared, and not just in what you call the Far Reaches. I haven't heard of any commercial vessels having that trouble—if they have, it's been far out—but then most owners have had sense enough to work their ships on shares, the way your Boston and New Bedford whalers did way back when."

My estimate of the situation was taking shape rapidly. In certain respects, it was more favorable than I'd expected— none of us had foreseen the degree of disorganization reigning in the world, the bold intransigence of smaller nations determined to assert their right to the freedom of space, and the rapid and apparently highly effective growth of a Free Space underground. One factor only went a long way to canceling out the obvious advantages—Whalen Borg was still alive and now had more power than ever. It helped to explain the persistent propaganda emphasis on Laure and her role in giving Saul's drive to the world, and told us that nowhere on Earth would we be completely out of danger, and that incessant vigilance would be the minimum price of our survival.

Henry Kwei must have read my mind. "The Republic of China has keen eyes, excellent ears, and—" He smiled. "— very sharp teeth, much sharper than the rest of the world knows. However, to carry out your mission—*our* mission—we're going to have to act swiftly, for the wider we cast our nets, the greater will the chances be of their coming to the notice of the wrong people. With your permission, Laure, I'd like to start disguising *Owl* immediately. In a couple of days, you won't know your ship. Ordinarily, I'd invite all of you to have dinner with me this evening, and I'd invite the President of the Republic and Admiral Leong, who's head of all our space activities. But these are not ordinary circumstances, and I feel you'll be safer keeping as low a profile as possible and staying aboard."

"But surely there's no reason why you can't have dinner with us here, is there, Henry? You can invite Chris and his wife, and Captain Placek can bring those of his people who used to work for me at Underseas. You'll be the first people Earthside to eat fish from another world—believe me, it's delicious. You can manage, can't you, Linda?"

Linda, justly proud of her kitchen skills, blushed and nodded, and Jamie and Sally Placek volunteered to help her.

"I'd be delighted to," said Kwei. "Perhaps tomorrow evening we can have a repeat performance, but with a Chinese feast brought in." He stood. "And now I'd better go ashore and get things moving. I'll be back in half an hour, and we'll still have the better part of the afternoon to work in."

By the time he returned, Laure and I and Franz had assembled our various lists, and he went to work with us directly. Item by item, he checked and rechecked the supplies we were sure we'd need, making suggestions, explaining why some might be a little difficult to obtain, why others would have to be purchased through the underground to avoid suspicion, and how his own Gilpin ships could pick some up in distant ports and places and deliver them to Taiwan in a matter of minutes.

"Supplies and equipment are going to be the least of your worries," he said finally. "There's very little on your lists that all sorts of non-space-traveling people don't use. The danger's going to start when you begin recruiting. Just how do you plan to go about it?"

"I'm afraid there's no alternative to direct contact in most cases," I answered. "Especially in today's atmosphere, people aren't going to come running when messages arrive second- or third-hand. For instance, Linda certainly is going to have to get to her big Swede personally, and we know that Jamie will have to deliver his father's microflexes to his uncle. Alec Macartney's a high-tech man with a lot to lose, and he's going to have to be shown what his brother's offering. We've prepared one-time videoflexes of Laure's World. They're automatically wiped after playing or if anybody tries to mess with them, and so are the straight message flexes. Then there are a couple of Bess Mayhew's friends to contact, plus others in California, and a relative of Tammy Uemura's and his family, together with another couple in Hawaii."

"They're going to be my job, and afterwards I'll get in touch with the final one in Colorado." Franz grinned. "Do I get to wear a great gray beard and travel with a Lower Slobovian passport?"

Kwei laughed. "No gray beard, and probably something like a Canadian passport for a starter—but I'm afraid that moustache is going to have to go."

Franz moaned.

"Now don't feel bad, Franz," soothed Laure. "It's a crying shame after all the years you've devoted to it, but they do grow back eventually if properly nurtured."

"Unlike heads," said Kwei grimly.

I'd been considering everything from our new perspective, and now suddenly I thought of an approach that might insure us against unforeseen pitfalls. "Would it be possible," I asked, "for your Free Space people to check out some of the names we've listed? Especially regarding their attitude to Freedom of Space, and who owes what to whom, and who has reason to fear the IPP. Most of them we—or at least some of us—know personally, but even there things can change. Could they do that for us?"

"Certainly, Commander. They know me well enough so that they won't even want to know who needs the information. A lot of them are people who'd be out in Gilpin's Space themselves if they weren't too old or didn't have family ties to hold them here, and who are willing to take risks to help others realize their dream. How long it'll take them to report, I don't know—probably we'll start hearing in just a day or two—but don't get impatient if a couple of weeks go by before you have reports on all of them."

"Henry, of course we will," said Laure, with a smile. "Perhaps we'd better start with those whom Franz is going to have to contact personally, so we can shave off his adornment and send him on his way. Oh yes, and also that big lumberjack of Linda's—"

"He's *not* a lumberjack, Mrs. Endicott," Linda broke in. "He takes care of all their big machines—you know, fixes them when they break down and all that. He even fixes radios." She flushed. "But he's a real good tree-topper too," she added proudly.

I was surprised. Somehow, we'd all rather stupidly pictured Lars as a not-too-bright Paul Bunyan type swinging a double-bitted axe. It was nice to know that he was turning out to be a big timber jack-of-all-trades. New planets can always use blacksmiths and mechanics and general fixer-uppers.

"If you and Mr. Andradi will give me a list of those you

want to know about as soon as possible, I'll get things rolling," Kwei promised. "As for this young lady's friend, I'm sure a phone call or two can at least locate him." He stood up. "I'll go ashore now and get the cosmetic work started on *Owl*. Commander Cormac, will you come with me? I'd like to have you check things over before we start in case there's anything you object to. But I can promise you no harm will come to *Owl*. Half the vessels we get in here are in for a thorough face-lifting, and my men are real experts."

"Henry," Laure said, "we're going to have to make arrangements regarding payment. I'm certain all my property in the United States has been seized long since, but my Swiss accounts are still intact, and I have strong reserves here on Taiwan and in Brazil.

"All in good time," he replied. "Even if you didn't have a penny, Laure, we all owe it to you. Money is no problem."

"And that goes double, Mrs. Endicott," declared Placek. "First thing I did after we'd satisfied our curiosity about Mars and Venus and one or two close stars was head right back to that wreck I located—remember, *Narwhal*?—and *Pussycat* burgled into her strongroom for us. Her safe was still intact and we hauled it aboard. Mrs. Endicott, it held close to two hundred grand in U.S. minted gold, even some of those fifty-dollar California private mintings. Believe me, they traded for a raft of Krugerrands. Even after paying the crew their shares, I've got more than enough for a few installments on my debt to you."

"Steve Placek," Laure said, "I *gave* you *Pussycat*."

"I know," he answered, "but that doesn't mean I don't owe you something in return, like shopping for you maybe."

He grinned at her, and she smiled back. Then Henry Kwei and I took off, and five minutes later we were going over a set of sketches for the alterations he'd made in *Pussycat*, and he swiftly indicated with a draftsman's pencil what he had in mind for *Owl*—and the changes were purely cosmetic, as he'd promised. The silhouette of the control tower was subtly changed; its viewports were made to appear narrower and, oddly, more numerous; a stub mast was added where there'd been none before; and a bold set of curlicues surrounding a fake registration number altered the entire feel of her forward. And none of it was even skin deep. The only genuine structural change was in her servos. Kwei said he'd remove their claws and substitute new ones of his own design, which were, he assured me, far more versatile and far stronger—compliments of the house. Then he called in his dock superintendent and a shop foreman, and went over everything again very quickly in Chinese. I could tell that it was all old hat for them, and as we made our way back to the ship, I saw men already hustling tools along the dock.

Laure had our lists ready for him when we returned. "Tomorrow," he said, "those of you who'll do the traveling can start getting measured for your disguises and your passports. Right now, before I start the ball rolling, I'm going to stop off at my office and call Chris. He'll want to come over right away, I know."

"That'll be fine, Henry. I remember him as a college kid, and I hope he does decide to join us. Besides, an extra ship will give us that much more cargo and passenger space."

He beamed. "I'll be back at dinnertime."

He left me worrying about whether his son, whom I'd never met, would really be able to cope in the Far Reaches—for certainly there'd be no way in which we could decently turn him down—and also whether a third ship might not overcomplicate problems headachey enough already.

I needn't have worried. When Chris Kwei turned up about a half-hour later, after we and the Placeks and the other Underseas people had swapped experiences and compared notes, instinct—that instinct the Far Reaches and Laure's World had awakened, which I still wasn't used to—told me instantly that he was absolutely solid. A little taller than his father, athletic and obviously in top shape, he had slightly wavy hair, always surprising in a Chinese. His manner was calm, forthright, and alertly intelligent.

He greeted Laure as warmly as Henry had, and she introduced him to us. *Pussycat*'s people, of course, knew him well. Henry had told him just enough that he could scarcely control his eagerness to hear more, and we spent what remained of the afternoon telling him about Laure's World and the plans we'd made for it and for ourselves, and letting *Owl* show him the video record. Once he had seen our neighbors of the reef, nothing could have deterred him from joining us.

When we sat down to dinner, there were fourteen of us at table, for Chris' wife had joined us and so had Latourette's, and the Placeks had brought his sister. Immediately, serious conversation ceased and celebration started. Toast after toast was proposed, and the wine, now that we were back on Earth and didn't have to worry about running out of it, flowed freely. We didn't forget the job ahead of us. Nor did we forget the danger we were in and the risks all of us were going to have to run. We shelved them. It was like R & R in time of war, and all the more enjoyable because of it.

When the party finally broke up shortly after eleven, we could still hear Henry's men working away at *Owl's* face-lift, and the fact that they kept on going through the night didn't disturb my sleep at all. On the two or three occasions when I woke and heard them, it was a reassuring sound, a guarantee that everything possible was being done to improve our chances. That night not one of us stood watch. Somehow we knew we could accept Placek's assurance that Henry Kwei's security system was impregnable.

3

WE KEPT BUSY—very busy. We reviewed our lists constantly, consulting Henry and Chris and Placek, and the Kweis did all the ordering and purchasing. Within hours, supplies started to arrive dockside, and Placek's crew took over the job of loading them, some on *Owl*, some on *Pussycat*. On the afternoon of the second day, Chris' own ship came in, a bit shorter than our two, rather more gracefully designed, and with very different servos for more delicate manipulation. She moored to the dock's extreme end, getting ready for her Gilpin drive.

Henry turned one of the dock offices over to us, and it was there that we interviewed people like the cosmetic artist who was going to disguise Franz and Linda, the expert forger whose job it was to provide them with convincing passports and other documents, and an occasional agent from the Free Space underground.

That underground was extremely efficient. Its first reports started to come in within forty-eight hours. They had located Linda's Swede, and he was indeed in Canada, but not in the North Woods at all. He had a job with a heavy equipment dealer in Ottawa and was considered a real expert. Linda promised us that she'd have no difficulty getting him to come along— all she had to do was say she'd marry him. The forger provided her with a Danish passport, complete with a record of her alleged travels showing that she'd been working for a Scandinavian firm in Melbourne for three years, and with credit cards and other identification. He took her passport photograph himself after the cosmetic man had finished with her. Her disguise was simplicity itself: a slight hair rinse; a very different hairdo; eyebrows tilted, darkened, narrowed; glasses she didn't need—that sort of thing. He also studied her distinguishing mannerisms, and coached her in avoiding them. With Laure's advice, Chris' wife got her an entire new wardrobe in none of her once-favorite styles and colors. Then she spent two full days responding to her new name, not responding when somebody called *Linda!* and generally being another person. When the experts agreed she was as ready as she'd ever be, a Gilpin ship dropped her at a remote airfield somewhere behind Suva, where a car was waiting for her. Three hours later, her plane left for Canada on schedule.

Getting Jamie off was even simpler. Someone in the underground got in touch with his uncle directly, using the special identifying phrases Jamie had given him, and told him that a Gilpin ship could deliver Jamie to the ketch on any reasonably radar-safe stretch of sea off his coast. All he had to do was set the time and place: the transfer would take seconds only—if they had to, they'd simply drop him off with a life jacket and Alec could throw him a line. Jamie said that'd be fine with him; he didn't mind a bit of wet. The message came back giving exact chart coordinates and setting a time after sunset on the following Saturday, and he was gone. Next day we heard that he'd arrived, and that all was well.

Franz, in the meantime, had to wait for clearances on the dozen or so people he was to contact. He and Laure occupied what little spare time they had accustoming *Pussycat*'s people as well as Chris and his wife and two kids, a boy and a girl, to the Structural Differential and to dream sessions. Laure had checked them all, and in her opinion none of them would have too much trouble in the Far Reaches. That didn't mean they wouldn't have rough going—just that they'd make it.

As for me, I spent most of my time checking purchases, thinking up new "absolute musts," helping the others when I could, and—I'm ashamed to say it—worrying.

A shipmaster *should* worry, I told myself, as one doubt after another assailed me, and new causes for worry kept appearing as though by black magic. I worried about the fact that we really knew next to nothing about Linda's Lars—despite the fact that on Laure's World and in the Far Reaches I'd never given it a second thought. I began to worry about those of Placek's crew whom I had not known at Underseas—there were only two of them—and about Henry's employees, and everything else my imagination could conjure up, including what might happen to Franz if even one of the people he was to contact ratted on him, and what might then become of us. After a couple of days of this, I decided to talk it over with Laure, and she, having listened patiently, suggested that I take a nap.

"Laure, are you serious?" I demanded. "What good would that do?"

"Take a nap," she repeated. "Pretend you're a cat. Relax totally, and think of Janet, only of Janet. Then see how you feel."

I didn't think much of her advice, but I took it. In my cabin, I laid down and consciously tried to let myself go limp. With my right hand, I touched my wedding ring, and let my memories flow spontaneously, from our first meeting, through our courtship, through the years that followed, all the way to our last night together on Laure's World. I began to doze—and suddenly, in that strange, crystal clear world between sleeping and waking, it was as though no distance separated us. First, I felt Janet's lips touch mine, ever so lightly, then her hand on my forehead; and then I heard her voice, *Geoffrey, Geoff! Listen to me. Your worries aren't entirely yours. They're mostly the mad voices of the world around you, almost like those in the Far Reaches. You don't have to let it torment you so. Don't let your guard down—you are among real dangers. But you can put those worries in their proper place so that they'll lose their power.*

Feeling her there beside me, I slept, and when I woke an hour later, my mind was alert, fully aware, but at ease. I went to Laure and told her of it, but she only smiled, unsurprised, and said that she was glad.

When I told Franz about it, later, he looked at me very seriously and told me that he, relaxed and at the point of sleep, felt as though he had never been away from Bess. "But my dreams of her," he said, actually embarrassed, "are—well, like those I used to have when I was about fourteen. And every time I realize she's laughing at me, but—but, dammit, it's fun anyway."

Finally the reports on Franz's contacts started coming in, and all but two were favorable. One of those, a tenured professor, had been purchased by the IPP's destruction of the man who had outpointed him for a major administrative appointment; another was a radio astronomer whose wife had denounced his space-oriented friends and colleagues in exchange for IPP's saving her delinquent son from a major felony conviction. I felt that we were lucky in each instance. Reports on the others were definitely encouraging. Tammy's cousin, a Sansei dental surgeon with a *hapahaole* wife and five sturdy children, built and flew model rockets as a hobby. Another in Hawaii, Peter Dougall, was a close friend of his; newly married, he was a high-tech man in optics, and belonged to at least two pro-space groups. At Stanford, there was a girl friend of Bess Mayhew's, described as brilliant, beautiful, and on the point of being fired from the University for her forthright political opinions; she was unmarried, but had a live-in boyfriend in her own department: vertebrate zoology. They were convention-going science-fiction buffs.

In addition, Franz was going to have to contact four friends of his: Andy Feuerbach, a rancher-agronomist in Colorado, Antonina Tarn, a veterinary student at U.C., Davis, and Ollie Taliaferro and Terry Ann Golding, both of whom worked for a leading computer outfit near San Jose. Feuerbach was married and had three offspring; the others were single. It meant that Franz was going to have to make at least seven and perhaps eight separate contacts, for in the atmosphere the IPP had created who would dare to trust an absolute stranger? Besides, there was always the possibility that one or another of our recruits would want to take a close friend or relative along, so he would have to interview those, too.

I didn't think it fair to him, and said so. "I know we've gone over all this before," I told him, "but the risk ought to be more fairly distributed. Is there any good reason why I can't help along?"

"Indeed there is, Commander, sir. It's because I know almost all these people, and you don't. Besides, if you went kiting off on my press gang detail, you'd more than double the chances of Br'er Breck getting us. Then you and *Owl* couldn't come plopping down out of Gilpin's Space to pick us up if we scream for you."

I argued that Placek could do that with *Pussycat,* but neither Franz nor Laure bought it, so—still feeling guilty—I gave it up, and we settled on working out as swift and effective a *modus operandi* as we could. With Henry's help, we outlined a communications network with the underground, providing as many fail-safe alternatives as possible. We decided that in a few cases, primarily where we were dealing with singles and childless couples, and where they could plausibly announce they were taking a few days' rest or vacation, they could make at least the first stages of the journey under their own power, probably to designated assembly points where we could pick them up when we picked up one or more of the families. Franz would have to pass the word to us via the underground. We discussed what each of them would be asked to bring along, and prepared lists of things we'd purchase for them to ensure against their overloading and wasting too much time in preparations. In the majority of cases, Henry assured us, the under ground could expedite any requests they'd make, using carefully selected commercial computer channels, where orders would arouse no suspicions even if monitored. Tentatively, we allowed six weeks for the operation, more than enough time for Henry to complete the conversion of his son's ship and for us to finish our buying and provisioning.

Or so we thought.

A day or so after Linda's departure, the disguise artist began to work on Franz. To the accompaniment of dreadful moans, off came the heroic moustache—not completely, to our surprise. Now, on Franz's upper lip, there was an almost pencil-thin line, too closely shaven, too carefully nurtured. "Lord God!" he exclaimed, when he first saw it in the mirror. "I look like a Buenos Aires gigolo!"

"Pre-cisely," agreed the disguise man, vastly pleased. "All the so-nice rich ladies will be thinking so, yes?"

"Yes, goddam it!"

The next step, almost as traumatic, was the cutting and taming of his ordinarily feral hair, parting it ever so tidily on one side, slicking it down with something smelly, and making his eyebrows decidedly less masculine. Somehow, too, the disguise artist managed to increase the angle at which his ears stuck out, and, with a subtle lotion, to shadow the skin under his lower lip so that he looked absolutely sullen, and to alter the appearance of his nostrils. Suddenly, he hardly looked like Franz at all, and I told him so. "My lad," I said, "you're going

to have to watch your step. Remember, we're depending on
you. You can't abandon us to become some ever-so-rich woman's mascot."

He answered me very rudely, then apologized to Laure for
it.

After that, the artist carefully coached him for a day or two,
just as he had Linda, only more so. He taught him how to
mince a little when he walked, how to pitch his voice a little
higher, how to avoid habitual mannerisms. He even insisted
that he start smoking cigarettes, which everyone knew he was
passionately against. Like Linda, too, he was provided with a
passport, Canadian in his case, a background of overseas em-
ployment, and a devoted aunt in Quebec, complete with well-
worn picture. She had only recently been installed in one of
the underground's safe-houses, and was to be one of his main
contacts. Finally, a Gilpin ship picked him up for Suva, where
he would take off by commercial airline for Hawaii, his first
stop.

His passport said he was an accountant—a profession few
people find interesting enough to ask too many questions about,
and one that provided him with a ready-made out for those
who did: He was just so damned tired of juggling books that
all he wanted was to run the few errands his boss had sent him
on, see a bit more of the wicked world, and take it easy for a
while. The messages he carried for Tammy and for Bess, as
well as his recordings of Laure's World, were all on special
microflexes, undetectable by ordinary airport and police search
devices. They could be set to wipe after one playing or if anyone
unauthorized tried to use them. They would play through any
video setup.

Naturally, we worried about Franz, for a great deal could
conceivably go wrong, but we told ourselves that he had a good
head and that he'd have the underground to fall back on in
emergencies. Anyhow, we had other fish to fry. Supplies kept
arriving. Work on Chris Kwei's neat little ship progressed rapidly. Then, too, we had people to consider—people who might
or might not be suitable. Oddly enough, when the parents
passed muster, the children inevitably did, too. We didn't have
to weed out any of Placek's folk, but when it came to checking
Chris' crew, we found that all but three, his Dutch nukepak
engineer, his captain, and his cook, were too uncertain, possibly
too Earthbound, to consider. That made no difference, really;

they had not been told what was in the wind, and Henry Kwei simply transferred them to non-space vessels.

Within a week, we began to get messages from Franz. He had stayed with Jerry Sakakura, Tammy's Sansei relative, for two days, and had found the whole family sick of the IPP, scared of the future, and—best of all—qualified. They fell in love with Laure's World at first sight. Luckily, they had been planning a vacation in Tahiti, talking about it to all their friends, and felt that if they announced they'd suddenly been offered bargain fares no one would question their leaving a couple of days early; other dental surgeons at the clinic would stand in for him. Franz made arrangements with the underground to pick up professional equipment and everything else that wasn't ordinary tourist luggage. They could be expected to arrive in a week or so. However, their friend Peter Dougall and his wife would have to make other arrangements. Under cover of a business trip to the mainland, which he could manage, they'd rendezvous with others in the Bay Area who had to be picked up directly by Gilpin ship.

Then, rather to our surprise, Linda showed up with her big Swede, Lars Nordström. She had had no difficulty persuading him, not only because she was marrying him, but also because he was well aware of the menace in Earth's future and of the hope and adventure promised by Laure's World. Laure took one look at him and knew that he would do: a powerful man, so relaxed that he seemed deceptively slow, so confident of his own strength and sanity that he radiated security. He had had only a sketchy formal education, but he spoke English with only a faint accent, and we found out later that he not only seemed to know something about everything, but could turn his hand to almost any task. He'd told his employers that he was running off to marry a girl from the old country; and they'd given him their blessing. Linda told us that they'd gone to Vancouver by train, then flown to Japan as tourists, then on to Taiwan. No one had subjected them to close questioning. Then, much embarrassed, she had explained that, well, they still weren't married. It was because—well, it was because—

Laure interrupted her. "My dear," she said, "obviously it was because there wasn't a ship's captain around to marry you." She turned to me. "Commander Cormac, please get your Gideon Bible."

I did perform the ceremony, but not then. We waited until

work was over and everyone could attend, and in the meantime, by one of Laure's organizing miracles, everyone had sent ashore for wedding presents and champagne and a terrific cake. I couldn't give them *Owl*'s best cabin for their honeymoon— the captain's was too instrumented—but we did the best we could.

Everyone felt that things were starting off auspiciously, and certainly during the next few days our morale was high. Chris especially was bubbling with enthusiasm. As soon as his drive was completed and installed aboard *Young Unicorn*, his ship, he insisted on taking off, not just for Gilpin's Space, but for the Far Reaches. He wanted me to come, but there was no way I could leave *Owl* and Laure, so Placek and Latourette went with him. They were gone five Earth-days, and Chris was so hyped on the Far Reaches—all he could talk about was Laure's World and its underwater beings—that he didn't even bother to take a look at Mars or Venus or even the outer planets; he just wanted to make sure he'd survive the tough spots. Now he was full of confidence, thinking of new equipment he could order, new ways he could help the rest of us. I told him about our plan to carry Alec's ketch as deckload, surrounding it with a metal cobweb to have it within the Gilpin field, and delighted, he told me he owned a yacht himself, a thirty-five-foot junk, specially built for him of teak and designed for the high seas, and with a mininuke auxiliary providing power for everything. At once, he started arranging with Placek to carry it as *Pussycat*'s deckload—his own ship was a bit too short—and the two of them, with Lars' active help, had a wonderful time designing a cradle for her and getting the metal webbing ready.

Then more news began to dribble in from Franz. He had flown from Hawaii to the Coast without incident, and his recruiting in the Bay Area had gone smoothly. All of them had been well chosen, and none had wanted to bring anyone else along, at least not anyone human; the vet student was bringing her two golden retrievers and a couple of the others had cats to contribute. His final message from the Bay said he'd be taking off for Denver next day.

A week went by, and we heard nothing from him. Jerry Sakakura and his family arrived safely, courtesy of the underground, and again we were able to corroborate prior judgment, in this case Tammy's and Malia's; they were good people. Of course, there was all the business of getting acquainted, of showing them more of Laure's World, and of starting to familiarize them with dream sessions and the Structural Differential. It would have been less trouble to have waited until everybody was assembled, and then go through it all without having to start over again with each arrival, but that we could not afford. We had no guarantee that there'd be any more arrivals.

In the meantime, disquieting news was reaching us. The UN had voted to form what they called a Space Defense Force of Gilpin ships contributed by the Security Council powers and those smaller nations they could browbeat into it. It was, of course, to be financed almost wholly by the United States, and was to be formed immediately. The first vessels were already assembling. The usual IPP and U.S.S.R. chorales accompanied all this, screaming of mysterious perils out of space, of self-seeking, evil men flouting the will of those enlightened individuals who were determined to have peace on Earth. Along with this, the Council published a free-distribution list of every known submarine on every nation's registration lists, with detailed descriptions, silhouettes, and a schedule of cash rewards for information regarding unregistered or falsely registered vessels and new subs being built. We wondered whether, covertly at least, they hadn't already started outlining "find and destroy" missions for the Space Defense Force.

I said as much to Steve Placek and, very much to my surprise and Laure's—for we had been longer in Gilpin's Space than anyone we knew of—we learned something about it that we might never have found out had we not returned to Earth. "They'll probably be stationing ships on permanent patrol off Earth," I said, "spotting unlicensed takeoffs, intercepting them before they reached adequate velocity, and shooting them down right there in Gilpin's Space."

Placek exchanged glances with Henry Kwei. They both chuckled. "Commander, you've had a lot more experience out there than the rest of us, but *Owl* has always been alone, so there's something you don't know and Saul Gilpin forgot to tell us."

"Come again?"

"Sir, *no* ship ever saw another ship in Gilpin's Space. If you and I shifted *Owl* and *Pussycat* into it right here and now, neither of us could see the other. Even if we didn't move out of Mr. Kwei's dock, we'd be invisible. It's weird! It's as if there wasn't just one Gilpin's Space, but—hell's fire!—an infinity of 'em. Maybe it's a single value-quantum in something that separates them. Maybe we'll never know. But that's how it is."

"In other words," Laure put in, "ships cannot follow one another in Gilpin's Space?"

"No way. Not unless they know where the other ship's going."

"And that," said Henry Kwei, "at least makes life a little easier for us and a bit harder for our adversaries—temporarily. We all know it's only a matter of time till they make it so tough on us independents that most of us will either have to sell out or toss in the towel. They'll use fear and hate propaganda, just as they are now, and political and economic pressure, and subversion, and open and covert military action. That's why we and the underground are doing all we can to get ourselves and our friends out there before their wall goes up. From what we've heard—and it makes sense—they'll probably turn a blind eye at least to some groups who really want to leave and not come back, those who aren't equipped, either intellectually or technically, to do anything but, hopefully, start semi-private societies on habitable planets. But they'll really clamp down on anybody more competent—anybody who could interfere with their plans for conquest or return to Earth with ideas or weapons that might overthrow them. That's why Fujiwara in Japan—Norisuke Fujiwara—is readying his fleet at top speed, and damn the expense."

"You mean that physicist-industrialist?" I said.

"The same. He, alone, is bigger than most of the conglomerates, and a hell of a lot sharper than their executives. They don't dare interfere with him, or perhaps they don't really want to, for when he leaves, chances are his empire will crumble and all his lovely fat markets'll be up for grabs. The way I've heard it, he's recruited thousands—every kind of skill a civilized society requires—and they're taking every sort of Far Eastern animal and bird, insect and tree and flower. He's a devout Buddhist, and his declared aim is to re-create the Japan of the Nara Period, Buddhism's brief Japanese Golden Age. But he's the only one who's daring to try anything as big as that, and as openly."

"The gossip is," said Placek, "that he either already has taken off or is just about to. I wish we had his clout."

"We may not need it," Laure told him with a smile. "We have been out there. We know we can cross the Far Reaches and survive. And we already have a world awaiting us."

4

MORE THAN TEN days went by after the arrival of the Sakakuras before the people of our West Coast contingent started dribbling in. Franz had not reported individually on each one, and we had been informed by the underground that communications from the mainland were always kept at a minimum for security reasons. If we heard nothing, we could assume all was well; if anything went really wrong, we'd hear immediately. Antonina Tarn, the veterinary student, was the first, and she surprised us by bringing, not only her two retrievers, but also a boyfriend—a forest ranger type who we knew immediately would have passed inspection if Franz had had an opportunity to inspect him. She had been unable to get in touch with him in time, and he had unexpectedly shown up only after Franz was gone. Ollie Taliaferro, long and chocolate brown and with a wry sense of humor, and Terry Ann Golding, petite and quiet, showed up together a couple of days later. All sorts of scientific and technical equipment followed them.

Everything had gone very smoothly, so smoothly that we began asking ourselves if anything was wrong, and whether so long a suspension of Murphy's Law was an ill omen. Then, finally, we did hear from Franz. He had been forced to speed up his schedule as much as possible, had visited Feuerbach just long enough to tell his story, leave his microflexes, and give him instructions how to get in touch with us through the underground. He was certain Feuerbach would come, and would explain in detail when he returned to Taiwan.

To our astonishment, he was back almost on the heels of his message. In Colorado, he had been recognized by a young woman he had known on the ski slopes, perhaps too well; she was wearing an IPP pin. He had done his best to convince her

she was mistaken, even showing her his Canadian passport,
but he wasn't at all sure she'd bought it. To be on the safe
side, he'd ridden the first available bus eighty or so miles to
Blackstrap, a half-abandoned cowtown near Feuerbach's. From
there, he'd phoned, and Feuerbach had picked him up. From
then on, he hadn't even waited to watch the flexes. He'd explained why he didn't want to risk a longer stay, and called an
underground cover-number. Then Feuerbach, a private pilot,
had flown him across the New Mexico border to a hidden
meadow, dropping him there. When night fell, a Gilpin ship
appeared, took him aboard, and so now here he was. He told
us that Feuerbach had been tremendously excited by the prospect of trading his Colorado acreage, under the vulture-shadow
of the IPP, for the unlimited, untouched pasturage of Laure's
World. On the flight, they talked about it; and he had left his
friend full of plans to take, not only his family, but if he possibly
could, Black Angus and Holstein and merino sheep embryos.
He'd been experimenting with bovine and ovine "bottle ba-
bies," and believed he had enough already started.

"We can count on him," Franz assured us, "and on his wife
and kids. I know them all, and I know them well. But we'd
better be sure the ship that picks him up has enough cargo
space. He thinks things out in detail, and he won't bring anything unnecessary, but he'll have a ton of stuff that is."

"Well, that's certainly going to have to be a Gilpin ship
pickup," I said. "How much time is he going to need?"

"He said two weeks, maybe a bit more. We'll probably get
a 'confirm' from him through the underground anytime now,
and then he'll give us a more precise idea. I know it'll be tough
waiting—" Franz grinned. He had dropped all the mannerisms
of his temporary persona, and now reminiscently he stroked
his upper lip. "—don't any of you worry me about it. I'm
going to be much too busy coaxing my moustache back. After
all, when we get home again, I want my Bess to recognize
me."

Early next morning, the media carried a report that Franz
Andradi, a renegade nuclear engineer and an accomplice of the
notorious Laure Endicott, might have been spotted in a Colorado restaurant by a woman who had once known him, a Mrs.
Carrie Worfell, wife of an IPP state assemblyman. The report
had not been confirmed, but the authorities were running down

all leads. It troubled all of us, naturally, even though Franz was certain they'd not be able to trace him to Feuerbach's.

We had already received word that Bess' Stanford friend would be in no position to take any long trips under her own power; she was being too closely watched and so was her boyfriend. (Franz told us that the underground had warned him not to contact her directly, and that the microflexes had been delivered to her surreptitiously.) The best she could do would be a weekend trip to Tahoe or some similar resort where people ordinarily wouldn't go if they were skipping the country, and that meant she and her lad would have to travel light. That fitted in well enough with Peter Dougall's plans, and we made arrangements to pick them up in a little clearing along a neglected logging road some miles from the lake.

"Somehow," Franz said, frowning a little, "I think this is a job we ought to do ourselves. After all, she's an old friend of Bess'. I'd not want to feel responsible if anything went wrong. Besides—well, I have a hunch."

I thought it over. We'd long since learned not to ignore each others' hunches, and besides, I was beginning to feel Earthbound, and I knew that even a short trip in *Owl* would do me good. "I don't see why not," I told him. "But it's Laure's ship. Laure, what do you think?"

"I think I understand," she answered. "Yes—if only you and Franz go, and if you promise to take no chances."

"We may need at least one more to help load. Any volunteers?"

"That's me!" offered Lars, shushing Placek, who was trying to get his oar in. "Don't listen to Steve here. He's already been every place."

Laure agreed that a third hand made sense; and two days later the three of us made the pickup, carefully setting *Owl*'s computer according to the underground's instructions, and coordinating our time precisely. In Gilpin's Space, it took us only minutes to reach California and the Sierra, and we hovered over the spectral image of the clearing for a quarter hour before I finally brought her down. I was concerned. We had picked up two very, very faint indications from the clearing, on the very edge of Gilpin Space perception, and I guessed them to be infrared traces, probably from two cars with their engines cooling, which was fine—but there *seemed* to be another from half a mile down the road. We weren't sure, but it suggested the possibility of a third car there, which was potentially bad medicine. So I waited until I could distinguish, not just the two cars in the clearing, but also the four people waiting there. Obviously, Dougall and his wife had made it.

"Get to the lock," I said to Franz and Lars. "Let's move."

We flicked out of Gilpin's Space a few feet from our passengers. The lock door opened. Lars shot the gangplank out and followed it. *"Hurry!"* Franz shouted. "Get aboard!"

They didn't hesitate. They ran. Lars heaved the two heaviest suitcases up after them; sucked the gangplank in. The lock slammed shut. And instantly I flicked her into Gilpin's Space again.

The missile hit almost exactly where we'd been. It hit with a flash and flare which, even in our silence showed us what would have happened had we been a moment late.

Then everybody came into the control tower, and even Lars was pale.

"I'm glad we came!" Franz whispered. "I'm glad we came ourselves."

"Amen!" I said.

We gave the new people orientation courses, went on with the training sessions, checked out the candidates Chris and Henry were considering for Chris' ship, and kept on stowing supplies, supplies, supplies. Feuerbach's confirmation came a couple of days later, with an estimate of weight allowance and cargo space, and we started shifting things around in anticipation. It's absolutely astounding how much a small vessel can hold if she's tubby enough and her people know the tricks of stowage.

Our shopping was made easier by Lars, who was on no one's wanted list and who had an almost unbelievably thorough knowledge of machinery. Most of the machines we'd bought were electric powered, with permanent batteries rechargable by nukepak, but he talked us also into loading two small steam-driven all-terrain vehicles and the makings of two complete water-power systems, pointing out that much of the stuff could be squeezed in as deckload. He and Chris ransacked Taipei together, hauling back not only absolute necessities we'd never thought of, but also a few rare Chinese porcelains, gem jade jewels for their ladies and for Laure, two bobtailed three-colored kittens which Chris' wife assured us were extremely lucky, and an evil-smelling unguent made in Singapore and decorated with an extravagantly whiskered mythological monster. Chris swore the Chinese characters on the jar said *Moustache Manure* and, roaring with laughter, they presented it to Franz, promising that, applied religiously night and morning, it would restore his growth as never before.

Now we were faced with a new problem—a critical one. Had the missile been fired by a couple of IPP hit men, given the job of wasting Ina Murdoch, Bess' friend—or was there more to it than that? Had Whalen Borg's people, in spite of our precautions, been able to bring in someone in Henry's organization, or even plant a mole among us? All we could do was sweat it out until the underground reported, but we heard from them only two days later. The word was that Ina and her boyfriend had definitely been targeted, but not initially for elimination. The missile had been fired only when it became obvious that they were escaping by Gilpin ship. Before that, it probably hadn't even been ready—a circumstance which may have saved our skins.

We felt better. All they could have seen was *Owl*'s new silhouette, from which she could never have been identified. But the incident left us even more keenly aware of how thin a wire we were all walking, and how fatally deep the gulf beneath us was.

It also left us with an even greater admiration for the faceless men and women who constituted the underground, and for the genius—whoever he might be—who had organized it and kept it going. Nobody talked about him. Nobody speculated as to his identity. And I think we all realized that, as Laure said, this was very much for the best.

We kept on working in the midst of our well-ordered chaos, waiting for a definite date from Andy Feuerbach. People were getting to know each other, forming spontaneous friendships— Chris Kwei and Linda's Lars were prime examples. Laure was delighted. "Look at them, Geoff!" she said, "I'll give you ten to one we'll have no trouble about who goes aboard which ship. The only ones who may not have a choice will be the Feuerbachs, once their stuff is loaded, and the Macartneys because they'll be the last picked up."

"You mean we'll take off directly after getting them?"

"I think so, Geoff. The less backing and forthing we do, the better our chances of seeing our world again."

We had heard very little from Alec Macartney, and that little had been extraordinarily guarded. The fact that the IPP was getting more and more followers in Britain was a good reason for anxiety, for even though Alec had always kept quiet politically, the fact that he was Jamie's brother was no secret. We did hear that, as unobtrusively as possible, he was making his preparations, but that they were taking longer than expected; and he doubted whether he'd be able to get Jamie all the sophisticated equipment on his shopping lists. He'd do his best, of course, but—

We heard from Feuerbach. His date was a day or two before we'd expected it, which was good news, and Placek volunteered to pick him up in *Pussycat*—and almost simultaneously the media reported that the UN's Space Defense Force had come up with a real breakthrough. They'd developed a surefire method of detecting the emergence of any Gilpin drive into normal space—instantly, they said—and they were going all out to equip their vessels, ground stations, and patrol-surveillance aircraft with it.

"Maybe they have," Placek commented, "but it's a lead-pipe cinch they won't have it installed in time to foul us up—if Feuerbach doesn't run into any delays, that is. And even when they do get it working, they're not going to run the risk of popping off missiles every time they pick up a blip, not until they have the world better controlled, that is. Anyhow, Commander, it's my turn. Franz knows the terrain. We'll be picking them up right on the ranch, won't we?"

"That's been the idea," Franz said. "He has too much stuff to haul it off anywhere."

"There!" Placek shouted. "That's the clincher. Commander, *Pussycat*'s much better equipped to load cargo in a hurry than *Owl* is, and we've done a hell of a lot more of it. It'd take you three times as long as it will us."

"He's right, Geoff," said Laure.

Before I could offer any argument, Henry Kwei spoke up. "As matters stand, you're defenseless, but there's no real reason why you should be. Somewhere around the yard here we have a spare laser turret for one of the Republic's patrol boats—a highly effective weapon. There's no reason why it can't be mounted either on *Owl* or *Pussycat*. The ship's nukepak can power it, and you'll be able to direct and fire it from your control tower."

"How long would installation take?"

"Twenty-four to thirty hours, at a guess."

The prospect of no longer being totally defenseless was an appealing one, and besides, the laser could also be extremely useful as a tool. I told him so. "Can we start right away?" I asked.

"Hey, listen!" interrupted Placek. "Weapons aren't my bag— no way. I wouldn't know what to do with it."

It was my turn to grin. "No, Steve, weaponry's not your bag—but it *is* mine, even though I'm a few years away from it. Let's get the thing installed on *Owl*, and when we make the pickup I'll ride shotgun for you. From Gilpin's Space, we can keep a pretty good eye on everything. I'll borrow Alwyss from you. If I recall correctly, he knows more about laser weapons than any of us."

We sent the message off to Feuerbach, setting the date for the day after we got the answer. He'd be ready, with his family and all his loot and clutter. He was sending his cook and three hired hands off, the first on a plausible vacation, the others on a cattle-trucking errand into Utah. He'd made arrangements for bonuses and severance pay when they found out he wasn't coming back. And did we have anybody with us who knew anything at all about critters? He'd need help with those embryos, and with a lot of fertile eggs.

"Commodore," asked Franz, "shall I tell Antonina Tarn she's been elected?"

He went off whistling "Old MacDonald Had a Farm."

Henry Kwei had already given preliminary orders for the laser installation; and I was not surprised when, less than twenty hours later, he reported that all was complete and set to go. Of course, we had to test fire it, which meant shifting into Gilpin's Space, getting far enough off Earth so no one would be likely to pester us when we ducked back into normal space, and let loose. It worked beautifully, and so, when we did set off on our expedition, we felt rather more secure than we had.

Besides Franz, Placek took Sousa and Latourette along, plus a Chinese crewman from Chris' ship who was a real expert on cargo stowage, and Antonina Tarn, very eager to get to work in her own field. I took only Lars and Alwyss, and Linda because she knew *Owl*'s computer setup thoroughly. We were scheduled to arrive after sundown, Placek and I coordinating our times to the second—after all, there was no way for us to communicate in Gilpin's Space. If he noticed anything suspicious coming up, he simply wouldn't flip into normal space. If I noticed anything—well, I'd have to make decisions on the spot.

A three-quarter moon was riding in the sky when we arrived, shining down on the spectral landscape with its ghostly trees and strange, ethereal mountains, and neither Linda on *Owl* nor *Pussycat* had any trouble finding Feuerbach's place. The ranch house stood on a knoll overlooking barns and outbuildings and corrals; it must have had a dozen or more rooms, and had been lovingly built out of hewn logs and fieldstone.

Our approach showed nothing except infrared from a flatbed and an all-terrain pickup parked close together under a group of trees behind the house, which was what we had been told to expect. Then, at the appointed instant, *Pussycat* showed up in front of them. Placek, of course, had set her down perfectly, and we, hovering there invisible, could do nothing but watch the swift and simultaneous opening of her large loading lock and her smaller access lock for personnel. We saw the gangplank extruded, and the powered loading ramp. Somebody, probably Placek, was outside talking to a group of people. The flatbed backed up, piled high with God-knows-what, and the loading servos went instantly to work.

"Vell, vell!" said Lars, deliberately parodying his own slight accent. "Ay bane poor Svedish boy with vun suitcase only." He shook his head. "What on earth does he want with all that stuff?"

"He wants it *off* Earth, dummy," Linda told him. "And when we get where we're going you're going to wish you'd brought just as much along."

The loading progressed smoothly and effectively. The level of the flatbed's load dropped rapidly. Meanwhile, a steady parade moved up and down the gangplank, carrying suitcases and boxes.

In less than fifteen minutes, the flatbed was unloaded, and the pickup took its place. Again the servos went to work. This time, though, we could see Antonina Tarn with Placek and a man whom we assumed was Feuerbach pointing out objects to be taken in by hand.

"Looks like they're moving in the someday-will-be live-stock," Lars remarked. Then, abruptly, he leaned forward. *"Hey, what's going on?"*

The work had stopped. Everyone on the ground was staring at a low range of hills perhaps a mile and a half away—and suddenly I saw Placek waving, pointing.

"Something's coming!" I said. "Let's get our ears on!" And I set *Owl* down higher on the knoll, beyond *Pussycat* and the trucks, where we were partly masked by second-growth trees and brush. We flipped into normal space. We listened—or rather *Owl* did. And we heard the flop-flop of an approaching copter, still far away, but flying low and coming fairly fast.

I raised *Pussycat* by radio and got Latourette, taking the chance that whoever the copter was wouldn't get on our frequency. "Tell Steve to get busy, Lee!" I told him. *"Hurry it up!* If we have to, we'll take care of this guy."

"Aye, aye!" he came back, and at once we saw the work resumed, furiously.

Now we could see the copter's running lights, I guessed three or four miles away, but still low enough so he couldn't see what was going on. We on *Owl* could see him, but we were masked and behind a military crest; I was sure he couldn't see us. Now he was closer, much closer.

"Commander, you want me to burn him?" Alwyss growled.

I frowned. I hated to take chances, but I thought of whoever was in the whirlybird. "Hold it!" I said. "Let's wait till we're sure he's seen what's happening. Running lit up like that he's probably Forest Service or the local sheriff looking for a pot plantation."

We waited, holding our breath—and suddenly, apparently for no good reason, the copter made a hundred-and-eighty-degree turn and scuttled off the way he'd come. There was no telling exactly what he'd seen, if anything, but he certainly couldn't have seen much. As far as we could tell, too, he was keeping radio silence.

I gave Placek the *all clear,* told him to hop to it, and in minutes the loading was completed and we were back in Gilpin's Space. A very few minutes more, and we were once again side by side in Henry's covered dock.

We were all very much relieved. We'd made it. Antonina told us that all the sometime critters were safely stowed away, and that they included, not only barnyard cattle, but also a few destined to become Arabian horses. Her eyes sparkled as she told it, saying that both she and Feuerbach hoped we wouldn't mind.

"If Laure's World doesn't, I won't," I promised her.

Next day, we found that we hadn't gotten away quite scot-free, but that night we celebrated.

5

THE FOLLOWING EVENING we learned from the media that our
helicopter pilot *had* been aware something was going on. He
had been on a routine patrol—someone had called in to report
smoke in a remote stand of timber—and he'd spotted something over at Feuerbach's, something he didn't think belonged—a Gilpin ship. Clearly, he'd glimpsed *Pussycat* at long
range just as she emerged into normal space. Immediately, he'd
dipped down to approach out of sight, and then thought better
of it because he'd heard what desperate characters those Free
Space people were, and high-tailed it home, too spooked even
to report by radio on the way. Anyhow, the cops and IPP people
rushed out, and found plenty of evidence. After all, nothing
as big and heavy as *Pussycat* can sit down on the grass without
leaving marks, and besides, Feuerbach and his whole family
were missing.

The media men couldn't get together on their story. Some
of them screamed that the Feuerbachs had been kidnapped.
Others were absolutely sure they'd been active anti-Individualists
who had conspired with Enemies of Earth. All that was routine.
However, one or two IPP commentators began to tie it in with
the recent disappearances of several others—they mentioned
the Lake Tahoe incident, and spoke darkly of various scientific
and professional people vanishing, from as far away as Hawaii,
they said. And they promised that very soon they'd name names.
Obviously, somebody had started putting two and two together,
and both Laure and I realized that because of it, any little
accidental slip might give them the right answer.

We decided to speed up proceedings as much as possible,
and to put up a bold and optimistic front for everybody's benefit. Everything now was getting readied rapidly. Chris and
Lars had designed an afterdeck cradle to hold Chris' yacht,

and Henry's men had built and installed it for them, complete with adequate lashings and a mast-high steel cobweb to extend the Gilpin field around her. Very carefully, *Pussycat* had submerged under her and lifted her. Then they'd lashed her down, and broken out the cobweb from the mainmast head and fastened it. They'd taken off immediately into Gilpin's Space, returning minutes later absolutely delighted to find everything intact. They couldn't wait to build a similar cradle to carry Alec's ketch on *Owl*'s afterdeck, and they had a splendid time bragging about the yacht races they'd have on the seas of Laure's World. They reminded us very practically that the two vessels would add notably to our cargo capacity.

I'd hoped that the media would forget about the Feuerbachs and the others who had disappeared, but they didn't; and even more disquieting, one of the IPP's prime mouthpieces dragged out the rumor of Franz having been sighted in Colorado and started hammering on that. The situation was getting unhealthier and unhealthier, and—as if all that wasn't enough—the Security Council announced that their Space Defense Force was to be under the joint command of an American and a Russian admiral. The Russian was someone named I. V. Plutkin. The American was Vice-Admiral Whalen Borg.

We reached the point where all we were waiting for now was a go-ahead from Alec—and now our communications from him were even more guarded than they had been. We gathered from the underground that he was almost certain he was being watched, that he'd stopped loading supplies, and that he was making a point of putting to sea each weekend, always leaving his wife and one or two kids ashore, and doing nothing but fishing. He'd also, as a cover, applied for a three-week vacation, to start in about a month. We worried. His situation was very different from ours in Taiwan. We could keep our kids either aboard ship or within the confines of Henry's huge facilities, but if he attempted to restrict his he would simply be advertising that he was up to something. A child's wrong word to the wrong person, and—

There was nothing we could do about it, so we kept on with the job at hand. Laure and Franz and I and Linda kept going over the people who were going with us, and finally we weeded out three whom we judged too risky: the wife of one of Chris' crewmen and her teenage son by a previous marriage, and Emily Brooke, an outwardly stable English woman chemist from Hongkong and a close friend of Chris' wife. We talked to Chris about them, and he decided reluctantly to leave the crewman, his wife and stepson behind with explanations, a good job with Henry, and a new bank account. The English-woman was another matter; they'd known her for years, and were absolutely sure she'd make it. Finally, against all our instincts, we withdrew our objections, cautioning Linda, who'd be going with them, to keep a special eye on her.

In the meantime, we went on with our daily sessions, fussed with our stowage, and settled who was going on which ship—as Laure had predicted, with no friction whatsoever. On *Owl,* we were borrowing Latourette and Alwyss because both were experienced seamen and we were going to have the tricky job of trying to pick up Alec's ketch. At best, it was going to be very iffy, and I'd never have considered it had it not been for her usefulness and cargo capacity. We were going to need either a perfectly smooth day—rare enough off the British Isles—or a safe harbor, which now would probably be even harder to come upon. Henry's men completed and installed a cradle very much like the one they'd made for Chris' junk, and we practiced with it until we figured that, even allowing for the ketch's differences, we could dive under her, surface, and have her lashed and cobwebbed in less than ten minutes. The job was simple enough, and all of it could be done either from *Owl's* deck or the ketch's, but still ten minutes was a hell of a long time. We made up our minds that, at the first sign of trouble, we'd jettison the ketch, cargo and all, and shift to Gilpin's Space.

We were going to be crowded aboard *Owl:* Laure and I, Latourette and Alwyss, the Sakakura family with Peter Dougall and his wife, and seven Macartneys counting young Jamie—twenty of us, but still not quite so crowded as the other vessels. Franz was going with Placek aboard *Pussycat.* After all the allocations had been made, we found that we totaled sixty-two men, women, and children, about equally divided between the two sexes, plus six or seven cats and two retrievers.

We waited for word from Alec, and Laure made arrange-ments to liquidate all her remaining Earthside assets, giving Henry Kwei her power of attorney to do so. The money, she said, after her debt to him was paid, was to go half and half to the Free Space underground and to the Republic of China, a gesture which Henry told her would be greatly appreciated.

"I'm keeping no reserve," she told him. "I'm certain it'll be years before any of us will dare to come back, even if we want to. Since I've been here with you, the IPP has captured three or four more countries. They don't have a majority in the Italian parliament, but they're now the strongest party, there and in Portugal. The junta that's taken over Greece is pure IPP. It's just a matter of time before they have the world encircled. It's probably lucky for Norisuke Fujiwara in Japan that he and his whole fleet took off when they did."

"Do you really think they'll throttle us completely?" Henry frowned.

"They may pretend their control's not complete. They'll probably let the pilgrim ships keep going out, after they've bled them white of everything they own, and then only those who're poor insurance risks. That'll last a while, but eventually, I think, a new breed of men will assert itself—those who not only can traverse the Far Reaches, but who'll thrive in them. Of course, even they will have their troubles, but they'll survive. How? Simply by bringing back such treasures from the stars that even the people who run the IPP, even the Security Council powers, will have to tolerate at least a few of them. I'm gambling, you see, that their own regimented officers and crews will never make it."

"And here on Taiwan, Laure? I cannot see myself selling out and starting over again somewhere else. And besides, I have my eldest son to think of. He'll be taking the firm over eventually."

"You ought to come with us, Henry, but I know you won't. So you'll just have to play it as it comes. *If* things more or less hold together, *if* the Republic of China does manage to stay free, I think you'll manage to stay free with it—not as free as you are now, but at least free to operate under whatever sort of totalitarian registration and licensing system they enforce."

Henry looked at her for a long, long minute. "Laure," he said at last, "whatever happens, I'll always know that Chris and Gwen and my grandchildren are safe with you. If you ever can, will you let me know?"

She promised him she would.

• • •

He waited—and three days later a Republic of China patrol boat intercepted and destroyed a long-range robot torp in Taipei harbor. It might have been aimed at Henry's dockyard—or it might not. We didn't know, and the unidentified submarine other patrol boats and aircraft sank half an hour later several miles off the coast would never tell us. But it didn't make our waiting any easier.

Then, two days after that, word finally came from Alec. It would have to be the coming weekend. The weather was promising; he didn't want to keep us waiting any longer; and he himself didn't dare to wait. He suggested a place and time, and the place was an isolated fishing harbor on the Cornish coast. As far as the underground knew, while it might have some sort of radar, it had nothing else, no military establishment, nothing seagoing more dangerous than a lifeboat and its volunteer crew. He'd set off on his usual fishing trip—but this time with the whole family aboard. He'd sail in late on the Saturday afternoon, go ashore in his skiff, buy a case of beer or ale, talk a bit with the natives. He'd expect us after sundown. He'd be anchored where there was depth enough for *Owl* to submerge safely. He and Jamie and his family wouldn't bring anything aboard except their bags; everything else would already be on the ketch.

Laure and I told Henry, and then set about our final inspections. We had planned an itinerary, and drilled the captains of the other two ships on it. The course for Laure's World had been fed into each ship's computer, not as a straight line, but tentatively in four stages. Laure had chosen three systems where we could rendezvous in normal space, and where we knew there were planets and their satellites on which to land. When the time came for us to pick up the Macartneys, Chris and Placek would take off ahead of us. Once they arrived at the first rendezvous point, they would shift into normal space, contact each other—and us, if we had made it. If we had not arrived, they were to land, compare notes, do what they could to help each other if necessary, and wait for us.

They were to wait only the equivalent of three Earth days. Then, if we still had not arrived, they were to give us up for lost and continue on.

It was not a pleasant prospect. Not even the bell at Lloyd's would toll for us, and there would be no way for us to tell those we had left on Laure's World what our fate had been—

except that in our hearts we, Laure and I, knew with a terrible certainty that they *would* know.

Busy with all our last-minute preparations, every once in a while I'd find myself confronted by the undeniable craziness of the operation we were going to attempt. The idea of diving under a forty-five-foot sailing vessel, making certain she was properly positioned to ride in her cradle, surfacing, and then not just lashing her down like a whaler's lifeboat but enveloping her in the wire cocoon that would enable her translation into Gilpin's Space—well, as a once-practical naval officer, I found myself shuddering at the thought. Yet it could not be avoided. On Laure's World, the ketch would be invaluable; so would whatever Alec had been able to load aboard. Even if we hadn't had a commitment to him and to his family, we still would have had to try it.

We were to pick them up at between 11:00 and 12:00 P.M. GMT, which meant early morning in Taiwan; and the night before Henry entertained us all at a farewell supper at which, for the first time, the President of the Republic and Admiral Leong were present, to wish us well, to thank Laure for her gift, and to assure us that the Republic, at least, would continue to assert the complete freedom of Gilpin's Space. A leave-taking on a long journey can be emotional enough; our leave-taking was of a different order. Everyone there, I know, was overawed by the vastness we were going to traverse, by its uncounted suns and worlds and beings, and by the knowledge that we were traveling, not just to a new and friendly world, but into an unknown forever. Few words were said. They had already been. Even Henry's parting with Chris and his grand-children was formal, almost muted. People shook hands more fervently than they ever had; they embraced people whom they had never embraced before. Even Franz didn't promise to send anyone a postcard. Next morning, everything was business. We, on *Owl*, waited until *Pussycat* and Chris' *Young Unicorn* had dissolved and disappeared. Then we too shifted into Gilpin's Space. My last view of the dock that had sheltered us was Henry's ghostly figure, standing there in its spectral ambience.

Presently, *Owl* was hovering motionless over the small harbor Alec had described to us.

From Gilpin's Space, its every detail was, as always, eerily visible. Several fishing boats and a yacht or two were tied up

to the single pier. Two or three similar vessels were anchored
or tied to buoys. Some showed a riding light, but that was all,
and I thanked our stars that no one was up partying. Alec's
ketch, *Morveth*, was anchored near the harbor's mouth, scarcely
moving in the slow, gentle sea-swell. Scattered cottages ashore
showed no lights at all. Everything looked almost too favorable.

"Standing by?" I said to Latourette and Alwyss, and they
nodded their readiness. So did Peter Dougall, who we'd found
had some sea experience. It was going to be their job to place
the two steel-cable tie-downs Henry had designed to hold the
ketch as securely as cables hold enormous logs on lumber
trucks, fasten them, tighten them down with turnbuckles, then
spread the all-important cobweb from the mainmast head.

"Going down," I said.

A moment later we were alongside *Morveth*, barely kissing
the surface of the water—and instantly, almost without a ripple,
we were in normal space. A summer stillness lay over the
harbor, its cottages, its cliffs. The scene was starlit, with what
remained of a pale moon. And suddenly, without warning or
rhyme or reason, I felt intensely that eyes were watching us,
unfriendly eyes.

Laure and I exchanged glances. "We'll have to hurry!" she
said grimly. "Geoff, I feel it, too."

Latourette threw the personnel lock open, extruded the gangplank so that its end rested on *Morveth* aft of her low midships
deckhouse. At once, Alec and his family were topside, bags,
bundles, and a cat-carrier in their hands.

"Get 'em all in, Alec," I told him, "fast as possible. We'll
get busy with the tie-downs."

My anxiety was intensifying, becoming irrationally acute.
Latourette and Alwyss jumped the three-foot gap between the
ships, and I followed them. Peter Dougall came after us with
the cobweb folded like a parachute. "Can you climb the mainmast?" I shouted at him.

"He won't need to!" Alec shouted back. "We've a halyard
ready!"

"Good man."

He joined Dougall and the other two.

"First the tie-downs," Alwyss said. "The web can wait till
she's out of the water."

I turned, leaving them on *Morveth*'s deck, made sure all
the Macartneys were safe inside, told Jamie to close the lock

and suck the gangplank back, then joined Laure in the control tower. When the lights said yes, I let *Owl* submerge. The dark water enfolded us, and I turned on our underwater lights. *Morveth's* graceful lines now were fully visible, and I saw, approvingly, that she was completely clean. I moved *Owl* ahead very carefully, brought the two ships into line, threw *Owl's* engine into reverse, and very, very slowly backed her until I judged that *Morveth's* bowsprit would come within a foot or two of our rear observation ports. Then, still very slowly, I began to surface. I felt *Morveth* touch her cradle, settle into it. I surfaced as quickly as I could.

Laure and I looked at each other. Everything was going beautifully.

And still everything was wrong.

"I'll give the boys a hand," I said. "The quicker we get this done the better."

I went out through the lock onto the wet deck, and Laure followed me. So did young Jamie, and Norman, the oldest of Alec's kids.

The world was silent, almost as silent as the still sea. Water dripped gently from *Morveth's* hull. Somewhere ashore a small dog yapped petulantly twice, and once again. Dougall and Latourette were swinging down onto *Owl's* deck. Alwyss was getting ready to pass them the tie-downs. I walked aft to where Alec had thrown over a Jacob's ladder, and I climbed it, the kids right with me. *Morveth's* standing rigging was of steel, and Alex was hoisting the packaged cobweb to the mainmast head; all we'd have to do when it was in place and the tie-downs secured was pull four ripcords, two amidships, one fore, one aft, make everything fast, and we'd be set.

From the direction of the pier, I heard—or thought I heard—the sound of oarlocks; and I tried to tell myself that probably some ancient fisherman ashore was getting curious. My anxiety was still upon me.

"Give us a hand with these lines!" Alec barked at the two boys. I took the one he handed me, and hurried aft, Jamie and Norman carrying theirs to port and starboard. "When I yell," I told them, "we'll all pull together. Then we'll get back onto *Owl's* deck and finish up."

I had called over my shoulder as I ran past *Morveth's* deck-house—so intent on what we were doing that my mind simply didn't register the soft, familiar, enormous sound that so suddenly broke the stillness. It didn't really register until I heard Laure's gasp and Alec's horrified, *"Good God, what's that?"*

Then I knew what the sound had been. It was the sound made by a Gilpin ship when, shifting into normal space, she settled on the water. I was not surprised. Somehow, I had known.

I stared out past *Morveth*'s stern, past *Owl*'s. Lying there, scarcely a hundred feet away, athwartships to us, was a vessel six or seven times as long as ours, and her winged control tower and the deck-domes that concealed her weaponry told me immediately exactly what she was—a Russian Tarantella-class sub, long since mothballed and now reactivated and converted. Any one of her weapons, obsolete though submarine warfare might be, could have destroyed us instantly. Of that there was no doubt. And there was no doubt that they had trapped us at our most helpless, when we couldn't possibly shift into Gilpin's Space or even reach our laser—which would have been suicide anyway.

She lay there, black and long and deadly, and we could hear her control tower lock opening. The moon's faint light showed us the Cyrillic characters on her tower, and over them, newly painted, *U.N.S.D.F.* Suddenly two searchlights blazed, fore and aft, flooding *Morveth* and *Owl* with brilliance and sharp shadows, and a third bright light turned on to illuminate the tower and the deck surrounding it. We could see that they'd broken out the UN flag. We could also see two men standing on the tower—and one of them, unmistakably, was Whalen Borg.

What does one think of when, abruptly, logic tells one all is lost? A few months before, I know I would have been filled with despair and black rage. Now I found myself completely cool, thinking first of my ship and of her people, thinking then of Janet and of Laure's World, thinking of all these with a fathomless regret—and believing none of it. I was completely cool, in total control of my mind and my decisions.

I saw Borg lift a bullhorn to his mouth. "Cormac!" he bellowed. "And you, Laure Endicott. You are under arrest—you and everyone aboard your vessel. Tell all your people to line up on deck. We will board, transfer you to our ship, and take over yours."

"Borg!" I shouted back. "Take a look at our registration

number and our silhouette. This is a Republic of China ship."

He laughed, and the man on the tower with him laughed as loudly. "We are familiar with false registrations, Mr. Cormac. Now you will do as the Admiral says!"

A boarding party was mustering just forward of the tower.

"Christ!" muttered Alwyss. "Commander, let me just get to our laser turret for one minute. Look, I can wipe those bastards out as fast as they can come up topside."

I grasped his arm, dug my fingers in. "Not a chance!" I whispered. "We'd all be dead—all, *Owl*, *Morveth*, Laure, the kids! *You* know what kind of stuff they've got aimed at us.

Alwyss' arm went limp; he turned away. *"Shit!"* he said under his breath.

"Laure Endicott!" bellowed Borg. "And you, Geoffrey Cormac! Our warrants are from the United Nations and the United States, with the latter taking precedence. As soon as we come alongside and board, I shall personally take you into custody—"

I looked at him across the water as, slowly, his ship began to turn. His face was not quite as full as it once had been, and it was pale. His voice had lost a little, too, in force and volume. But all the old venom was still there, and more.

Then Laure's voice rang out, icily clear. "Admiral Borg, Commander Cormac and I will surrender. We have no choice. But there is no reason why you should take our crew, or the people who, as you know, have taken passage with us."

Borg's answering laugh was not nice to hear. I saw him leave the tower for the deck—

And then it happened. It happened so fast that even after it was over I scarcely could believe what I had seen. Abeam of *Owl*, a third vessel had appeared, soundlessly. It did not speak to the Russian submarine. From a projection like a stubby bowsprit on its tower, a vague blue nimbus blossomed, took shape, flew forward growing as it flew. Another followed it scarcely a yard away. Another and another and another. Swelling, glowing, intensifying. I saw the first one strike directly on the tower, then almost simultaneously the rest. One hoarse, terrible cry came from the sub—and that was all. Otherwise, there had been no sound at all.

And where that four-hundred-foot ship of war had been, there now was nothing—nothing except the roiled surface of the sea.

I looked at the new arrival, and recognized her.

She was *Cupid's Arrow.*

She came alongside. Her personnel lock opened. There, in the moonlight, stood Saul Gilpin, decked out in his squirrel-tail moustache and a Dutch barge-captain's cap.

"Hello, Auntie Laure!" he called out. "Here I am—*meus ex kachina.*"

In the distance I heard the oarlocks again—frantically fast this time.

I stood there tongue-tied, trying to unwind, and I learned later that all the rest of us had reacted similarly—all except Laure.

"Why, hello Saul!" she called back to him. "What a *nice* surprise! But you should know that *meus,* in latin, means *mine,* not *me.*"

"Come, come!" he answered. *"Ma chérie,* surely you'd not niggle me out of such a lovely pun on a point of grammar? And anyhow, isn't it good to know that there's more than one way to throw a Gilpin ship right out of normal space?"

"Thank God there is!" Laure said. "Thank God!"

"You can thank me, too," he replied modestly. The two vessels touched, and he jumped across to *Owl,* and then he was in Laure's arms, and she was kissing him.

Then everybody was swarming over him.

"Saul," I said when finally I could make myself heard, "what's become of her, of that Rusky sub?"

Moments passed before he answered me, his voice subdued. "That was something I hoped I'd never have to do," he said. "She's in Gilpin's Space, but it's not her own. She's going to have a time getting back."

"And Borg?"

"He's there, too. Or part of him, that is. Remember how my cables looked when you first found out I'd stolen *Cupid's Arrow?* That's what the field's edge does." He worried the ends of his moustache. "Anyhow, he's not coming back, ever. But I'm sorry for those others on deck with him, the poor sods. Those below decks are probably all right. The locks probably closed automatically. But look—we can't just stand here. Any time now you're likely to have visitors, and we'd best not be here when they arrive. So finish lashing down your pick-a-back—"

"Let's get crackin'!" shouted Latourette.

From a pocket of his pea jacket, Saul fetched a microflex, handed it to me. "Geoff, go up and feed this into your computer. It'll take you where I'm going. I'll flip off now and wait for you." He patted Laure's cheek. "See you in a few minutes, Auntie Laure. We'll have a grand reunion."

He jumped back to *Cupid's Arrow,* and before we'd finished the job on *Morveth,* he and his ship had disappeared.

Just before we ourselves flipped back into Gilpin's Space, we heard approaching engines in the sky.

6

OWL BORE US westward, across the broad Atlantic, over the Appalachians and the Mississippi and the plains of Texas, all at what, for Gilpin's Space, was a sluggard's speed. At first, everybody talked at once. How had Saul known where to find us? How had he known we were in dire straits? How had he managed to get there in the nick of time?

"If you asked him those questions," Laure said, "he'd probably answer you the way he did me—*meus ex kachina*. A very Saulish answer. I'm going to accuse him of only coming to our rescue so he could use his dreadful pun. We never thought that *Cupid's Arrow*, like *Owl* and *Pussycat*, was designed and equipped to keep in touch with her sister ships automatically. Saul must have been aware of us ever since we hit the Solar System. He'll probably explain how he knew we needed him when we get where we're going."

"And where might that be?" asked Molly, Alec's wife.

"At a guess, I'd say probably in Hopi country," Laure told her.

"Well, I hope there won't be any Russian submarines waiting for us there." Molly shivered. "I still haven't gotten over that last one."

Laure was right. High over Northern Arizona, above a landscape riven by vast canyons and shadowed by sheer escarpments thrown up by ancient cataclysms, *Owl* slowed, stopped dead, dropped. She dropped into a canyon that was a jagged slash in the Earth's crust, its Gilpin ghost even more impressive than its reality ever could have been. Then, momentarily, she hovered. In the canyon's wall, directly ahead of us, I saw what seemed to be a huge shallow cave, perhaps a hundred feet from top to bottom at its vertical maximum and half a dozen times as long. *Owl* headed directly into it, and we saw that the shallowness was an illusion. From our point of entry, the cave turned sharply to the right, burrowing through the striations of the solid rock. There was only the false light of Gilpin's Space, very faint now. The cave turned left again, expanding both horizontally and vertically, and suddenly everything became clearly visible. Ahead of us I saw *Cupid's Arrow* and another Gilpin ship. *Owl*'s computer signaled me to take over the controls. I set her down and shifted into normal space.

Saul and his Lillian, his daughter and her husband, the two Hopi who had appeared on our screen with him on the way out, and a dozen people whom we'd never met were there to welcome us.

Our lock was opened. Our gangplank was extruded. Laure leading, we stepped out, all of us, onto the rock floor of the cave. The light, soft and indirect, came from the vessels resting there. Otherwise, as far as we could see, the cave was completely empty.

Again, Laure and Saul kissed. For a long moment, he held her at arms' length. "Laure, Laure!" he whispered. "My God, how wonderfully you've changed—no, not *changed*. You're still yourself, but it's as though you never were yourself before, not fully. But now—"

Shaking his head, he let her go. Polly Esther hugged her, then Lillian. After that, it was my turn. And then there were introductions all around.

"This cavern," Saul told us, "is my headquarters, *our* headquarters—for the moment, that is. This means it's headquarters for the Free Space underground—" He teased his squirrel-tail and grinned. "No pun intended."

"So *that's* who's been running the Free Space operation," said Laure. "Saul, we never suspected you of such administrative practicality."

He bowed.

"Also, it's as secure as any cave can be," he went on, "and close to Hopi country—quite handy, lovely Laure, for consulting the kachinas. People have climbed up here, of course, in the past, but there's been nothing to interest archaeologists, and even less to interest spelunkers, so officially it's not been worth looking at. What'll happen if the Powers really have developed a drive detector—well, we'll solve that problem when it comes to us. But I'm not too worried, at least where *Cupid's Arrow* is concerned. Remember what I told you about

Louisa when you saw us on your screen? She's psychic, Laure. If trouble's coming, she can always tell."

And so, I thought, *can Laure, and I myself, and all of us who have been there and back again, perhaps not as clearly as Louisa, but definitely—yes, very definitely.*

Saul pointed at the third ship. "That's *Sundowner.* Bart Crankshaw, who you just met, owns her and he and she used to do all sorts of interesting things around the Java Sea, but now he's giving full time to the underground. Like all of us, he has his reasons. 'E's an Aussie, don'tcher know? Speaks pure Stryne, 'e does."

"Absolutely." Crankshaw laughed. "I speak it fluently when I have to. Usually, however, I prefer to imitate the more intelligible sort of BBC announcer."

He was tall, gray-haired, in his later fifties.

"It was Bart's ship, mostly, that shuttled your people to and from Suva and here and there. He and his gang have to be on their way. But he did want to meet you first."

"It's not often one meets a lady who is not only very brave and very beautiful, but to whom the world owes so much. Mrs. Endicott, wherever in this Universe you're going. I—we, all of us—wish you well."

Laure thanked him. She said good-bye to his small crew one by one—somehow she had managed to remember every name. Then they boarded their vessel. Almost at once, she vanished.

"And now," said Saul, *"mi chère matante,* we can hardly wait to hear about your travels. Come, I know you have liquor in *Owl*'s wardroom, but it's going to have to last you, so we'll fetch some over from *Cupid's Arrow.*"

"I love you, Saul," Laure declared, "and we'd all love to drink your liquor, but before we do I want to know why you're here on this sick old Earth instead of out in the Far Reaches, and how you ever managed to find out about the Macartneys and our picking up their ketch."

"We couldn't stay in Space—" Abruptly Saul was intensely serious. "—because, Laure, it was I who started this, and I felt I owed something to everyone who became involved. That is why I—and a lot of others—started the underground. That's why I've helped to keep it going—"

Lillian pinched him. "What he means is that he runs the show. Very effectively, I must say. It's doing so well that any day now he ought to be able to let someone else take over, and then—then we can do what you did and find ourselves a fresh, new world!"

"My dear," said Laure, "you won't need to find one. You can come to ours."

"We'll have to take a raincheck for now, but believe me, we'll be there, if I have to drag Saul by his whiskers."

"I think I know how you found out we'd come back, Saul— *Pussycat* called us before we even knew we'd sent a signal. But how did you ever learn we were picking *Morveth* up?"

He chuckled. "You're right about *Owl* keeping me informed, but as for your last question—" He hesitated. "—I rather hate to tell you, but the Macartneys have a small boy named Robin, and small boys aren't very good at keeping secrets. Of course, they only tell them to their closest special friends, and always make them promise not to tell a soul. He just couldn't manage to keep the news about his exciting cousin Jamie under his hat, and—well, the IPP put two and two together—"

"Why, that little brute!" growled Alec. "So that's why we were being so closely watched. I didn't dare load half my stuff—not even the electron microscope. And then that ambush! Well, just wait till we get him in the cabin. I'll teach him to go giving the whole thing away!"

Saul smiled gently. "Speak to him by all means," he said, "but softly, softly. Don't forget, Alec Macartney, that where Auntie Laure is taking you survival won't depend on keeping secrets. Everything will be different. All those subliminal and psychic pressures that weigh so heavily on us here on Earth will be gone completely. I wish I could go with you."

"You can," said Laure. "Saul, you've laid the foundation. Now men like your friend Crankshaw, men like Henry Kwei— they can keep things going. All of you aboard *Cupid's Arrow* really should come with us, if for no other reason—" She smiled at Lillian. "—then just because you snubbed us ever since our return, even though you knew very well we were here. I do believe you'd still not be speaking to us if it weren't for our giving you such a splendid chance to use your awful pun."

"Madame," said Saul gravely, "the first rule of the Free Space underground is that we make no contacts unless they're absolutely necessary—not even with our sisters and our cousins and our aunts. That's one reason we're still functioning. I'm

deeply hurt by your imputation. However, out of the goodness
of my heart, I shall give you the opportunity to wash your
mouth out either with Wild Turkey or with a comparable Scotch."
He took her arm. *"En avant!* Let's board your ship. The booze
and snacks will follow, and we can talk, and you can show us
your tourist photos of your world."

We crowded into *Owl*'s wardroom, and some of Saul's people
brought liquor over, and sandwiches, and for a little while we
ate and drank and answered questions. Then it came time for
Laure to tell them of her world. She brought the screen to life.
"I'm afraid," she told them, "that tourist pictures are what
you're going to get." Then, as she had for Henry Kwei and
the others, she showed them one brief sequence after another,
from our first landing to our settlement on Mutton Island: the
fauna and flora, continents and archipelagoes, forests and
mountains and the frozen poles. When it was over, there was
utter silence. I myself was almost overwhelmed by the sudden
intensity of my yearning for Laure's World, for its untouched
magnificence and cleanliness, and above all for Janet. I sat
there as silent as the rest.

Louisa was the first to speak. She spoke in a very low voice,
to Saul, and in Hopi.

He listened to her, obviously disturbed, tearing at his moustache. He did not reply.

Laure, sitting next to Paul, asked him what she'd said.

"She spoke to him of a Hopi prophesy," he replied. "It isn't
a happy one. She said, 'Saul, you are one of us. You are
our—' brother is as close as I can come to it. 'You should not
be one of those who waits until the Blue Star Kachina dances.
No, neither you nor Paul nor I.'"

Finally Saul answered her, in Hopi and very somberly, and
again Paul translated. "He has repeated that the responsibility
is his. The drive he invented and gave the world is now a
weapon. He is afraid that, because of it, the Blue Star Kachina
may dance before his time."

"And what must happen when the Blue Star Kachina dances?"
Laure asked.

"Disaster," Paul replied. "But, I, too, think he is mistaken
when he blames himself. That kachina will not dance until a
new blue star flares in the daylight sky."

"A supernova?" I broke in. "Even if the prophesy is right,

that may be tomorrow or it may not happen for a hundred thousand years. Anyhow, Saul—" I raised my voice, and he turned, listening to me. "—you did not give the world a weapon. You gave it an instrument of power, and any instrument of power *can* be a weapon: a pitchfork, chain saw, tractor, aircraft. You gave the world an instrument of power—and a safety valve. How many thousands have already taken off for space? How many more are going to escape before the Powers really can clamp down? And will they ever succeed in stopping *every-body?* And will they even want to? I don't think so. Neither does Henry Kwei. Neither does Laure. Saul, how do you know the whole thing might not have blown up already if you *hadn't* given us the drive?"

There we all sat, in *Owl*'s convivial wardroom, the ship's screen only just turned off; and I knew that later on, en route to Laure's World, we'd have to offer an explanation to the Macartneys and those others who didn't know Saul as we did.

He stared at me for a moment. "Geoffrey—" he began.

"Call me *Commodore!*" I snapped.

That brought back a bit of his usual self. His ears twitched, and he almost smiled. "It's not just the world, Commodore," he said. "No, indeed. In a way—spiritually, you might say— I am a Hopi. They're my people. How can I leave them at a time of crisis, hey?"

Louisa answered him, again in Hopi.

"Dear Louisa—" He shook his head. "She's telling me that almost all the old Hopi beliefs and rituals have decayed, that almost nobody follows them anymore. She says that if she and Paul feel free to leave, why can't I? Well, there are those I must consult—"

He stopped. Suddenly he stood. He held his glass on high. "A toast!" he cried. "Enough of questions, of dismal proph- ecies! Enough of Gentle Saul's cruel conscience! Let it torment him after you are gone. Come now, let's drink to Laure—and to her world!"

Everyone echoed him, but I overheard Louisa whispering to Laure. "For the Hopi, what will be will be. There are still enough who follow the old ways, if the prophesy must be fulfilled. We shall talk to him, Paul and I, but if he stays we can't abandon him."

"Does your—your second-sight tell you nothing?" Laure whispered back.

"Not yet," Louisa answered. "No, not yet."

For another half-hour, we drank and talked, and neither Laure nor I tried again to argue Saul into a change of heart, knowing him too well for that."

Then came the good-byes, embraces, kisses, a tear or two or three. They were very quiet good-byes, for everyone realized that, in minutes, we would have left Old Earth irrevocably behind, and within hours and days light-years would separate us.

But I saw Laure, before I parted company with them, give Lillian and Louisa a dozen microflexes. "Take these," she said. "Show them to him—especially those that deal with Vee Vee and the Gnat and the beings of the reef."

Lillian took them, and touched her lightly on the cheek, and Louisa, standing by, said something in her native tongue which I knew was a blessing.

Moments later, we were back in Gilpin's Space, threading through the cave into the canyon—then up, and out, with the threatened Earth left far behind.

When we reached the planet designated as our first rendez-vous, *Pussycat* and *Young Unicorn* were already there, *Pussycat* and Chris' junk-yacht deckload all secure. They had had their problems in the Far Reaches, as everybody does, but again our system of selection—or perhaps I should say our developed instincts—proved out. So, again, did the Senoi sessions and training with the Structural Differential. Everyone aboard both ships had profited by our experience, even the few who, with Placek, already had ventured into the Far Reaches. When terrors struck them out of the vastnesses, they—and their relatives and friends—knew how to cope. Besides, we'd learned that we veterans had acquired some measure of Laure's protective power, a power which, while it worked unconsciously, did at least take some of the edge from the alien emotions that cut at us. Aboard *Pussycat,* Franz took the night watch, usually with Placek; aboard *Young Unicorn,* Linda did the same, with Lars—who had turned out to be that rare bird, a Far Reaches natural—backing her up.

Each assault, each seeming emergency successfully coped with, gave them renewed assurance. There were only three exceptions: Molly Brooke, on *Young Unicorn,* of whom we had been so dubious, and Antonina Tarn's two retrievers on *Pussycat*. Molly had turned out to be a second Rhoda, totally vulnerable, slightly paranoid. But the two dogs were a tragedy.

Almost as soon as *Pussycat* entered the Far Reaches, they began to howl spasmodically. They tried crazily to run away. Sometimes they growled and snapped. More often they did their best to hide. Antonina, weeping, had started to talk about putting them to sleep. "Christ!" she said. "The poor bastards! I should've understood—me, going to be a vet!—I should've realized that dogs don't have the sense of individuality most people have—most people and all cats. They're too dependent. Look! We've been here on this planet almost two days now, and they're still cringing-crawling. They won't eat. They'll barely drink their water. What the hell are we going to do?"

"It's damn lucky nobody brought Dobermans," Placek grunted. "Why don't you let Mrs. Endicott have a look at them?"

"Yes," said Laure, "I'd like to."

I went with her to Antonina's cabin. The dogs were wretched, their coats staring, eyes bloodshot, thick sputum drooling from the lax corners of their mouths.

Laure knelt before them, and they cringed from her.

"Give them a little time," she said. "Leave me alone with them for a bit."

We went out, I and Placek and Antonina, and had a beer together, and in about ten minutes Laure joined us.

"They're quieter now," she said, smiling again. "But what can we *do?*" asked Antonina, not encouraged.

"Something very simple, really. Franz and I will trade places. He'll move over to *Owl*. I'll go with you in *Pussycat* and Jamie Macartney can come with me—he's very nice with animals. Jamie and I will stand the night watches, and the dogs can sleep in the control tower with us. The rest of the time, they can be either in my cabin or in yours. Antonina, I'm sure they'll be all right."

Antonina looked relieved and pleased—and at the same time a little hurt. Laure patted her hand, and told her she understood. "Don't worry," she said, "they won't stop being your dogs."

Molly was something else again. Like Rhoda, she wanted to return to Earth; unlike Rhoda, she had no one of her own to lean on, not the way Rhoda could lean on Dan. Laure had several talks with her, with Chris, and with Chris' Gwen, without any acceptable solution being found. The girl wasn't just neurotic; it seemed almost as though she was deliberately being difficult, and Chris spent half his time apologizing for her.

"Well, I suppose there's only one thing we can do," said Laure finally. "Perhaps the same medicine will do for girl and dog. We'll shuffle people around a bit, and she can move over to *Pussycat*—perhaps with one of Chris' kids—she's fond of them. I think I can protect her adequately at night, and Sally Placek can take care of her in the daytime. If we're lucky, maybe she'll fall in love with somebody."

It took another day for all of us to talk her into it, but finally the transfers were made, and another couple—Bess' Stanford friend and her young man—moved into her cabin on *Young Unicorn*.

Sighing with relief, but with our fingers crossed, we took off again. Franz and I held down the night watch aboard *Owl* together, and spent a pleasant time playing chess, at which he usually beat me, and gin rummy, at which I always beat him, and telling each other how wonderful it'd be to get back to a civilized world and our girls.

When we made our second landing a few days later, we found that all had gone very well indeed. Molly had simmered down; almost all her tension had disappeared, and strangely, too, she and the dogs had found a common emotional ground. Now they were sleeping in her cabin, quietly and peacefully, when Laure and Jamie were on watch, and only occasionally, during daytime naps, showed any signs of their previous terror and confusion.

Laure and Franz and I talked matters over. "It's gone a lot better than I'd ever have expected," Franz declared. "We've learned a lot, and a lot of what we've learned's rubbed off. Do we really need to make that third rendezvous?"

"Why don't we make it conditional?" I suggested. "On *Owl*, we'll be going slower, simply because the Macartneys had no preparatory training and we're having to give it all to them en route. Tell Chris and Placek that we'll take *Owl* to the designated spot, and that if they decide they have to land they can wait for us there. If they aren't there when we arrive, we'll know they didn't run into anything they needed help with—"

"Or ran into a hell of a lot more than they could handle?" Franz said. "Or is that just the Magyar in me talking?"

"I think you've been humming 'Gloomy Sunday' to yourself again," Laure told him. "What do you think Bess would say?"

Franz grinned. He felt his lip, where his moustache was struggling to regain its former luxuriance. "Promise you won't tell?"

Laure laughed. "Yes, Franz, I promise."

"You, too, Commander?"

"*Commodore*," I corrected him. "All right, me too."

We talked it over with the others, and they agreed to try and make the run straight through: and when *Owl* did finally reach the third rendezvous, nobody was there.

"All's well," I said. "I feel it—it's almost as if Laure told me."

"She did," Franz answered. "She told me, too."

We continued our slow passage for the sake of the Macartneys, and we encountered nothing we couldn't cope with easily. We did not resent the extra time, but somehow all we could think of now was getting back to Laure's World and those we loved and had risked losing for all time. When we passed through what I always thought of as the inspection point, where it had seemed as though some vast intelligence had vetted us and found us good, those of us who had passed through before experienced it for a few moments only, but others, like the Macartneys, told us that it had seemed to last for an eternity, and that—even as we ourselves—they never would feel quite the same again.

Finally, then, we entered our new world's null zone, and hours later, from Gilpin's Space, we looked down on all its glories, glowing ghostlike there, awaiting us.

It was late afternoon when we came down over Mutton Island, dropping as swiftly as I dared—

There were *four* vessels there.

One of them, Chris' junk, floated on the tranquil bay. The other three had landed near our settlement.

We could see people gathering there, hurrying.

"*Three?*" Franz exclaimed. "What's that third vessel doing here?"

I set *Owl* down gently. I flipped her into normal space. "My God, Franz, don't you recognize her? That's *Cupid's Arrow!*"

We threw the lock open, shot the gangplank out. Together, Laure and Janet came running up as I rushed out. I took them both into my arms. Bess was close behind them. So was Saul, his squirrel-tail as ravaged as before, Vee Vee and the Gnat clinging to his hands.

"Thank God! Thank God!" sobbed Janet.

"Thank God indeed!" I echoed, kissing her again and again. I looked at Saul, reached out to slap him on the back. "Now it's complete. We have our world, our loves, our friends!"

"Yes," he said. "And we shall have our own kachinas."